P9-APE-451

PERCHANCE TO DREAM

Perchance to Dream

EDITED BY
DAMON KNIGHT

DOUBLEDAY & COMPANY, INC., GARDEN CITY, NEW YORK, 1972

Grateful acknowledgment is made for permission to reprint material from the following publications:

"Mr. Arcularis" by Conrad Aiken. Reprinted by permission of The World Publishing Company from *The Collected Short Stories of Conrad Aiken* by Conrad Aiken. Copyright © 1922, 1923, 1924, 1925, 1927, 1928, 1929, 1930, 1931, 1932, 1933, 1934, 1935, 1941, 1950, 1952, 1953, 1955, 1956, 1957, 1958, 1959, 1960 by Conrad Aiken.

"An Occurrence at Owl Creek Bridge" by Ambrose Bierce from *The Collected Writings of Ambrose Bierce*, Citadel Press, Inc. New York, 1946.

"The Circular Ruins" by Jorge Luis Borges. From the book *The Aleph and Other Stories* 1933–1969 by Jorge Luis Borges. Edited and trans. by Norman Thomas di Giovanni in collaboration with the author. Eng. trans. copyright © 1968, 1969, 1970 by Emece Editores, S.A. and Norman Thomas di Giovanni; copyright © 1970 by Jorge Luis Borges, Adolfo Bio-Casares and Norman Thomas di Giovanni. Published by E. P. Dutton & Co., Inc. and used with their permission.

"Interpretation of a Dream" by John Collier. Copyright 1951 by *The New Yorker* Magazine, reprinted by permission of the Harold Matson Company, Inc.

"The End of the Party" by Graham Greene. From *Twenty-one Stories* by Graham Greene. Copyright 1947 by Graham Greene. All rights reserved. Reprinted by permission of The Viking Press, Inc.

"The Brushwood Boy" by Rudyard Kipling. From the book *The Day's Work* by Rudyard Kipling. Reprinted by permission of Macmillan Co. of Canada Ltd., and Mrs. George Bambridge.

"Dream's End" by Henry Kuttner. Copyright 1947 by Henry Kuttner. Reprinted by permission of the Harold Matson Company, Inc.

"The Secret Songs" by Fritz Leiber. Copyright © 1962 by Mercury Press, Inc. Reprinted by permission of Robert P. Mills, Ltd.

"Lord Mountdrago" by W. Somerset Maugham. Copyright 1939 by W. Somerset Maugham from *The Mixture as Before* by W. Somerset Maugham. Reprinted by permission of Doubleday & Company, Inc. and A. P. Watt & Son.

"A Friend to Alexander" by James Thurber, copyright 1942 by James Thurber. Copyright © 1970 by Helen W. Thurber and Rosemary Thurber Sauers. From *My World and Welcome to It*, published by Harcourt Brace Jovanovich, Inc. Originally printed by *The New Yorker*.

"Under the Knife" by H. G. Wells from *The Short Stories of H. G. Wells*. Published by St. Martin's Press, 1971. Reprinted by permission of Collins-Knowlton-Wing, Inc., and The Estate of the Late H. G. Wells.

Contents

Introduction   vii

A Friend to Alexander, *James Thurber*   1

The End of the Party, *Graham Greene*   12

Dream's End, *Henry Kuttner*   23

An Occurrence at Owl Creek Bridge, *Ambrose Bierce*   40

Under the Knife, *H. G. Wells*   52

The Dream of a Ridiculous Man, *Fyodor Dostoevsky*   68

The Brushwood Boy, *Rudyard Kipling*   92

Lord Mountdrago, *W. Somerset Maugham*   130

Mr. Arcularis, *Conrad Aiken*   158

Interpretation of a Dream, *John Collier*   181

The Secret Songs, *Fritz Leiber*   189

The Circular Ruins, *Jorge Luis Borges*   202

Sometimes a thousand twangling instruments
Will hum about mine ears; and sometimes voices,
That, if I then had wak'd after long sleep,
Will make me sleep again: and then, in dreaming,
The clouds methought would open and show riches
Ready to drop on me; that, when I wak'd
I cried to dream again.

The Tempest, Act III, Scene 2

To sleep: perchance to dream: ay, there's the rub;
For in that sleep of death what dreams may come
When we have shuffled off this mortal coil,
Must give us pause.

Hamlet, Act III, Scene 1

Introduction

Dreams, according to the *Encyclopaedia Britannica,* are "illusory or hallucinatory experiences" which may take place sleeping or waking; and therefore, the encyclopedist rather quaintly concludes, a mirage must be considered "a species of dream." Sane people are able to distinguish between dream and reality; insane people are not; but this rule holds only in daylight. In sleep, "normal" people mistake the dream for reality, so that an insane person might be defined as one who behaves in the daytime as we all do at night.

The Victorians, by way of distinguishing themselves from their primitive ancestors, chose to regard dreams as nonsensical,* and it is from them that we get the most common literary attitude toward dreams. Every other culture considers them of great importance. Instances of premonitory dreams are well documented. Poems and stories sometimes come to their authors in dreams; the most familiar examples are Coleridge's *Kubla Khan* and Robert Louis Stevenson's *Strange Case of Dr. Jekyll and Mr. Hyde.* (In each case the author was interrupted: Stevenson during the dream itself [he said to his wife, "Why did you wake me? I was dreaming a fine bogey tale"] and Coleridge [by a person from Porlock] while he was engaged in setting down the poem he had dreamed.) Scientific problems have been solved in the same way, for instance the structure of the benzene ring by Friedrich August Kikule von Stradonitz, who dreamed of a snake swallowing its own tail. In recent years it has been discovered that dreaming is not an aberration or a mere indulgence of the sleeping brain, but a physiological necessity: people who are allowed to sleep but prevented from dreaming develop symptoms of stress, and eventually begin to hallucinate. Modern depth psychology was founded on the interpretation of dreams; yet in spite of all that has been written and said, we are still as far from understanding why we dream what we dream as the authors of the *Old Gypsy Dream Book.*

"Dreams, as we all know, are very queer things . . ." Dostoevsky wrote that, but it might as well have been any of the other authors

---

* As in Lewis Carroll's *Sylvie and Bruno:*
> He thought he saw a Buffalo
> Upon the chimney-piece:
> He looked again, and found it was
> His sister's husband's niece.

in this book. Notice how in Dostoevsky's story and in Wells's, the flight into cosmic space is made as a natural extension of the dream world, fifty or a hundred years before we brought it into the realm of everyday life. Both authors insist on the truth and importance of the dream; Dostoevsky says, "If once one has recognised the truth and seen it, you know that it is the truth and that there is no other and there cannot be, whether you are asleep or awake."

James Thurber, Henry Kuttner, and Jorge Luis Borges, each in his different way, question the distinction between sleeping and waking. One of these authors, and one other—I don't want to be more precise, lest I spoil your pleasure—suggest that death is a dream, or that dreaming continues after death.

Images of darkness abound in these stories. It is hard to say which is more frightening, the psychic roller-coaster of Kuttner's *Dream's End,* inexorably whirling the reader toward "the black, thundering abyss," or the understated terror of the child in Graham Greene's *The End of the Party.* But not all the stories are so alarming. Thurber's and Collier's are very funny (and Collier's, incidentally, is a perfect parody, whether so intended or not, of Maugham's *Lord Mountdrago*).

There are dreams within dreams in these stories; there are dreams that last only a moment in Ambrose Bierce's *An Occurrence at Owl Creek Bridge,* and dreams that last half a lifetime in Kipling's *The Brushwood Boy.* There are walking dreams in Aiken's *Mr. Arcularis,* and drug dreams in Leiber's *The Secret Songs.*

These are stories that I have read and loved over a period of thirty years. They seem to belong here together.

DAMON KNIGHT
Madeira Beach, Florida
April 14, 1972

A *Friend* to *Alexander*

JAMES THURBER

~~~~~~

"I have taken to dreaming about Aaron Burr every night," Andrews said.

"What for?" said Mrs. Andrews.

"How do I know what for?" Andrews snarled. "What for, the woman says."

Mrs. Andrews did not flare up; she simply looked at her husband as he lay on the chaise longue in her bedroom in his heavy blue dressing gown, smoking a cigarette. Although he had just got out of bed, he looked haggard and tired. He kept biting his lower lip between puffs.

"Aaron Burr is a funny person to be dreaming about nowadays—I mean with all the countries, in the world threatening each other. I wish you would go and see Dr. Fox," said Mrs. Andrews, taking her thumb from between the pages of her mystery novel and tossing the book toward the foot of her bed. She sat up straighter against her pillow. "Maybe haliver oil or B_1 is what you need," she said. "B_1 does wonders for people. I don't see why you see *him* in your dreams. *Where* do you see him?"

"Oh, places; in Washington Square or Bowling Green or on Broadway. I'll be talking to a woman in a victoria, a woman holding a white lace parasol, and suddenly there will be Burr, bowing and smiling and smelling like a carnation, telling his stories about France and getting off his insults."

Mrs. Andrews lighted a cigarette, although she rarely smoked until after lunch. "Who is the woman in the victoria?" she asked.

"What? How do I know? You know about people in dreams, don't you? They are nobody at all, or everybody."

"You see Aaron Burr plainly enough, though. I mean he isn't nobody or everybody."

"All right, all right," said Andrews. "You have me there. But I don't know who the woman is, and I don't care. Maybe it's Madame Jumel or Mittens Willett or a girl I knew in high school. That's not important."

"Who is Mittens Willett?" asked Mrs. Andrews.

"She was a famous New York actress in her day, fifty years ago or so. She's buried in an old cemetery on Second Avenue."

"That's very sad," said Mrs. Andrews.

"Why is it?" demanded Andrews, who was now pacing up and down the deep-red carpet.

"I mean she probably died young," said Mrs. Andrews. "Almost all women did in those days."

Andrews ignored her and walked over to a window and looked out at a neat, bleak street in the Fifties. "He's a vile, cynical cad," said Andrews, suddenly turning away from the window. "I was standing talking to Alexander Hamilton when Burr stepped up and slapped him in the face. When I looked at Hamilton, who do you suppose he was?"

"I don't know," said Mrs. Andrews. "Who was he?"

"He was my brother, the one who was killed by that drunkard in the cemetery."

Mrs. Andrews had never got that story straight and she

didn't want to go into it again now; the facts in the tragic case and her way of getting them mixed up always drove Andrews into a white-faced fury. "I don't think we ought to dwell on your nightmare," said Mrs. Andrews. "I think we ought to get out more. We could go to the country for weekends."

Andrews wasn't listening; he was back at the window, staring out into the street again.

"I wish he'd go back to France and stay there," Andrews snapped out suddenly the next morning at breakfast.

"Who, dear?" said his wife. "Oh, you mean Aaron Burr. Did you dream about him again? I don't see why you dream about him all the time. Don't you think you ought to take some Luminal?"

"No," said Andrews. "I don't know. Last night he kept shoving Alexander around."

"Alexander?"

"Hamilton. God knows I'm familiar enough with him to call him by his first name. He hides behind my coattails every night, or tries to."

"I was thinking we might go to the Old Drovers' Inn this weekend," said Mrs. Andrews. "You like it there."

"Hamilton has become not only my brother Walter but practically every other guy I have ever liked," said Andrews. "That's natural."

"Of course it is," she said. They got up from the table. "I do wish you'd go to Dr. Fox."

"I'm going to the zoo," he said, "and feed popcorn to the rhinoceros. That makes things seem right, for a little while, anyway."

It was two nights later at five o'clock in the morning that Andrews bumbled into his wife's bedroom in pajamas and bare feet, his hair in his eyes, his eyes wild. "He got him!" he croaked. "He got him! The bastard got him. Alexander fired into the air, he fired in the air and smiled at him, just like Wal-

ter, and that fiend from hell took deliberate aim—I saw him
—I saw him take deliberate aim—he killed him in cold blood,
the foul scum!"

Mrs. Andrews, not quite awake, was fumbling in the box
containing the Nembutal while her husband ranted on. She
made him take two of the little capsules, between his sobs.

Andrews didn't want to go to see Dr. Fox but he went to
humor his wife. Dr. Fox leaned back in his swivel chair behind
his desk and looked at Andrews. "Now, just what seems to be
the trouble?" he asked.

"Nothing seems to be the trouble," said Andrews.

The doctor looked at Mrs. Andrews. "He has nightmares,"
she said.

"You look a little underweight, perhaps," said the doctor.
"Are you eating well, getting enough exercise?"

"I'm not underweight," said Andrews. "I eat the way I always have and get the same exercise."

At this, Mrs. Andrews sat straighter in her chair and began
to talk, while her husband lighted a cigarette. "You see, I think
he's worried about something," she said, "because he always
has this same dream. It's about his brother Walter, who was
killed in a cemetery by a drunken man, only it isn't *really* about
him."

The doctor did the best he could with this information. He
cleared his throat, tapped on the glass top of his desk with
the fingers of his right hand, and said, "Very few people are
actually *killed* in cemeteries." Andrews stared at the doctor
coldly and said nothing. "I wonder if you would mind stepping
into the next room," the doctor said to him.

"Well, I hope you're satisfied," Andrews snapped at his wife as
they left the doctor's office a half hour later. "You heard what
he said. There's nothing the matter with me at all."

"I'm glad your heart is so fine," she told him. "He said it
was fine, you know."

"Sure," said Andrews. "It's fine. Everything's fine." They got into a cab and drove home in silence.

"I was just thinking," said Mrs. Andrews, as the cab stopped in front of their apartment building, "I was just thinking that now that Alexander Hamilton is dead, you won't see anything more of Aaron Burr." The cab driver, who was handing Andrews change for a dollar bill, dropped a quarter.

Mrs. Andrews was wrong. Aaron Burr did not depart from her husband's dreams. Andrews said nothing about it for several mornings, but she could tell. He brooded over his breakfast, did not answer any of her questions, and jumped in his chair if she dropped a knife or spoon. "Are you still dreaming about that man?" she asked him finally.

"I wish I hadn't told you about it," he said. "Forget it, will you?"

"I can't forget it with you going on this way," she said. "I think you ought to see a psychiatrist. What does he do now?"

"What does who do now?" Andrews asked.

"Aaron Burr," she said. "I don't see why he keeps coming into your dreams now."

Andrews finished his coffee and stood up. "He goes around bragging that he did it with his eyes closed," he snarled. "He says he didn't even look. He claims he can hit the ace of spades at thirty paces blindfolded. Furthermore, since you asked what he does, he jostles me at parties now."

Mrs. Andrews stood up too and put her hand on her husband's shoulder. "I think you should stay out of this, Harry," she said. "It wasn't any business of yours, anyway, and it happened so long ago."

"I'm not getting into anything," said Andrews, his voice rising to a shout. "It's getting into me. Can't you see that?"

"I see that I've got to get you away from here," she said. "Maybe if you slept someplace else for a few nights, you wouldn't dream about him any more. Let's go to the country tomorrow. Let's go to the Lime Rock Lodge."

Andrews stood for a long while without answering her. "Why can't we go and visit the Crowleys?" he said finally. "They live in the country. Bob has a pistol and we could do a little target shooting."

"What do you want to shoot a pistol for?" she asked quickly. "I should think you'd want to get away from that."

"Yeh," he said, "sure," and there was a far-off look in his eyes. "Sure."

When they drove into the driveway of the Crowleys' house, several miles north of New Milford, late the next afternoon, Andrews was whistling "Bye-Bye Blackbird." Mrs. Andrews sighed contentedly and then, as her husband stopped the car, she began looking around wildly. "My bag!" she cried. "Did I forget to bring my bag?" He laughed his old, normal laugh for the first time in many days as he found the bag and handed it to her, and then, for the first time in many days, he leaned over and kissed her.

The Crowleys came out of the house and engulfed their guests in questions and exclamations. "How you been?" said Bob Crowley to Andrews, heartily putting an arm around his shoulder.

"Never better," said Andrews, "never better. Boy, is it good to be here!"

They were swept into the house to a shakerful of Bob Crowley's icy Martinis. Mrs. Andrews stole a happy glance over the edge of her glass at her husband's relaxed face.

When Mrs. Andrews awoke the next morning, her husband lay rigidly on his back in the bed next to hers, staring at the ceiling. "Oh, God," said Mrs. Andrews.

Andrews didn't move his head. "One Henry Andrews, an architect," he said suddenly in a mocking tone. "One Henry Andrews, an architect."

"What's the matter, Harry?" she asked. "Why don't you go back to sleep? It's only eight o'clock."

"That's what he calls me!" shouted Andrews. " 'One Henry Andrews, an architect,' he keeps saying in his nasty little sneering voice. 'One Henry Andrews, an architect.' "

"Please don't yell!" said Mrs. Andrews. "You'll wake the whole house. It's early. People want to sleep."

Andrews lowered his voice a little. "I'm beneath him," he snarled. "I'm just anybody. I'm a man in a gray suit. 'Be on your good behavior, my good man,' he says to me, 'or I shall have one of my lackeys give you a taste of the riding crop.' "

Mrs. Andrews sat up in bed. "Why should he say that to you?" she asked. "He wasn't such a great man, was he? I mean, didn't he try to sell Louisiana to the French, or something, behind Washington's back?"

"He was a scoundrel," said Andrews, "but a very brilliant mind."

Mrs. Andrews lay down again. "I was in hopes you weren't going to dream about him any more," she said. "I thought if I brought you up here—"

"It's him or me," said Andrews grimly. "I can't stand this forever."

"Neither can I," Mrs. Andrews said, and there was a hint of tears in her voice.

Andrews and his host spent most of the afternoon, as Mrs. Andrews had expected, shooting at targets on the edge of the wood behind the Crowley studio. After the first few rounds, Andrews surprised Crowley by standing with his back to the huge hulk of dead tree trunk on which the target was nailed, walking thirty paces ahead in a stiff-legged, stern-faced manner, with his revolver held at arm's length above his head, then turning suddenly and firing.

Crowley dropped to the ground, uninjured but scared. "What the hell's the big idea, Harry?" he yelled.

Andrews didn't say anything, but started to walk back to the tree again. Once more he stood with his back to the target and began stepping off the thirty paces.

"I think they kept their arm hanging straight down," Bob called to him. "I don't think they stuck it up in the air."

Andrews, still counting to himself, lowered his arm, and this time, as he turned at the thirtieth step, he whirled and fired from his hip, three times in rapid succession.

"Hey!" said Crowley.

Two of the shots missed the tree but the last one hit it, about two feet under the target. Crowley looked at his house guest oddly as Andrews began to walk back to the tree again, without a word, his lips tight, his eyes bright, his breath coming fast.

"What the hell?" Crowley said to himself. "Look, it's my turn," he called, but Andrews turned, then stalked ahead, unheeding. This time when he wheeled and fired, his eyes were closed.

"Good God Almighty, man!" said Crowley from the grass, where he lay flat on his stomach. "Hey, give me that gun, will you?" he demanded, getting to his feet.

Andrews let him take it. "I need a lot more practice, I guess," he said.

"Not with me standing around," said Crowley. "Come on, let's go back to the house and shake up a drink. I've got the jumps."

"I need a lot more practice," said Andrews again.

He got his practice next morning just as the sun came up and the light was hard and the air was cold. He had crawled softly out of bed, dressed silently, and crept out of the room. He knew where Crowley kept the target pistol and the cartridges. There would be a target on the tree trunk, just as high as a man's heart. Mrs. Andrews heard the shots first and sat sharply upright in bed, crying "Harry!" almost before she was awake.

Then she heard more shots. She got up, put on a dressing gown, and went to the Crowleys' door. She heard them moving about in their room. Alice opened the door and stepped out into the hall when Mrs. Andrews knocked. "Is Harry all right?" asked Mrs. Andrews. "Where is he? What is he doing?"

"He's out shooting behind the studio, Bob says," Alice told her. "Bob'll go out and get him. Maybe he had a nightmare, or walked in his sleep."

"No," said Mrs. Andrews, "he never walks in his sleep. He's awake."

"Let's go down and put on some coffee," said Alice. "He'll need some."

Crowley came out of the bedroom and joined the women in the hallway. "I'll need some too," he said. "Good morning, Bess. I'll bring him back. What the hell's the matter with him, anyway?" He was down the stairs and gone before she could answer. She was glad of that.

"Come on," said Alice, taking her arm. They went down to the kitchen.

Mrs. Crowley found the butler in the kitchen, just standing there. "It's all right, Madison," she said. "You go back to bed. Tell Clotheta it's all right. Mr. Andrews is just shooting. He couldn't sleep."

"Yes, Ma'am," mumbled Madison, and went back to tell his wife that they said it was all right.

"It can't be right," said Clotheta, "shootin' pistols at this time of night."

"Hush up," Madison told her. He was shivering as he climbed back into bed.

"I wish dat man would go 'way from heah," grumbled Clotheta. "He's got a bad look to his eyes."

Andrews brightened Clotheta's life by going away late that afternoon. When he and his wife got in their car and drove off, the Crowleys slumped into chairs and looked at each other and said, "Well." Crowley got up finally to mix a drink. "What do you think is the matter with Harry?" he asked.

"I don't know," said his wife. "It's what Clotheta would call the shoots, I suppose."

"He said a funny thing when I went out and got him this morning," Crowley told her.

"I could stand a funny thing," she said.

"I asked him what the hell he was doing there in the freezing air with only his pants and shirt and shoes on. 'I'll get him one of these nights,' he said."

"Why don't you sleep in my room tonight?" Mrs. Andrews asked her husband as he finished his Scotch-and-water nightcap.

"You'd keep shaking me all night to keep me awake," he said. "You're afraid to let me meet him. Why do you always think everybody else is better than I am? I can outshoot him the best day he ever lived. Furthermore, I have a modern pistol. He has to use an old-fashioned single-shot muzzle-loader." Andrews laughed nastily.

"Is that quite fair?" his wife asked after a moment of thoughtful silence.

He jumped up from his chair. "What do I care if it's fair or not?" he snarled.

She got up too. "Don't be mad with me, Harry," she said. There were tears in her eyes.

"I'm sorry, darling," he said, taking her in his arms.

"I'm very unhappy," she sobbed.

"I'm sorry, darling," he said again. "Don't you worry about me. I'll be all right. I'll be fine." She was crying too wildly to say anything more.

When she kissed him good night later on she knew it was really goodbye. Women have a way of telling when you aren't coming back.

"Extraordinary," said Dr. Fox the next morning, letting Andrews' dead left hand fall back upon the bed. "His heart was as sound as a dollar when I examined him the other day. It has just stopped as if he had been shot."

Mrs. Andrews, through her tears, was looking at her dead husband's right hand. The three fingers next to the index finger were closed in stiffly on the palm, as if gripping the handle of a pistol. The taut thumb was doing its part to hold that invisible handle tightly and unwaveringly. But it was the index finger that Mrs. Andrews' eyes stayed on longest. It was only slightly curved inward, as if it were just about to press the trigger of the pistol. "Harry never even fired a shot," wailed Mrs. Andrews. "Aaron Burr killed him the way he killed Hamilton. Aaron Burr shot him through the heart. I knew he would. I knew he would."

Dr. Fox put an arm about the hysterical woman and led her from the room. "She is crazy," he said to himself. "Stark, raving crazy."

The End of the Party

GRAHAM GREENE

~~~~~~

Peter Morton woke with a start to face the first light. Through the window he could see a bare bough dropping across a frame of silver. Rain tapped against the glass. It was January the fifth.

He looked across a table, on which a night-light had guttered into a pool of water, at the other bed. Francis Morton was still asleep, and Peter lay down again with his eyes on his brother. It amused him to imagine that it was himself whom he watched, the same hair, the same eyes, the same lips and line of cheek. But the thought soon palled, and the mind went back to the fact which lent the day importance. It was the fifth of January. He could hardly believe that a year had passed since Mrs. Henne-Falcon had given her last children's party.

Francis turned suddenly upon his back and threw an arm across his face, blocking his mouth. Peter's heart began to beat fast, not with pleasure now but with uneasiness. He sat up and called across the table, "Wake up." Francis's shoulders shook and he waved a clenched fist in the air, but his eyes remained closed. To Peter Morton the whole room seemed suddenly to darken, and he had the impression of a great bird swooping. He cried again, "Wake up," and once more there was silver light and the touch of rain on the windows. Francis rubbed his eyes. "Did you call out?" he asked.

"You are having a bad dream," Peter said with confidence. Already experience had taught him how far their minds reflected each other. But he was the elder, by a matter of minutes, and that brief extra interval of light, while his brother still struggled in pain and darkness, had given him self-reliance and an instinct of protection towards the other who was afraid of so many things.

"I dreamed that I was dead," Francis said.

"What was it like?" Peter asked with curiosity.

"I can't remember," Francis said, and his eyes turned with relief to the silver of day, as he allowed the fragmentary memories to fade.

"You dreamed of a big bird."

"Did I?" Francis accepted his brother's knowledge without question, and for a little the two lay silent in bed facing each other, the same green eyes, the same nose tilting at the tip, the same firm lips parted, and the same premature modelling of the chin. The fifth of January, Peter thought again, his mind drifting idly from the image of cakes to the prizes which might be won. Egg-and-spoon races, spearing apples in basins of water, blindman's-buff.

"I don't want to go," Francis said suddenly. "I suppose Joyce will be there . . . Mabel Warren." Hateful to him, the thought of a party shared with those two. They were older then he. Joyce was eleven and Mabel Warren thirteen. Their long pigtails swung superciliously to a masculine stride. Their sex humiliated him, as they watched him fumble with his egg, from under lowered scornful lids. And last year . . . he turned his face away from Peter, his cheeks scarlet.

"What's the matter?" Peter asked.

"Oh, nothing. I don't think I'm well. I've got a cold. I oughtn't to go to the party."

Peter was puzzled. "But, Francis, is it a bad cold?"

"It will be a bad cold if I go to the party. Perhaps I shall die."

"Then you mustn't go," Peter said with decision, prepared to solve all difficulties with one plain sentence, and Francis let his nerves relax in a delicious relief, ready to leave everything to Peter. But though he was grateful he did not turn his face towards his brother. His cheeks still bore the badge of a shameful memory, of the game of hide-and-seek last year in the darkened house, and of how he had screamed when Mabel Warren put her hand suddenly upon his arm. He had not heard her coming. Girls were like that. Their shoes never squeaked. No boards whined under their tread. They slunk like cats on padded claws. When the nurse came in with hot water Francis lay tranquil, leaving everything to Peter. Peter said, "Nurse, Francis has got a cold."

The tall starched woman laid the towels across the cans and said, without turning, "The washing won't be back till tomorrow. You must lend him some of your handkerchiefs."

"But, Nurse," Peter asked, "hadn't he better stay in bed?"

"We'll take him for a good walk this morning," the nurse said. "Wind'll blow away the germs. Get up now, both of you," and she closed the door behind her.

"I'm sorry," Peter said, and then, worried at the sight of a face creased again by misery and foreboding, "Why don't you just stay in bed? I'll tell mother you felt too ill to get up." But such a rebellion against destiny was not in Francis's power. Besides, if he stayed in bed they would come up and tap his chest and put a thermometer in his mouth and look at his tongue, and they would discover that he was malingering. It was true that he felt ill, a sick empty sensation in his stomach and a rapidly beating heart, but he knew that the cause was only fear, fear of the party, fear of being made to hide by himself in the dark, uncompanioned by Peter and with no night-light to make a blessed breach.

"No, I'll get up," he said, and then with sudden desperation, "But I won't go to Mrs. Henne-Falcon's party. I swear on the Bible I won't." Now surely all would be well, he thought. God would not allow him to break so solemn an oath. He would show him a way. There was all the morning before him and all the afternoon until four o'clock. No need to worry now when the grass was still crisp with the early frost. Anything might happen. He might cut himself or break his leg or really catch a bad cold. God would manage somehow.

He had such confidence in God that when at breakfast his mother said, "I hear you have a cold, Francis," he made light of it. "We should have heard more about it," his mother said with irony, "if there was not a party this evening," and Francis smiled uneasily, amazed and daunted by her ignorance of him. His happiness would have lasted longer if, out for a walk that morning, he had not met Joyce. He was alone with his nurse, for Peter had leave to finish a rabbit-hutch in the woodshed. If Peter had been there he would have cared less; the nurse was Peter's nurse also, but now it was as though she were employed only for his sake, because he could not be trusted to go for a walk alone. Joyce was only two years older and she was by herself.

She came striding towards them, pigtails flapping. She glanced scornfully at Francis and spoke with ostentation to the nurse. "Hello, Nurse. Are you bringing Francis to the party this evening? Mabel and I are coming." And she was off again down the street in the direction of Mabel Warren's home, consciously alone and self-sufficient in the long empty road. "Such a nice girl," the nurse said. But Francis was silent, feeling again the jump-jump of his heart, realizing how soon the hour of the party would arrive. God had done nothing for him, and the minutes flew.

They flew too quickly to plan any evasion, or even to prepare his heart for the coming ordeal. Panic nearly overcame him when, all unready, he found himself standing on the doorstep, with coat-collar turned up against a cold wind, and the nurse's electric torch making a short luminous trail through the darkness. Behind him were the lights of the hall and the sound of a servant laying the table for dinner, which his mother and father would eat alone. He was nearly overcome by a desire to run back into the house and call out to his mother that he would not go to the party, that he dared not go. They could not make him go. He could almost hear himself saying those final words, breaking down for ever, as he knew instinctively, the barrier of ignorance that saved his mind from his parents' knowledge. "I'm afraid of going. I won't go. I daren't go. They'll make me hide in the dark, and I'm afraid of the dark. I'll scream and scream and scream." He could see the expression of amazement on his mother's face, and then the cold confidence of a grown-up's retort. "Don't be silly. You must go. We've accepted Mrs. Henne-Falcon's invitation."

But they couldn't make him go; hesitating on the door-step while the nurse's feet crunched across the frost-covered grass to the gate, he knew that. He would answer, "You can say I'm ill. I won't go. I'm afraid of the dark." And his mother, "Don't be silly. You know there's nothing to be afraid of in the dark." But he knew the falsity of that reasoning; he knew how they taught also that there was nothing to fear in death, and how fearfully they avoided the idea of it. But they couldn't make him go to the party. "I'll scream. I'll scream."

"Francis, come along." He heard the nurse's voice across the dimly phosphorescent lawn and saw the small yellow circle of her torch wheel from tree to shrub and back to tree again. "I'm coming," he called with despair, leaving the lighted door-

way of the house; he couldn't bring himself to lay bare his last
secrets and end reserve between his mother and himself, for
there was still in the last resort a further appeal possible to
Mrs. Henne-Falcon. He comforted himself with that, as he
advanced steadily across the hall, very small, towards her enormous bulk. His heart beat unevenly, but he had control
now over his voice, as he said with meticulous accent, "Good
evening, Mrs. Henne-Falcon. It was very good of you to ask
me to your party." With his strained face lifted towards the
curve of her breasts, and his polite set speech, he was like an
old withered man. For Francis mixed very little with other
children. As a twin he was in many ways an only child. To
address Peter was to speak to his own image in a mirror, an
image a little altered by a flaw in the glass, so as to throw
back less a likeness of what he was than of what he wished
to be, what he would be without his unreasoning fear of darkness, footsteps of strangers, the flight of bats in dusk-filled gardens.

"Sweet child," said Mrs. Henne-Falcon absent-mindedly, before, with a wave of her arms, as though the children were a
flock of chickens, she whirled them into her set programme
of entertainments: egg-and-spoon races, three-legged races, the
spearing of apples, games which held for Francis nothing worse
than humiliation. And in the frequent intervals when nothing
was required of him and he could stand alone in corners as
far removed as possible from Mabel Warren's scornful gaze,
he was able to plan how he might avoid the approaching terror
of the dark. He knew there was nothing to fear until after
tea, and not until he was sitting down in a pool of yellow
radiance cast by the ten candles on Colin Henne-Falcon's
birthday cake did he become fully conscious of the imminence
of what he feared. Through the confusion of his brain, now
assailed suddenly by a dozen contradictory plans, he heard

Joyce's high voice down the table. "After tea we are going to play hide-and-seek in the dark."

"Oh, no," Peter said, watching Francis's troubled face with pity and an imperfect understanding, "don't let's. We play that every year."

"But it's in the programme," cried Mabel Warren. "I saw it myself. I looked over Mrs. Henne-Falcon's shoulder. Five o'clock, tea. A quarter to six to half-past, hide-and-seek in the dark. It's all written down in the programme."

Peter did not argue, for if hide-and-seek had been inserted in Mrs. Henne-Falcon's programme, nothing which he could say could avert it. He asked for another piece of birthday cake and sipped his tea slowly. Perhaps it might be possible to delay the game for a quarter of an hour, allow Francis at least a few extra minutes to form a plan, but even in that Peter failed, for children were already leaving the table in twos and threes. It was his third failure, and again, the reflection of an image in another's mind, he saw a great bird darken his brother's face with its wings. But he upbraided himself silently for his folly, and finished his cake encouraged by the memory of that adult refrain, "There's nothing to fear in the dark." The last to leave the table, the brothers came together to the hall to meet the mustering and impatient eyes of Mrs. Henne-Falcon.

"And now," she said, "we will play hide-and-seek in the dark."

Peter watched his brother and saw, as he had expected, the lips tighten. Francis, he knew, had feared this moment from the beginning of the party, had tried to meet it with courage and had abandoned the attempt. He must have prayed desperately for cunning to evade the game, which was now welcomed with cries of excitement by all the other children. "Oh, do let's." "We must pick sides." "Is any of the house out of bounds?" "Where shall home be?"

"I think," said Francis Morton, approaching Mrs. Henne-Falcon, his eyes focused unwaveringly on her exuberant breasts, "it will be no use my playing. My nurse will be calling for me very soon."

"Oh, but your nurse can wait, Francis," said Mrs. Henne-Falcon absent-mindedly, while she clapped her hands together to summon to her side a few children who were already straying up the wide staircase to upper floors. "Your mother will never mind."

That had been the limit of Francis's cunning. He had refused to believe that so well prepared an excuse could fail. All that he could say now, still in the precise tone which other children hated, thinking it a symbol of conceit, was, "I think I had better not play." He stood motionless, retaining, though afraid, unmoved features. But the knowledge of his terror, or the reflection of the terror itself, reached his brother's brain. For the moment, Peter Morton could have cried aloud with the fear of bright lights going out, leaving him alone in an island of dark surrounded by the gentle lapping of strange footsteps. Then he remembered that the fear was not his own, but his brother's. He said impulsively to Mrs. Henne-Falcon, "Please. I don't think Francis should play. The dark makes him jump so." They were the wrong words. Six children began to sing, "Cowardy, cowardy custard," turning torturing faces with the vacancy of wide sunflowers towards Francis Morton.

Without looking at his brother, Francis said, "Of course I will play. I am not afraid. I only thought . . ." But he was already forgotten by his human tormentors and was able in loneliness to contemplate the approach of the spiritual, the more unbounded, torture. The children scrambled round Mrs. Henne-Falcon, their shrill voices pecking at her with questions and suggestions. "Yes, anywhere in the house. We will turn out all the lights. Yes, you can hide in the cupboards. You must stay hidden as long as you can. There will be no home."

Peter, too, stood apart, ashamed of the clumsy manner in which he had tried to help his brother. Now he could feel, creeping in at the corners of his brain, all Francis's resentment of his championing. Several children ran upstairs, and the lights on the top floor went out. Then darkness came down like the wings of a bat and settled on the landing. Others began to put out the lights at the edge of the hall, till the children were all gathered in the central radiance of the chandelier, while the bats squatted round on hooded wings and waited for that, too, to be extinguished.

"You and Francis are on the hiding side," a tall girl said, and then the light was gone, and the carpet wavered under his feet with the sibilance of footfalls, like small cold draughts, creeping away into corners.

"Where's Francis?" he wondered. "If I join him he'll be less frightened of all these sounds." "These sounds" were the casing of silence. The squeak of a loose board, the cautious closing of a cupboard door, the whine of a finger drawn along polished wood.

Peter stood in the centre of the dark deserted floor, not listening but waiting for the idea of his brother's whereabouts to enter his brain. But Francis crouched with fingers on his ears, eyes uselessly closed, mind numbed against impressions, and only a sense of strain could cross the gap of dark. Then a voice called "Coming," and as though his brother's self-possession had been shattered by the sudden cry, Peter Morton jumped with his fear. But it was not his own fear. What in his brother was a burning panic, admitting no ideas except those which added to the flame, was in him an altruistic emotion that left the reason unimpaired. "Where, if I were Francis, should I hide?" Such, roughly, was his thought. And because he was, if not Francis himself, at least a mirror to him, the answer was immediate. "Between the oak bookcase on the left of the study door and the leather settee." Peter Morton was unsurprised by the swiftness of the response. Between the twins there could be no jargon of telepathy. They had been together in the womb, and they could not be parted.

Peter Morton tiptoed towards Francis's hiding place. Occasionally a board rattled, and because he feared to be caught by one of the soft questers through the dark, he bent and untied his laces. A tag struck the floor and the metallic sound set a host of cautious feet moving in his direction. But by that time he was in his stockings and would have laughed inwardly at the pursuit had not the noise of someone stumbling on his abandoned shoes made his heart trip in the reflection of another's surprise. No more boards revealed Peter Morton's progress. On stockinged feet he moved silently and unerringly towards his object. Instinct told him that he was near the wall, and, extending a hand, he laid the fingers across his brother's face.

Francis did not cry out, but the leap of his own heart revealed to Peter a proportion of Francis's terror. "It's all right," he whispered, feeling down the squatting figure until he captured a clenched hand. "It's only me. I'll stay with you." And grasping the other tightly, he listened to the cascade of whispers his utterance had caused to fall. A hand touched the bookcase close to Peter's head and he was aware of how Francis's fear continued in spite of his presence. It was less intense, more bearable, he hoped, but it remained. He knew that it was his brother's fear and not his own that he experienced. The dark to him was only an absence of light; the groping hand that of a familiar child. Patiently he waited to be found.

He did not speak again, for between Francis and himself touch was the most intimate communion. By way of joined hands thought could flow more swiftly than lips could shape themselves round words. He could experience the whole progress of his brother's emotion, from the leap of panic at the unexpected contact to the steady pulse of fear, which now went on and on with the regularity of a heart-beat. Peter Morton thought with intensity, "I am here. You needn't be afraid. The lights will go on again soon. That rustle, that movement is nothing to fear. Only Joyce, only Mabel Warren." He bombarded the drooping form with thoughts of safety, but he was conscious that the fear continued. "They are beginning to whisper together. They are tired of looking for us. The lights will go on soon. We shall have won. Don't be afraid. That was only someone on the stairs. I believe it's Mrs. Henne-Falcon. Listen. They are feeling for the lights." Feet moving on a carpet, hands brushing a wall, a curtain pulled apart, a clicking handle, the opening of a cupboard door. In the case above their heads a loose book shifted under a touch. "Only Joyce, only Mabel Warren, only Mrs. Henne-Falcon," a crescendo of reassuring thought before the chandelier burst, like a fruit tree, into bloom.

The voices of the children rose shrilly into the radiance. "Where's Peter?" "Have you looked upstairs?" "Where's Francis?" but they were silenced again by Mrs. Henne-Falcon's scream. But she was not the first to notice Francis Morton's stillness, where he had collapsed against the wall at the touch of his brother's hand. Peter continued to hold the clenched fingers in an arid and puzzled grief. It was not merely that his brother was dead. His brain, too young to realize the full paradox, yet wondered with an obscure self-pity why it was that the pulse of his brother's fear went on and on, when Francis was now where he had been always told there was no more terror and no more darkness.

Dream's End

HENRY KUTTNER

The sanitarium was never quiet. Even when night brought comparative stillness, there was an anticipatory tension in the air—for cyclic mental disorders are as inevitable, though not as regular, as the swing of a merry-go-round.

Earlier that evening Gregson, in Ward 13, had moved into the downswing of his manic-depressive curve, and there had been trouble. Before the orderlies could buckle him into a restraining jacket, he had managed to break the arm of a "frozen" catatonic patient, who had made no sound even as the bone snapped.

Under apomorphine, Gregson subsided. After a few days he would be at the bottom of his psychic curve, dumb, motionless, and disinterested. Nothing would be able to rouse him then, for a while.

Dr. Robert Bruno, Chief of Staff, waited till the nurse had gone out with the no longer sterile hypodermic. Then he nodded at the orderly.

"All right. Prepare the patient. I want him in Surgery Three in half an hour."

He went out into the corridor, a tall, quiet man with cool blue eyes and firm lips. Dr. Kenneth Morrissey was waiting for him. The younger man looked troubled.

"Surgery, Doctor?"

"Come on," Bruno said. "We've got to get ready. How's Wheeler?"

"Simple fracture of the radius, I think. I'm having plates made."

"Turn him over to one of the other doctors," Bruno suggested. "I need your help." He used his key on the locked door. "Gregson's in good shape for the experiment."

Morrissey didn't answer. Bruno laughed a little.

"What's bothering you, Ken?"

"It's the word experiment," Morrissey said.

"Pentothal narcosynthesis was an experiment when they first tried it. So is this—empathy surrogate. If there's a risk, I'll be taking it, not Gregson."

"You can't be sure."

They stepped into the elevator.

"I *am* sure," Bruno said, with odd emphasis. "That's been my rule all my life. I make sure. I've got to *be* sure before I undertake anything new. This experiment can't possibly fail. I don't run risks with patients."

"Well—"

"Come in here." Bruno led the way from the elevator to an examination room. "I want a final check-up. Try my blood-pressure." He stripped off his white coat and deftly wound the pneumatic rubber around his arm.

"I've explained the whole situation to Gregson's wife," Bruno went on as Morrissey squeezed the bulb. "She's signed the authorization papers. She knows it's the only chance to cure Gregson. After all, Ken, the man's been insane for seven years. Cerebral deterioration's beginning to set in."

"Cellular, you mean? Um-m. I'm not worried about that. Blood-pressure okay. Heart—"

Morrissey picked up a stethoscope. After a while he nodded.

"A physician hasn't any right to be afraid of the dark," Bruno said.

"A physician isn't charting unmapped territory," Morrissey said abruptly. "You can dissect a cadaver, but you can't do that to the psyche. As a psychiatrist you should be the first to admit that we don't know all there is to know about the mind. Would you take a transfusion from a meningitis patient?"

Bruno chuckled. "Witchcraft, Ken—pure witchcraft! The germ theory of psychosis! Afraid I'll catch Gregson's insanity? I hate to disillusion you, but episodic disorders aren't contagious."

"Just because you can't see a bug doesn't mean it isn't there," Morrissey growled. "What about a filterable virus? A few years ago nobody could conceive of liquid life."

"Next you'll be going back to Elizabethan times and talking about spleen and humors." Bruno resumed his shirt and coat. He sobered. "In a way, though, this *is* a transfusion. The only type of transfusion possible. I'll admit no one knows all there is to know about psychoses. Nobody knows what makes a man think, either. But that's where physics is beginning to meet medicine. Witchcraft and medicine isolated digitalin when they met. And scientists are beginning to know the nature of thought—an electronic pattern of energy."

"Empirical!"

"Compare not the brain, but the mind itself, to a uranium pile," Bruno said. "The potentialities for atomic explosion are in the mind because you can't make a high-specialized colloid for thinking without approaching the danger level. It's the price humans pay for being *homo sapiens*. In a uranium pile you've got boron-steel bars as dampers, to absorb the neutrons before they can get out of control. In the mind, those dampers are purely psychic, naturally—but they're what keep a man sane."

"You can prove anything by symbolism," Morrissey said sourly. "And you can't stick bars of boron-steel in Gregson's skull."

"Yes, I can," Bruno said. "In effect."

"But those dampers are—*ideas!* Thoughts! You can't—"

"What is a thought?" Bruno asked.

Morrissey grimaced and followed the Chief of Staff out.

"You can chart a thought on the encephalograph—" he said stubbornly.

"Because it's a radiation. What causes that radiation? Energy emitted by certain electronic patterns. What causes electronic patterns? The basic physical structure of matter. What causes uranium to throw off neutrons under special conditions? Same answer. If a uranium pile starts to get out of control, you can damp it, if you move fast, with boron or cadmium."

"If you move fast. Why use Gregson? He's been insane for years."

"If he'd been insane for only a week, we couldn't prove it was the empathy surrogate that cured him. You're just arguing to dodge the responsibility. If you don't want to help me, I'll get somebody else."

"It would take weeks to train another man," Morrissey said. "No, I'll operate. Only—have you thought of the possible effect on your own mind?"

"Certainly," Bruno said. "Why the devil do you suppose I've been running exhaustive psychological tests on myself? I'm completely oriented, I'm so normal that my mind must be full of boron dampers." He paused at the door of his office. "Barbara's here. I'll meet you in Surgery."

Morrissey's shoulders slumped. Bruno smiled slightly and

opened the door. His wife was sitting on a leather couch, idly turning the pages of a psychiatric review.

"Studying?" Bruno said. "Want a job as a nurse?"

"Hello, darling," she said, tossing the magazine aside.

She came toward him quickly. She was small and dark and, Bruno thought academically, extremely pretty. Then his thoughts stopped being academic as he kissed her.

"What's up?"

"You're doing that operation tonight, aren't you? I wanted to wish you luck."

"How'd you know?"

"Bob," she said, "we've been married long enough so I can read your mind a little. I don't know what the operation is, but I know it's important. So—for luck!"

She kissed him again. Then, with a smile and a nod, she slipped out and was gone. Dr. Robert Bruno sighed, not unhappily, and sat behind his desk. He used the annunciator to check the sanitarium's routine, made certain everything was running smoothly, and clicked his tongue with satisfaction.

Now—the experiment. . . .

Surgery Three had some new equipment for the experiment. Bruno's collaborator, Andrew Parsons, the atomic physicist, was there, small and untidy, with a scowling, wrinkled face that looked incongruous under the surgeon's cap. There was to be no real surgery; trepanning wasn't necessary, but aseptic precautions were taken as a matter of course.

The anesthetist and two other nurses stood ready, and Morrissey, in his white gown, seemed to have forgotten his worry and had settled down to his usual quiet competence. Gregson was on one of the tables, already prepped and unconscious. Intravenous anesthesia would presently supplement the apomorphine in his system, as it would also be administered to Bruno himself.

Ferguson and Dale, two other doctors, were present. At worst quick cerebral surgery might be necessary, if anything went badly amiss. But nothing could, Bruno thought. Nothing could.

He glanced at the sleek, shining machines, with their attachments and registering dials. Not medical equipment, of course. They were in Parsons' line; he had planned and built them. But the idea had been Bruno's to begin with, and Bruno's psychiatric knowledge had complemented Parson's technology. Two branches of science had met, and the result would be—a specific for insanity.

Two spots on Bruno's head had been shaved clean. Parsons carefully affixed electrodes, which were already in place on Gregson's skull.

"Remember," Parsons said, "you should be as relaxed as possible."

"You took no sedative, Doctor," Morrissey said.

"I don't need one. The anesthetic will be enough."

The nurses moved with silent competence about the table. The emergency oxygen apparatus was tested. The adrenalin was checked; the sterilizer steamed on its table. Bruno emptied his mind and relaxed as a nurse swabbed his arm with alcohol.

Superimposure of the electronic mental matrix of sanity . . . psychic rapport . . . the pattern of his sanity-dampers would be fixed unalterably in the twisted, warped mind of the manic-depressive.

He felt the sting of the needle. Automatically he began counting. One. Two. Three. . . .

He opened his eyes. The face of Morrissey, intent and abstracted, hung over him. Beyond Morrissey was the bright ceiling fluorescent, glaring down with a brilliance that made Bruno blink. His arm stung slightly but otherwise there were no after effects.

"Can you hear me, Doctor?" Morrissey said.

Bruno nodded. "Yes. I'm awake now." His tongue was a little thick. That was natural. "Gregson?"

But Morrissey's face was growing smaller. No, it was receding. The ceiling light shrank. *He was falling—*

He shot down with blinding rapidity. White walls rushed up past him. Morrissey's face receded to a shining dot far above. It grew darker as he fell. Winds screamed, and there was a slow, gradually increasing thundering like an echo resounding from the floor of this monstrous abyss.

Down and down, faster and faster, with the white walls fading to gray and to black, till he was blind, till he was deafened with that roaring echo.

Visibility returned. Everything was out of focus. He blinked, swallowed, and made out the rectangular shape of a bedside screen. There was something else, white and irregular.

"Are you awake, Doctor?"

"Hello, Harwood," Bruno said to the nurse. "How long have I been out?"

"About two hours. I'll call Dr. Morrissey."

She stepped out of the room. Bruno flexed his muscles experimentally. He felt all right. Not even a headache. His vision was normal now. He instinctively reached for his wrist and began counting the pulse. Through the window he could see the slow motion of a branch, the leaves fluttering in a gentle wind. Footsteps sounded.

"Congratulations," Morrissey said, coming to the bed. "Gregson's in shock, but he's already beginning to come out of it. No prognosis yet, but I'll bet a cookie you've done it."

Bruno let out his breath in a long sigh. "You think so?"

Morrissey laughed. "Don't tell me you weren't sure!"

"I'm always sure," Bruno said. "Just the same, confirmation's always pleasant. I'm thirsty as the devil. Get me some ice, Ken, will you?"

"All right." Morrissey leaned out of the door and called

the nurse. Then he came back and lowered the Venetian blind. "Sun in your eyes. That better? How do you feel, or need I ask?"

"Quite normal. No ill effects at all. Say, you'd better notify Barbara I'm alive."

"I already have. She's coming over. Meanwhile, Parsons is outside. Want to see him?"

"Sure."

The physicist must have been near the door, for he appeared almost instantly.

"I'll have to depend on you now," he said. "Psychiatric examinations are out of my line, but Dr. Morrissey tells me we've apparently succeeded."

"We can't be sure yet," Bruno said cautiously, reaching for cracked ice. "I'm keeping my fingers crossed."

"How do you feel?"

"If there's a healthier specimen in this hospital than Dr. Bruno," Morrissey said, "I've yet to hear of it. I'll be back. I've got to check a patient." He went out.

Bruno lay back on his pillow.

"I'll be up and around tomorrow," he said, "and I'll want to make some tests on Gregson then. Meanwhile, I'll relax— for a change. One good thing about this place; the routine's so perfect that you can unhitch yourself completely and let yourself rest, if you want to. A dependable staff."

The Venetian blind clattered in the wind. Parsons grunted and went toward it, taking hold of the cord.

He raised the blind and stood there, his back to Bruno. But it was dark outside the window.

"The sun was in my eyes," Bruno said. "Wait a minute! That was only a little while ago. Parsons, something's wrong!"

"What?" Parsons asked, without turning.

"Morrissey said I was unconscious for only two hours. And I took anesthesia at half-past nine. At night! But the sun was shining in that window when I woke up, a few minutes ago!"

"It's night now," Parsons said.

"It can't be. Get Morrissey. I want to—"

But Parsons suddenly leaned forward and opened the window. Then he jumped out and vanished.

"*Morrissey!*" Bruno shouted.

Morrissey came in. He didn't look at Bruno. He walked quickly across the room and jumped out of the window into the darkness.

Ferguson and Dale entered, still in their operating gowns. They followed Morrissey through the window.

Bruno hoisted himself up. Three nurses came through the door. An intern and an orderly followed. Then others.

In nightmare procession the staff filed into Bruno's room. In deadly silence they walked to the window and jumped out.

The blankets slipped down from Bruno's body. He saw them sail slowly toward the window—

The bed was tilting! No—the room itself was turning, revolving, till Bruno clung frantically to the head-board while gravity dragged him inexorably toward a window that now gaped directly below him.

The bed fell. It spilled Bruno out. He saw the oblong of the window opening like a mouth to swallow him. He plunged through into utter blackness, into an echoing, roaring hell of night and thunder. . . .

"Oh, good God!" Bruno moaned. "What a dream! Morrissey, get me a sedative!"

The psychiatrist laughed. "You've had a dream-within-a-dream before, haven't you, Doctor? It sounds unnerving, but now you've told me all about it. The catharsis is better than a barbiturate."

"I suppose so." Bruno lay back in the bed.

This wasn't the room he had dreamed about. It was much

larger, and outside the windows was normal darkness. Morrissey had said that the anesthetic had lasted for several hours.

"Anyway, I'm jittery," Bruno said.

"I didn't know you had any nerves. . . . Here, Harwood."
Morrissey turned to the nurse and scribbled down a few sym-
bols on a pad. "There. We'll get your sedative. Don't you want
to know about Gregson?"

"I'd forgotten about him completely," Bruno acknowledged.
"Can you tell anything definite yet?"

"We caught him on the downcurve of the depressive cycle,
remember? Well, he isn't talking yet, but there's a touch of
euphoria. The elation will wear off. One thing, you've broken
the cycle. His mind isn't adjusted yet to those—damper bars
you put in 'em, but off-hand, I'd say it looks pretty good."

"What does Parsons think?"

"He's immersed in calculations. Said he'd be around to see
you as soon as you woke up. Here's that sedative."

Bruno accepted the capsules from the nurse and washed
them down with water.

"Thanks. I'd rather rest a bit. I must have unconsciously
piled up quite a lot of tension."

"So I gather," Morrissey said drily. "Well, here's the bell-
cord. Anything else?"

"Just rest." Bruno hesitated. "Oh—one thing." He extended
his arm. "Pinch it."

Morrissey stared and chuckled.

"Still not sure you're awake? I can assure you you are, Doctor.
I'm not going to jump out of the window. And it's still night,
you'll notice."

When Bruno didn't move, Morrissey pinched up a fold of
the other's forearm between thumb and finger.

"Ouch!" Bruno said. "Thanks."

"Any time," Morrissey said cheerfully. "Get some rest now.
I'll be back."

He went out with the nurse. Bruno blew out his breath and let his gaze wander around the room. Everything looked perfectly solid and normal. No black, thundering abyss lurked under the floor. An unpleasant dream!

He reached for pad and pencil and made careful notes on the curious double-delusion before he let himself relax. Then he felt the sedative creeping slowly along his nerves, a warm, pleasant sensation that he was glad to encourage. He didn't want to think. Later would be time enough. The empathy surrogate experiment, Gregson, the physicist Parsons, Barbara—later!

He drowsed. It seemed only a moment before he opened his eyes to see sunlight beyond the window. Brief panic touched him, then he looked at his wrist-watch and was reassured to see that it said eleven o'clock. He could hear the muffled sounds of the ordinary hospital routine going on outside door and window. Presently, feeling refreshed, he got up and dressed.

In Nurse Harwood's office he telephoned Morrissey, exchanged brief greetings, and then went to his own office to shower and shave.

He telephoned Barbara.

"Hello, there," she said. "Morrissey notified me you were doing all right. So I thought I'd wait till you woke up."

"I'm awake now. Suppose I come over to the house for lunch?"

"Swell. I'll be waiting."

"Half an hour, then?"

"Half an hour. I'm glad you called, Bob. I was worried."

"You needn't have been."

"Was your experiment a success?"

"Can't tell yet. Keep your fingers crossed."

Ten minutes later Bruno's fingers were still crossed as he examined Gregson. Parsons and Morrissey were present. The physicist kept making notes, but Morrissey stood silent and watchful.

There was very little to be seen as yet. Gregson lay in his bed, the shaved spots on his head white against the dark hair, his features relaxed and peaceful. The typical anxiety expression was gone. Bruno opened the man's eyes and flashed his light into them. Contraction of the pupils seemed normal.

"Can you hear me, Gregson?"

Gregson's lips moved. But he said nothing.

"It's all right. You're feeling fine, aren't you? You're not worried about anything, are you?"

"Headache," Gregson said. "Bad headache."

"We'll give you something for that. Now try to sleep."

Outside, in the corridor, Bruno tried hard to repress his exultation. Parsons blinked at him, scowling.

"Can you tell anything yet?"

Bruno checked himself. "No. It's too soon. But—"

"The manic-depressive phase is passed," Morrissey put in. "He seems rational. And he hasn't been for three years."

"Those damper bars—" Bruno smiled. "Well, we'll have to wait and see. We can't write up a report yet. He's certainly oriented. We'll give him a chance to rest. More tests later. I don't want to jump the gun."

But with Barbara he let himself be more enthusiastic.

"We've done it, Barbara! Found a specific for insanity."

She leaned across the table to pour coffee.

"I thought there were so many types of psychosis that the treatment varied considerably."

"Well, that's true, but we've never got to the real basis of the trouble before. You can cure a cold by rest therapy, force fluids and aspirin, but cold vaccine gets directly to the root of the trouble. Some types of insanity have been thought incurable, but tetanus was incurable till we got a vaccine for it. The empathy surrogate therapy is the lowest common denominator. It works on the electronic structure of the mind, and unless there's physical deterioration, as in advanced paresis, our treatment should work beautifully."

"So that's what you were working on," Barbara said. "Bob, you don't know how glad I am that it's successful."

"Well—we hope. We're almost sure. But—"

"You can take a vacation now? You've been working so hard!"

"A few more weeks, and I'll be ready. I've got to collate my notes. I can't run out on Parsons at this stage. But very soon, I promise."

He looked up to see her smile. Suddenly he stiffened. Her smile was broadening, stretching, the lower lip dropping till all her teeth showed. The lower lids of her eyes hung . . . stretched. . . .

Her nose lengthened.

Her eyes slowly crawled out of their sockets and lengthened on dreadful stalks down her cheeks.

She melted down and out of sight beneath the table.

The table began to sink.

And now everything around him was melting. Under him the chair became plastic and then fluid. The floor was a bowl, and the walls were dripping down into it, into a shining whirlpool at the center.

He slipped helplessly along that slope till the pool engulfed him, in a chaos of thunder and confusion and sickening horror.

The winds bellowed. . . . The empty drop closed around him. . . . He fell in darkness. . . .

This time, when he woke, he wasn't sure. The panic had not left him. He learned, later, that he had been semi-delirious for eight days, and only Morrissey's unceasing attention had kept him reasonably quiet. Then there were weeks of convalescence, and a vacation, and it seemed a long time before he came back from Florida, tanned and healthy, to resume his duties.

Even then, though, there was the fear.

When he drove toward the blocky buildings of the sanitarium he felt a touch of it brush him. He reached for Barbara's hand, and felt some comfort in the assurance of her nearness. She had been helpful, too, though she had not understood.

Every day after that, when he left her, there was a fleeting apprehension lest he never see her again. To forget the uncertainty of his footing, the ground that was no longer absolutely solid, he plunged into the hospital's routine. And gradually, after more weeks, the terror began to leave him.

Gregson had been cured. He was still under precautionary observation, but all traces of his psychosis seemed to have vanished. There were still minor neuroses, the natural result of the past six years of abnormal restraint, but they were disappearing under proper therapy. The empathy surrogate treatment was successful. Yet, for a while, Bruno refused to attempt more experiments.

Parsons was displeased. He was anxious to chart a graph on the process, and one trial did not provide enough evidence. Bruno kept putting the physicist off with promises. It eventually ended in a minor spat which Morrissey halted by pointing out that Dr. Robert Bruno was, technically, his own patient, and was not yet ready for further research on the dangerous subject.

Parsons, furious, went off. Bruno followed Morrissey into the latter's office and sat down in one of the more comfortable chairs. It was mid-afternoon, and beyond the windows the drowsy hum of summer made a peaceful counterpoint to the conversation.

"Cigarette, Ken?"

"Thanks. . . . Look, Bob." The two men had drawn closer

together in the last weeks. Morrissey no longer addressed his Chief of Staff with the formal "Doctor." "I've been collating the facts of your case, and I think I've got at the root of the trouble. Do you want to hear my diagnosis?"

"Candidly, I don't," Bruno said, closing his eyes and inhaling smoke. "I'd prefer to forget it. But I know I can't. That would be psychically ruinous."

"You had a cyclic self-containing dream—I suppose you could call it that. You dreamed you were dreaming you were dreaming. You know what your trouble is?"

"Well?"

"You're not sure you're awake now."

"Oh, I'm sure enough," Bruno said. "Most of the time."

"You've got to be sure all the time. Or else make yourself believe that it doesn't matter whether you're dreaming or waking."

"Doesn't matter! Ken! To know that everything may melt away under my feet at any time, and to think that doesn't matter! That's impossible!"

"Then you've got to be sure you're awake. Those hallucinations you had are over. Weeks have passed."

"Hallucinatory time is elastic and subjective."

"It's a defense mechanism—you know that, I suppose?"

"Defense against what?"

Morrissey moistened his lips. "Remember, I'm the psychiatrist and you're the patient. You were psychoanalyzed when you studied psychiatry, but you didn't get all the devils out of your subconscious. Hang it, Bob, you know very well that most psychiatrists take up the work because they're attracted to it for pathological reasons—neuroses of their own. Why did you always insist that you were so utterly sure of everything?"

"I always made sure."

"Compensation. To allow for a basic unsureness and insecurity in your own make-up. Consciously you were sure the empathy surrogate treatment would work, but your unconscious mind wasn't so certain. You never let yourself know that, though. But it came out under stress—the therapy itself."

"Go on," Bruno said slowly.

Morrissey tapped the papers on his desk.

"I know my diagnosis is pretty accurate, but you can decide that for yourself. You can tell, perhaps, better than I can. The frontiers of the mind are *terra incognita.* Your simile of a uranium pile was better than you'd realized. When critical mass is approached, there's danger. And the damper bars in your own mind—what did Parsons' machine do to them?"

"I am quite sane," Bruno said. "I think."

"Sure you are, now. You're getting over that explosion. You'd been building up an anxiety neurosis, and the therapy made it blow off. Just how, I don't understand. The electronic patterns of the mind aren't in my field. All I know is that the experiment with Gregson removed the safety blocks from your mind, and you lost control for a while. Thus the hallucinations, which simply followed the path of least resistance. Point One: You're afraid of insecurity and unsureness, and you always have been. Thus your dream follows a familiarly symbolic pattern. At any time the sureness of waking may vanish. Point Two: As long as you think you're dreaming, you're dodging responsibility!"

"Good Lord, Ken!" Bruno said. "I just want to be sure I'm awake!"

"And there's absolutely no way you can be sure of that," Morrissey said. "The conviction must come from your own mind and be subjective. No objective proof is possible. Otherwise, if you fail to convince yourself, the anxiety neurosis will grow back into a psychosis, and—" He shrugged.

"It sounds logical," Bruno said. "I'm beginning to see it pretty clearly. I think, perhaps, this clarification is what I needed."

"Do you think you're dreaming now?"

"Not at the moment—certainly."

"Swell," Morrissey said. "Because the conglobulation of the psych between the forever and upstriding kaleeno bystixing forinder saan—"

Bruno jumped up. "Ken!" he said, dry-throated. "Stop it!"

"Fylixar catween baleeza—"

"*Stop it!*"

"BYZINDERKONA REPSTILLING AND ALWAYS ALWAYS ALWAYS NEVER KNOWING NEVER KNOWING NEVER KNOWING—"

The words came out in great whirling shining globes. They raced past Bruno's head with a screaming hiss. They bombarded him. They carried him back into a thundering, windy abyss of blackness and terror.

Morrissey stepped back from the bed and asked: "Can you understand me now?"

Dr. Robert Bruno managed to nod.

"Good," Morrissey said. "You were out for about three hours. But everything's going nicely. You'll be up and around pretty soon. There's plenty to be done. Barbara wants to see you—and Parsons."

"Ken," Bruno said, "wait a minute. Am I awake now? I mean, really awake?"

Morrissey stared and grinned.

"Sure," he said. "I can guarantee that."

But Bruno did not answer. His gaze moved to the windows, to the solidity of the walls and ceiling, to the reality of his own hands and arms.

Never knowing?

He looked at Morrissey, waiting for Morrissey to vanish, and the black pit to open again beneath him.

An Occurrence at Owl Creek Bridge

AMBROSE BIERCE

~~~~~~

I

A man stood upon a railroad bridge in northern Alabama, looking down into the swift water twenty feet below. The man's hands were behind his back, the wrists bound with a cord. A rope closely encircled his neck. It was attached to a stout cross-timber above his head and the slack fell to the level of his knees. Some loose boards laid upon the sleepers supporting the metals of the railway supplied a footing for him and his executioners—two private soldiers of the Federal army, directed by a sergeant who in civil life may have been a deputy sheriff. At a short remove upon the same temporary platform was an officer in the uniform of his rank, armed. He was a captain. A sentinel at each end of the bridge stood with his rifle in the position known as "support," that is to say, vertical in front of the left shoulder, the hammer resting on the forearm thrown straight across the chest—a formal and unnatural position, enforcing an erect carriage of the body. It did not appear to be the duty of these two men to know what was occurring at the centre of the bridge; they merely blockaded the two ends of the foot planking that traversed it.

Beyond one of the sentinels nobody was in sight; the railroad ran straight away into a forest for a hundred yards, then, curving, was lost to view. Doubtless there was an outpost farther along. The other bank of the stream was open ground—a gentle acclivity topped with a stockade of vertical tree trunks, loopholed for rifles, with a single embrasure through which protruded the muzzle of a brass cannon commanding the bridge. Midway of the slope between bridge and fort were the spectators—a single company of infantry in line, at "parade rest," the butts of the rifles on the ground, the barrels inclining slightly backward against the right shoulder, the hands crossed upon the stock. A lieutenant stood at the right of the line, the point of his sword upon the ground, his left hand resting upon his right. Excepting the group of four at the centre of the bridge, not a man moved. The company faced the bridge, staring stonily, motionless. The sentinels, facing the banks of the stream, might have been statues to adorn the bridge. The captain stood with folded arms, silent, observing the work of his subordinates, but making no sign. Death is a dignitary who when he comes announced is to be received with formal manifestations of respect, even by those most familiar with him. In the code of military etiquette silence and fixity are forms of deference.

The man who was engaged in being hanged was apparently about thirty-five years of age. He was a civilian, if one might judge from his habit, which was that of a planter. His features were good—a straight nose, firm mouth, broad forehead, from which his long, dark hair was combed straight back, falling behind his ears to the collar of his well-fitting frock-coat. He wore a mustache and pointed beard, but no whiskers; his eyes were large and dark gray, and had a kindly expression which one would hardly have expected in one whose neck was in the hemp. Evidently this was no vulgar assassin. The liberal military code makes provision for hanging many kinds of persons, and gentlemen are not excluded.

The preparations being complete, the two private soldiers stepped aside and each drew away the plank upon which he had been standing. The sergeant turned to the captain, saluted and placed himself immediately behind that officer, who in turn moved apart one pace. These movements left the condemned man and the sergeant standing on the two ends of the same plank, which spanned three of the cross-ties of the bridge. The end upon which the civilian stood almost, but not quite, reached a fourth. This plank had been held in place by the weight of the captain; it was now held by that of the sergeant. At a signal from the former the latter would step aside, the plank would tilt and the condemned man go down between two ties. The arrangement commended itself to his judgment as simple and effective. His face had not been covered nor his eyes bandaged. He looked a moment at his "unsteadfast footing," then let his gaze wander to the swirling water of the stream racing madly beneath his feet. A piece of dancing driftwood caught his attention and his eyes followed it down the current. How slowly it appeared to move! What a sluggish stream!

He closed his eyes in order to fix his last thoughts upon his wife and children. The water, touched to gold by the early sun, the brooding mists under the banks at some distance down the stream, the fort, the soldiers, the piece of drift—all had distracted him. And now he became conscious of a new disturbance. Striking through the thought of his dear ones was a sound which he could neither ignore nor understand, a sharp, distinct, metallic percussion like the stroke of a blacksmith's hammer upon the anvil; it had the same ringing quality. He wondered what it was, and whether immeasurably distant or near by—it seemed both. Its recurrence was regular, but as slow as the tolling of a death knell. He awaited each stroke with impatience and—he knew not why—apprehension. The intervals of silence grew progressively longer; the delays became maddening. With their greater infrequency the sounds increased in strength and sharpness. They hurt his ear like the thrust of a knife; he feared he would shriek. What he heard was the ticking of his watch.

He unclosed his eyes and saw again the water below him. "If I could free my hands," he thought, "I might throw off the noose and spring into the stream. By diving I could evade the bullets and, swimming vigorously, reach the bank, take to the woods and get away home. My home, thank God, is as yet outside their lines; my wife and little ones are still beyond the invader's farthest advance."

As these thoughts, which have here to be set down in words, were flashed into the doomed man's brain rather than evolved from it the captain nodded to the sergeant. The sergeant stepped aside.

II

Peyton Farquhar was a well-to-do planter, of an old and highly respected Alabama family. Being a slave owner and like other slave owners a politician he was naturally an original secessionist and ardently devoted to the Southern cause. Circumstances of an imperious nature, which it is unnecessary to relate here, had prevented him from taking service with the gallant army that had fought the disastrous campaigns ending with the fall of Corinth, and he chafed under the inglorious restraint, longing for the release of his energies, the larger life of the soldier, the opportunity for distinction. That opportunity, he felt, would come, as it comes to all in war time. Meanwhile he did what he could. No service was too humble for him to perform in aid of the South, no adventure too perilous for him to undertake if consistent with the character of a civilian who was at heart a soldier, and who in good faith and without too much qualification assented to at least a part of the frankly villainous dictum that all is fair in love and war.

One evening while Farquhar and his wife were sitting on a rustic bench near the entrance to his grounds, a gray-clad soldier rode up to the gate and asked for a drink of water. Mrs. Farquhar was only too happy to serve him with her own white hands. While she was fetching the water her husband approached the dusty horseman and inquired eagerly for news from the front.

"The Yanks are repairing the railroads," said the man, "and are getting ready for another advance. They have reached the Owl Creek bridge, put it in order and built a stockade on the north bank. The commandant has issued an order, which is posted everywhere, declaring that any civilian caught interfering with the railroad, its bridges, tunnels or trains will be summarily hanged. I saw the order."

"How far is it to the Owl Creek bridge?" Farquhar asked.

"About thirty miles."

"Is there no force on this side the creek?"

"Only a picket post half a mile out, on the railroad, and a single sentinel at this end of the bridge."

"Suppose a man—a civilian and student of hanging—should elude the picket post and perhaps get the better of the sentinel," said Farquhar, smiling, "what could he accomplish?"

The soldier reflected. "I was there a month ago," he replied. "I observed that the flood of last winter had lodged a great quantity of driftwood against the wooden pier at this end of the bridge. It is now dry and would burn like tow."

The lady had now brought the water, which the soldier drank. He thanked her ceremoniously, bowed to her husband and rode away. An hour later, after nightfall, he repassed the plantation, going northward in the direction from which he had come. He was a Federal scout.

III

As Peyton Farquhar fell straight downward through the bridge he lost consciousness and was as one already dead. From this state he was awakened—ages later, it seemed to him—by the pain of a sharp pressure upon his throat, followed by a sense of suffocation. Keen, poignant agonies seemed to shoot from his neck downward through every fibre of his body and limbs. These pains appeared to flash along well-defined lines of ramification and to beat with an inconceivably rapid periodicity. They seemed like streams of pulsating fire heating him to an intolerable temperature. As to his head, he was conscious of nothing but a feeling of fulness—of congestion. These sensations were unaccompanied by thought. The intellectual part of his nature was already effaced; he had power only to feel, and feeling was torment. He was conscious of motion. Encompassed in a luminous cloud, of which he was now merely the fiery heart, without material substance, he swung through unthinkable arcs of oscillation, like a vast pendulum. Then all at once, with terrible suddenness, the light about him shot upward with the noise of a loud plash; a frightful roaring was in his ears, and all was cold and dark. The power of thought was restored; he knew that the rope had broken and he had fallen into the stream. There was no additional strangulation; the noose about his neck was already suffocating him and kept the water from his lungs. To die of hanging at the bottom of a river!—the idea seemed to him ludicrous. He opened his eyes in the darkness and saw above him a gleam of light, but how distant, how inaccessible! He was still sinking, for the light became fainter and fainter until it was a mere glimmer. Then it began to grow and brighten, and he knew that he was rising toward the surface—knew it with reluctance, for he was now very comfortable. "To be hanged and drowned," he thought, "that is not so bad; but I do not wish to be shot. No; I will not be shot; that is not fair."

He was not conscious of an effort, but a sharp pain in his wrist apprised him that he was trying to free his hands. He gave the struggle his attention, as an idler might observe the feat of a juggler, without interest in the outcome. What splendid effort!—what magnificent, what superhuman strength! Ah, that was a fine endeavor! Bravo! The cord fell away; his arms parted and floated upward, the hands dimly seen on each side in the growing light. He watched them with a new interest as first one and then the other pounced upon the noose at his neck. They tore it away and thrust it fiercely aside, its undulations resembling those of a water-snake. "Put it back, put it back!" He thought he shouted these words to his hands, for the undoing of the noose had been succeeded by the direst pang that he had yet experienced. His neck ached horribly; his brain was on fire; his heart, which had been fluttering faintly, gave a great leap, trying to force itself out at his mouth. His whole body was racked and wrenched with an insupportable anguish! But his disobedient hands gave no heed to the command. They beat the water vigorously with quick, downward strokes, forcing him to the surface. He felt his head emerge; his eyes were blinded by the sunlight; his chest expanded convulsively, and with a supreme and crowning agony his lungs engulfed a great draught of air, which instantly he expelled in a shriek!

He was now in full possession of his physical senses. They

were, indeed, preternaturally keen and alert. Something in the awful disturbance of his organic system had so exalted and refined them that they made record of things never before perceived. He felt the ripples upon his face and heard their separate sounds as they struck. He looked at the forest on the bank of the stream, saw the individual trees, the leaves and the veining of each leaf—saw the very insects upon them: the locusts, the brilliant-bodied flies, the gray spiders stretching their webs from twig to twig. He noted the prismatic colors in all the dewdrops upon a million blades of grass. The humming of the gnats that danced above the eddies of the stream, the beating of the dragon-flies' wings, the strokes of the water-spiders' legs, like oars which had lifted their boat—all these made audible music. A fish slid along beneath his eyes and he heard the rush of its body parting the water.

He had come to the surface facing down the stream; in a moment the visible world seemed to wheel slowly round, himself the pivotal point, and he saw the bridge, the fort, the soldiers upon the bridge, the captain, the sergeant, the two privates, his executioners. They were in silhouette against the blue sky. They shouted and gesticulated, pointing at him. The captain had drawn his pistol, but did not fire; the others were unarmed. Their movements were grotesque and horrible, their forms gigantic.

Suddenly he heard a sharp report and something struck the water smartly within a few inches of his head, spattering his face with spray. He heard a second report, and saw one of the sentinels with his rifle at his shoulder, a light cloud of blue smoke rising from the muzzle. The man in the water saw the eye of the man on the bridge gazing into his own through the sights of the rifle. He observed that it was a gray eye and remembered having read that gray eyes were keenest, and that all famous marksmen had them. Nevertheless, this one had missed.

A counter-swirl had caught Farquhar and turned him half

round; he was again looking into the forest on the bank opposite the fort. The sound of a clear, high voice in a monotonous sing-song now rang out behind him and came across the water with a distinctness that pierced and subdued all other sounds, even the beating of the ripples in his ears. Although no soldier, he had frequented camps enough to know the dread significance of that deliberate, drawling, aspirated chant; the lieutenant on shore was taking a part in the morning's work. How coldly and piti-lessly—with what an even, calm intonation, presaging, and en-forcing tranquillity in the men—with what accurately meas-ured intervals fell those cruel words:

"Attention, company! . . . Shoulder arms! . . . Ready! . . . Aim! . . . Fire!"

Farquhar dived—dived as deeply as he could. The water roared in his ears like the voice of Niagara, yet he heard the dulled thunder of the volley and, rising again toward the surface, met shining bits of metal, singularly flattened, oscillating slowly downward. Some of them touched him on the face and hands, then fell away, continuing their descent. One lodged between his collar and neck; it was uncomfortably warm and he snatched it out.

As he rose to the surface, gasping for breath, he saw that he had been a long time under water; he was perceptibly farther down stream—nearer to safety. The soldiers had almost finished reloading; the metal ramrods flashed all at once in the sunshine as they were drawn from the barrels, turned in the air, and thrust into their sockets. The two sentinels fired again, independently and ineffectually.

The hunted man saw all this over his shoulder; he was now swimming vigorously with the current. His brain was as ener-getic as his arms and legs; he thought with the rapidity of light-ning.

"The officer," he reasoned, "will not make that martinet's error a second time. It is as easy to dodge a volley as a single shot.

He has probably already given the command to fire at will. God help me, I cannot dodge them all!"

An appalling plash within two yards of him was followed by a loud, rushing sound, *diminuendo*, which seemed to travel back through the air to the fort and died in an explosion which stirred the very river to its deeps! A rising sheet of water curved over him, fell down upon him, blinded him, strangled him! The cannon had taken a hand in the game. As he shook his head free from the commotion of the smitten water he heard the deflected shot humming through the air ahead, and in an instant it was cracking and smashing the branches in the forest beyond.

"They will not do that again," he thought; "the next time they will use a charge of grape. I must keep my eye upon the gun; the smoke will apprise me—the report arrives too late; it lags behind the missile. That is a good gun."

Suddenly he felt himself whirled round and round—spinning like a top. The water, the banks, the forests, the now distant bridge, fort and men—all were commingled and blurred. Objects were represented by their colors only; circular horizontal streaks of color—that was all he saw. He had been caught in a vortex and was being whirled on with a velocity of advance and gyration that made him giddy and sick. In a few moments he was flung upon the gravel at the foot of the left bank of the stream —the southern bank—and behind a projecting point which concealed him from his enemies. The sudden arrest of his motion, the abrasion of one of his hands on the gravel, restored him, and he wept with delight. He dug his fingers into the sand, threw it over himself in handfuls and audibly blessed it. It looked like diamonds, rubies, emeralds; he could think of nothing beautiful which it did not resemble. The trees upon the bank were giant garden plants; he noted a definite order in their arrangement, inhaled the fragrance of their blooms. A strange, roseate light shone through the spaces among their trunks and the wind made in their branches the music of aeolian harps. He had no wish to perfect his escape—was content to remain in that enchanting spot until retaken.

A whiz and rattle of grapeshot among the branches high above his head roused him from his dream. The baffled cannoneer had fired him a random farewell. He sprang to his feet, rushed up the sloping bank, and plunged into the forest.

All that day he traveled, laying his course by the rounding sun. The forest seemed interminable; nowhere did he discover a break in it, not even a woodman's road. He had not known that he lived in so wild a region. There was something uncanny in the revelation.

By nightfall he was fatigued, footsore, famishing. The thought of his wife and children urged him on. At last he found a road which led him in what he knew to be the right direction. It was as wide and straight as a city street, yet it seemed untraveled. No fields bordered it, no dwelling anywhere. Not so much as the barking of a dog suggested human habitation. The black bodies of the trees formed a straight wall on both sides, terminating on the horizon in a point, like a diagram in a lesson in perspective. Overhead, as he looked up through this rift in the wood, shone great golden stars looking unfamiliar and grouped in strange constellations. He was sure they were arranged in some order which had a secret and malign significance. The wood on either side was full of singular noises, among which—once, twice, and again—he distinctly heard whispers in an unknown tongue.

His neck was in pain and lifting his hand to it he found it horribly swollen. He knew that it had a circle of black where the rope had bruised it. His eyes felt congested; he could no longer close them. His tongue was swollen with thirst; he relieved its fever by thrusting it forward from between his teeth into the cold air. How softly the turf had carpeted the untraveled avenue—he could no longer feel the roadway beneath his feet!

Doubtless, despite his suffering, he had fallen asleep while walking, for now he sees another scene—perhaps he has merely recovered from a delirium. He stands at the gate of his own home. All is as he left it, and all bright and beautiful in the morning sunshine. He must have traveled the entire night. As he pushes open the gate and passes up the wide white walk, he sees a flutter of female garments; his wife, looking fresh and cool and sweet, steps down from the veranda to meet him. At the bottom of the steps she stands waiting, with a smile of ineffable joy, an attitude of matchless grace and dignity. Ah, how beautiful she is! He springs forward with extended arms. As he is about to clasp her he feels a stunning blow upon the back of the neck; a blinding white light blazes all about him with a sound like the shock of a cannon—then all is darkness and silence!

Peyton Farquhar was dead; his body, with a broken neck, swung gently from side to side beneath the timbers of the Owl Creek bridge.

Under the Knife

H. G. WELLS

~~~~~~

"What if I die under it?" The thought recurred again and again, as I walked home from Haddon's. It was a purely personal question. I was spared the deep anxieties of a married man, and I knew there were few of my intimate friends but would find my death troublesome chiefly on account of their duty of regret. I was surprised indeed, and perhaps a little humiliated, as I turned the matter over, to think how few could possibly exceed the conventional requirement. Things came before me stripped of glamour, in a clear dry light, during that walk from Haddon's house over Primrose Hill. There were the friends of my youth: I perceived now that our affection was a tradition, which we foregathered rather laboriously to maintain. There were the rivals and helpers of my later career: I suppose I had been cold-blooded or undemonstrative—one perhaps implies the other. It may be that even the capacity for friendship is a question of physique. There had been a time in my own life when I had grieved bitterly enough at the loss of a friend; but as I walked home that afternoon the emotional side of my imagination was dormant. I could not pity myself, nor feel sorry for my friends, nor conceive of them as grieving for me.

I was interested in this deadness of my emotional nature— no doubt a concomitant of my stagnating physiology; and my thoughts wandered off along the line it suggested. Once before, in my hot youth, I had suffered a sudden loss of blood, and had been within an ace of death. I remembered now that my affections as well as my passions had drained out of me, leaving scarce anything but a tranquil resignation, a dreg of self-pity. It had been weeks before the old ambitions and tendernesses and all the complex moral interplay of a man had reasserted themselves. It occurred to me that the real meaning of this numbness might be a gradual slipping away from the pleasure-pain guidance of the animal man. It has been proven, I take it, as thoroughly as anything can be proven in this world, that the higher emotions, the moral feelings, even the subtle unselfishness of love, are evolved from the elemental desires and fears of the simple animal: they are the harness in which man's mental freedom goes. And it may be that as death overshadows us, as our possibility of acting diminishes, this complex growth of balanced impulse, propensity and aversion, whose interplay inspires our acts, goes with it. Leaving what?

I was suddenly brought back to reality by an imminent collision with the butcher-boy's tray. I found that I was crossing the bridge over the Regent's Park Canal, which runs parallel with that in the Zoological Gardens. The boy in blue had been looking over his shoulder at a black barge advancing slowly, towed by a gaunt white horse. In the Gardens a nurse was leading three happy little children over the bridge. The trees were bright green; the spring hopefulness was still unstained by the dusts of summer; the sky in the water was bright and clear, but broken by long waves, by quivering bands of black, as the barge drove through. The breeze was stirring; but it did not stir me as the spring breeze used to do.

Was this dulness of feeling in itself an anticipation? It was curious that I could reason and follow out a network of suggestion as clearly as ever: so, at least, it seemed to me. It was calmness rather than dulness that was coming upon me. Was there any ground for the belief in the presentiment of death? Did a man near to death begin instinctively to withdraw himself from the meshes of matter and sense, even before the cold hand was laid upon his? I felt strangely isolated—isolated without regret—from the life and existence about me. The children playing in the sun and gathering strength and experience for the business of life, the park-keeper gossiping with a nurse-maid, the nursing mother, the young couple intent upon each other as they passed me, the trees by the wayside spreading new pleading leaves to the sunlight, the stir in their branches—I had been part of it all, but I had nearly done with it now.

Some way down the Broad Walk I perceived that I was tired, and that my feet were heavy. It was hot that afternoon, and I turned aside and sat down on one of the green chairs that line the way. In a minute I had dozed into a dream, and the tide of my thoughts washed up a vision of the resurrection. I was still sitting in the chair, but I thought myself actually dead, withered, tattered, dried, one eye (I saw) pecked out by birds. "Awake!" cried a voice; and incontinently the dust of the path and the mould under the grass became insurgent. I had never before thought of Regent's Park as a cemetery, but now, through the trees, stretching as far as eye could see, I beheld a flat plain of writhing graves and heeling tombstones. There seemed to be some trouble: the rising dead appeared to stifle as they struggled upward, they bled in their struggles, the red flesh was torn away from the white bones. "Awake!" cried a voice; but I determined I would not rise to such horrors. "Awake!" They would not let me alone. "Wike up!" said an angry voice. A cockney angel! The man who sells the tickets was shaking me, demanding my penny.

I paid my penny, pocketed my ticket, yawned, stretched my legs, and, feeling now rather less torpid, got up and walked on towards Langham Place. I speedily lost myself again in a shifting maze of thoughts about death. Going across Marylebone Road into that crescent at the end of Langham Place, I had the narrowest escape from the shaft of a cab, and went on my way with a palpitating heart and a bruised shoulder. It struck me that it would have been curious if my meditations on my death on the morrow had led to my death that day.

But I will not weary you with more of my experiences that day and the next. I knew more and more certainly that I should die under the operation; at times I think I was inclined to pose to myself. The doctors were coming at eleven, and I did not get up. It seemed scarce worth while to trouble about washing and dressing, and though I read my newspapers and the letters that came by the first post, I did not find them very interesting. There was a friendly note from Addison, my old school-friend, calling my attention to two discrepancies and a printer's error in my new book, with one from Langridge venting some vexation over Minton. The rest were business communications. I breakfasted in bed. The glow of pain at my side seemed more massive. I knew it was pain, and yet, if you can understand, I did not find it very painful. I had been awake and hot and thirsty in the night, but in the morning bed felt comfortable. In the night-time I had lain thinking of things that were past; in the morning I dozed over the question of immortality. Haddon came, punctual to the minute, with a neat black bag; and Mowbray soon followed. Their arrival stirred me up a little. I began to take a more personal interest in the proceedings. Haddon moved the little octagonal table close to the bedside, and, with his broad back to me, began taking things out of his bag. I heard the light click of steel upon steel. My imagination, I found, was not altogether stagnant. "Will you hurt me much?" I said in an off-hand tone.

"Not a bit," Haddon answered over his shoulder. "We shall chloroform you. Your heart's as sound as a bell." And as he spoke, I had a whiff of the pungent sweetness of the anaesthetic.

They stretched me out, with a convenient exposure of my side, and, almost before I realised what was happening, the chloroform was being administered. It stings the nostrils, and there is a suffocating sensation at first. I knew I should die— that this was the end of consciousness for me. And suddenly I felt that I was not prepared for death: I had a vague sense of a duty overlooked—I knew not what. What was it I had not done? I could think of nothing more to do, nothing desirable left in life; and yet I had the strangest disinclination to death. And the physical sensation was painfully oppressive. Of course the doctors did not know they were going to kill me. Possibly I struggled. Then I fell motionless, and a great silence, a monstrous silence, and an impenetrable blackness came upon me.

There must have been an interval of absolute unconsciousness, seconds or minutes. Then with a chilly, unemotional clearness, I perceived that I was not yet dead. I was still in my body; but all the multitudinous sensations that come sweeping from it to make up the background of consciousness had gone, leaving me free of it all. No, not free of it all; for as yet something still held me to the poor stark flesh upon the bed—held me yet not so closely that I did not feel myself external to it, independent of it, straining away from it. I do not think I saw, I do not think I heard; but I perceived all that was going on, and it was as if I both heard and saw. Haddon was bending over me, Mowbray behind me; the scalpel—it was a large scalpel—was cutting my flesh at the side under the flying ribs. It was interesting to see myself cut like cheese, without a pang, without even a qualm. The interest was much of a quality with that one might feel in a game of chess between strangers. Haddon's face was firm and his hand steady; but I was surprised to perceive (*how* I know not) that he was feeling the gravest doubt as to his own wisdom in the conduct of the operation. Mowbray's thoughts, too, I could see. He was thinking that Haddon's manner showed too much of the specialist. New suggestions came up like bubbles through a stream of frothing meditation, and burst one after another in the little bright spot of his consciousness. He could not help noticing and admiring Haddon's swift dexterity, in spite of his envious quality and his disposition to detract. I saw my liver exposed. I was puzzled at my own condition. I did not feel that I was dead, but I was different in some way from my living self. The grey depression, that had weighed on me for a year or more and coloured all my thoughts, was gone. I perceived and thought without any emotional tint at all. I wondered if everyone perceived things in this way under chloroform, and forgot it again when he came out of it. It would be inconvenient to look into some heads, and not forget.

Although I did not think that I was dead, I still perceived quite clearly that I was soon to die. This brought me back to the consideration of Haddon's proceedings. I looked into his mind, and saw that he was afraid of cutting a branch of the portal vein. My attention was distracted from details by the curious changes going on in his mind. His consciousness was like the quivering little spot of light which is thrown by the mirror of a galvanometer. His thoughts ran under it like a stream, some through the focus bright and distinct, some shadowy in the half-light of the edge. Just now the little glow was steady; but the least movement on Mowbray's part, the slightest sound from outside, even a faint difference in the slow movement of the living flesh he was cutting, set the light-spot shivering and spinning. A new sense-impression came rushing up through the flow of thoughts; and lo! the light-spot jerked away towards it, swifter than a frightened fish. It was wonderful to think that upon that unstable, fitful thing depended all the complex motions of the man; that for the next five minutes, therefore, my life hung upon its movements. And he was growing more and more nervous in his work. It was as if a little picture of a cut vein grew brighter, and struggled to oust from his brain another picture of a cut falling short of the mark. He was afraid: his dread of cutting too little was battling with his dread of cutting too far.

Then, suddenly, like an escape of water from under a lock-gate, a great uprush of horrible realisation set all his thoughts swirling, and simultaneously I perceived that the vein was cut. He started back with a hoarse exclamation, and I saw the brown-purple blood gather in a swift bead, and run trickling. He was horrified. He pitched the red-stained scalpel on to the octagonal table; and instantly both doctors flung themselves upon me, making hasty and ill-conceived efforts to remedy the disaster. "Ice!" said Mowbray, gasping. But I knew that I was killed, though my body still clung to me.

I will not describe their belated endeavours to save me, though I perceived every detail. My perceptions were sharper and swifter than they had ever been in life; my thoughts rushed through my mind with incredible swiftness, but with perfect definition. I can only compare their crowded clarity to the effects of a reasonable dose of opium. In a moment it would all be over, and I should be free. I knew I was immortal, but what would happen I did not know. Should I drift off presently, like a puff of smoke from a gun, in some kind of half-material body, an attenuated version of my material self? Should I find myself suddenly among the innumerable hosts of the dead, and know the world about me for the phantasmagoria it had always seemed? Should I drift to some spiritualistic séance, and there make foolish, incomprehensible attempts to affect a purblind medium? It was a state of unemotional curiosity, of colourless expectation. And then I realised a growing stress upon me, a feeling as though some huge human magnet was drawing me upward out of my body. The stress grew and grew. I seemed an atom for which monstrous forces were fighting. For one brief, terrible moment sensation came back to me. That feeling of falling headlong which comes in nightmares, that feeling a thousand times intensified, that and a black horror swept across my thoughts in a torrent. Then the two doctors, the naked body with its cut side, the little room, swept away from under me and vanished, as a speck of foam vanishes down an eddy.

I was in mid-air. Far below was the West End of London, receding rapidly,—for I seemed to be flying swiftly upward,— and as it receded, passing westward like a panorama, I could see, through the faint haze of smoke, the innumerable roofs chimney-set, the narrow roadways, stippled with people and conveyances, the little specks of squares, and the church steeples like thorns sticking out of the fabric. But it spun away as the earth rotated on its axis, and in a few seconds (as it seemed) I was over the scattered clumps of town about Ealing, the little Thames a thread of blue to the south, and the Chiltern Hills and the North Downs coming up like the rim of a basin, far away and faint with haze. Up I rushed. And at first I had not the faintest conception what this headlong rush upward could mean.

Every moment the circle of scenery beneath me grew wider and wider, and the details of town and field, of hill and valley, got more and more hazy and pale and indistinct, a luminous grey was mingled more and more with the blue of the hills and the green of the open meadows; and a little patch of cloud, low and far to the west, shone ever more dazzlingly white. Above, as the veil of atmosphere between myself and outer space grew thinner, the sky, which had been a fair springtime blue at first, grew deeper and richer in colour, passing steadily through the intervening shades, until presently it was as dark as the blue sky of midnight, and presently as black as the blackness of a frosty starlight, and at last as black as no blackness I had ever beheld. And first one star, and then many, and at last an innumerable host broke out upon the sky: more stars than anyone has ever seen from the face of the earth. For the blueness of the sky is the light of the sun and stars sifted and spread abroad blindingly: there is diffused light even in the darkest skies of winter, and we do not see the stars by day only because of the dazzling irradiation of the sun. But now I saw things—I know not how; assuredly with no mortal eyes—and that defect of bedazzlement blinded me no longer. The sun was incredibly strange and wonderful. The body of it was a disc of blinding white light: not yellowish, as it seems to those who live upon the earth, but livid white, all streaked with scarlet streaks and rimmed about with a fringe of writhing tongues of red fire. And shooting half-way across the heavens from either side of it and brighter than the Milky Way, were two pinions of silver white, making it look more like those winged globes I have seen in Egyptian sculpture than anything else I can remember upon earth. These I knew for the solar corona, though I had never seen anything of it but a picture during the days of my earthly life.

When my attention came back to the earth again, I saw that it had fallen very far away from me. Field and town were long since indistinguishable, and all the varied hues of the country were merging into a uniform bright grey, broken only by the brilliant white of the clouds that lay scattered in flocculent masses over Ireland and the west of England. For now I could see the outlines of the north of France and Ireland, and all this Island of Britain, save where Scotland passed over the horizon to the north, or where the coast was blurred or obliterated by cloud. The sea was a dull grey, and darker than the land; and the whole panorama was rotating slowly towards the east.

All this had happened so swiftly that until I was some thousand miles or so from the earth I had no thought for myself. But now I perceived I had neither hands nor feet, neither parts nor organs, and that I felt neither alarm nor pain. All about me I perceived that the vacancy (for I had already left the air behind) was cold beyond the imagination of man; but it troubled me not. The sun's rays shot through the void, powerless to light or heat until they should strike on matter in their course. I saw things with a serene self-forgetfulness, even as if I were God. And down below there, rushing away from me,—countless miles in a second,—where a little dark spot on the grey marked the position of London, two doctors were struggling to restore life to the poor hacked and outworn shell I had abandoned. I felt then such release, such serenity as I can compare to no mortal delight I have ever known.

It was only after I had perceived all these things that the meaning of that headlong rush of the earth grew into comprehension. Yet it was so simple, so obvious, that I was amazed at my never anticipating the thing that was happening to me. I had suddenly been cut adrift from matter: all that was material of me was there upon earth, whirling away through space, held to the earth by gravitation, partaking of the earth-inertia, moving in its wreath of epicycles round the sun, and with the sun and the planets on their vast march through space. But the immaterial has no inertia, feels nothing of the pull of matter for matter: where it parts from its garment of flesh, there it remains (so far as space concerns it any longer) immovable in space. *I* was not leaving the earth: the earth was leaving *me*, and not only the earth but the whole solar system was streaming past. And about me in space, invisible to me, scattered in the wake of the earth upon its journey, there must be an innumerable multitude of souls, stripped like myself of the material, stripped like myself of the passions of the individual and the generous emotions of the gregarious brute, naked intelligences, things of new-

born wonder and thought, marvelling at the strange release that
had suddenly come on them!

As I receded faster and faster from the strange white sun in
the black heavens, and from the broad and shining earth upon
which my being had begun, I seemed to grow in some incredible manner vast: vast as regards this world I had left, vast as
regards the moments and periods of a human life. Very soon I
saw the full circle of the earth, slightly gibbous, like the moon
when she nears her full, but very large; and the silvery shape of
America was now in the noonday blaze wherein (as it seemed)
little England had been basking but a few minutes ago. At first
the earth was large, and shone in the heavens, filling a great part
of them; but every moment she grew smaller and more distant.
As she shrank, the broad moon in its third quarter crept into
view over the rim of her disc. I looked for the constellations.
Only that part of Aries directly behind the sun and the Lion,
which the earth covered, were hidden. I recognised the tortuous,
tattered band of the Milky Way with Vega very bright between
sun and earth; and Sirius and Orion shone splendid against the
unfathomable blackness in the opposite quarter of the heavens.
The Pole Star was overhead, and the Great Bear hung over the
circle of the earth. And away beneath and beyond the shining
corona of the sun were strange groupings of stars I had never
seen in my life—notably a dagger-shaped group that I knew for
the Southern Cross. All these were no larger than when they
had shone on earth, but the little stars that one scarce sees shone
now against the setting of black vacancy as brightly as the first-
magnitudes had done, while the larger worlds were points of in-
describable glory and colour. Aldebaran was a spot of blood-red
fire, and Sirius condensed to one point the light of innumerable sapphires. And they shone steadily: they did not scintillate,
they were calmly glorious. My impressions had an adamantine
hardness and brightness: there was no blurring softness, no
atmosphere, nothing but infinite darkness set with the myriads

of these acute and brilliant points and specks of light. Presently, when I looked again, the little earth seemed no bigger than the sun, and it dwindled and turned as I looked, until in a second's space (as it seemed to me), it was halved; and so it went on swiftly dwindling. Far away in the opposite direction, a little pinkish pin's head of light, shining steadily, was the planet Mars. I swam motionless in vacancy, and, without a trace of terror or astonishment, watched the speck of cosmic dust we call the world fall away from me.

Presently it dawned upon me that my sense of duration had changed; that my mind was moving not faster but infinitely slower, that between each separate impression there was a period of many days. The moon spun once round the earth as I noted this; and I perceived clearly the motion of Mars in his orbit. Moreover, it appeared as if the time between thought and thought grew steadily greater, until at last a thousand years was but a moment in my perception.

At first the constellations had shone motionless against the black background of infinite space; but presently it seemed as though the group of stars about Hercules and the Scorpion was contracting, while Orion and Aldebaran and their neighbours were scattering apart. Flashing suddenly out of the darkness there came a flying multitude of particles of rock, glittering like dust-specks in a sunbeam, and encompassed in a faintly luminous cloud. They swirled all about me, and vanished again in a twinkling far behind. And then I saw that a bright spot of light, that shone a little to one side of my path, was growing very rapidly larger, and perceived that it was the planet Saturn rushing towards me. Larger and larger it grew, swallowing up the heavens behind it, and hiding every moment a fresh multitude of stars. I perceived its flattened, whirling body, its disc-like belt, and seven of its little satellites. It grew and grew, till it towered enormous; and then I plunged amid a streaming multitude of clashing stones and dancing dust-particles and gas-eddies, and saw for a moment the mighty triple belt like three concentric arches of moonlight above me, its shadow black on the boiling tumult below. These things happened in one-tenth of the time it takes to tell them. The planet went by like a flash of lightning; for a few seconds it blotted out the sun, and there and then became a mere black, dwindling, winged patch against the light. The earth, the mother mote of my being, I could no longer see.

So with a stately swiftness, in the profoundest silence, the solar system fell from me as it had been a garment, until the sun was a mere star amid the multitude of stars, with its eddy of planet-specks lost in the confused glittering of the remoter light. I was no longer a denizen of the solar system: I had come to the outer Universe, I seemed to grasp and comprehend the whole world of matter. Ever more swiftly the stars closed in about the spot where Antares and Vega had vanished in a phosphorescent haze, until that part of the sky had the semblance of a whirling mass of nebulae, and ever before me yawned vaster gaps of vacant blackness, and the stars shone fewer and fewer. It seemed as if I moved towards a point between Orion's belt and sword; and the void about that region opened vaster and vaster every second, an incredible gulf of nothingness into which I was falling. Faster and ever faster the universe rushed by, a hurry of whirling motes at last, speeding silently into the void. Stars glowing brighter and brighter, with their circling planets catching the light in a ghostly fashion as I neared them, shone out and vanished again into inexistence; faint comets, clusters of meteorites, winking specks of matter, eddying light-points whizzed past, some perhaps a hundred millions of miles or so from me at most, few nearer, travelling with unimaginable rapidity, shooting constellations, momentary darts of fire, through that black, enormous night. More than anything else it was like a dusty draught, sunbeam-lit. Broader and wider and deeper grew the starless space, the vacant Beyond, into which I was being drawn. At last a quarter of the heavens was black and blank, and the whole headlong rush of stellar universe closed in behind me like a veil of light that is gathered together. It drove away from me like a monstrous jack-o'-lantern driven by the wind. I had come out into the wilderness of space. Ever the vacant blackness grew broader, until the hosts of the stars seemed only like a swarm of fiery specks hurrying away from me, inconceivably remote, and the darkness, the nothingness and emptiness, was about me on every side. Soon the little universe of matter, the cage of points in which I had begun to be, was dwindling, now to a whirling disc of luminous glittering, and now to one minute disc of hazy light. In a little while it would shrink to a point, and at last would vanish altogether.

Suddenly feeling came back to me—feeling in the shape of overwhelming terror; such a dread of those dark vastitudes as no words can describe, a passionate resurgence of sympathy and social desire. Were there other souls, invisible to me as I to them, about me in the blackness? or was I indeed, even as I felt, alone? Had I passed out of being into something that was neither being nor not-being? The covering of the body, the covering of matter, had been torn from me, and the hallucinations of companionship and security. Everything was black and silent. I had ceased to be. I was nothing. There was nothing, save only that infinitesimal dot of light that dwindled in the gulf. I strained myself to hear and see, and for a while there was naught but infinite silence, intolerable darkness, horror, and despair.

Then I saw that about the spot of light into which the whole world of matter had shrunk there was a faint glow. And in a band on either side of that the darkness was not absolute. I watched it for ages, as it seemed to me, and through the long waiting the haze grew imperceptibly more distinct. And then about the band appeared an irregular cloud of the faintest, palest brown. I felt a passionate impatience; but the things grew brighter so slowly that they scarce seemed to change. What was unfolding itself? What was this strange reddish dawn in the interminable night of space?

The cloud's shape was grotesque. It seemed to be looped along its lower side into four projecting masses, and, above, it ended in a straight line. What phantom was it? I felt assured I had seen that figure before; but I could not think what, nor where, nor when it was. Then the realisation rushed upon me. *It was a clenched Hand.* I was alone in space, alone with this huge, shadowy Hand, upon which the whole Universe of Matter lay like an unconsidered speck of dust. It seemed as though I watched it through vast periods of time. On the forefinger glittered a ring; and the universe from which I had come was but a spot of light upon the ring's curvature. And the thing that the Hand gripped had the likeness of a black rod. Through a long eternity I watched this Hand, with the ring and the rod, marvelling and fearing and waiting helplessly on what might follow. It seemed as though nothing could follow: that I should watch for ever, seeing only the Hand and the thing it held, and understanding nothing of its import. Was the whole universe but a refracting speck upon some greater Being? Were our worlds but the atoms of another universe, and those again of another, and so on through an endless progression? And what was I? Was I indeed immaterial? A vague persuasion of a body gathering about me came into my suspense. The abysmal darkness about the Hand filled with impalpable suggestions, with uncertain, fluctuating shapes.

Then, suddenly, came a sound, like the sound of a tolling bell: faint, as if infinitely far; muffled, as though heard through thick swathings of darkness: a deep, vibrating resonance, with vast gulfs of silence between each stroke. And the Hand appeared to tighten on the rod. And I saw far above the Hand, towards the apex of the darkness, a circle of dim phosphorescence, a ghostly sphere whence these sounds came throbbing;

and at the last stroke the Hand vanished, for the hour had come, and I heard a noise of many waters. But the black rod remained as a great band across the sky. And then a voice, which seemed to run to the uttermost parts of space, spoke, saying, "There will be no more pain."

At that an almost intolerable gladness and radiance rushed in upon me, and I saw the circle shining white and bright, and the rod black and shining, and many things else distinct and clear. And the circle was the face of the clock, and the rod the rail of my bed. Haddon was standing at the foot, against the rail, with a small pair of scissors on his fingers; and the hands of my clock on the mantel over his shoulder were clasped together over the hour of twelve. Mowbray was washing something in a basin at the octagonal table, and at my side I felt a subdued feeling that could scarce be spoken of as pain.

The operation had not killed me. And I perceived, suddenly, that the dull melancholy of half a year was lifted from my mind.

The Dream of a Ridiculous Man

FYODOR DOSTOEVSKY

I

I am a ridiculous person. Now they call me a madman. That would be a promotion if it were not that I remain as ridiculous in their eyes as before. But now I do not resent it, they are all dear to me now, even when they laugh at me—and, indeed, it is just then that they are particularly dear to me. I could join in their laughter—not exactly at myself, but through affection for them, if I did not feel so sad as I look at them. Sad because they do not know the truth and I do know it. Oh, how hard it is to be the only one who knows the truth! But they won't understand that. No, they won't understand it.

In old days I used to be miserable at seeming ridiculous. Not seeming, but being. I have always been ridiculous, and I have known it, perhaps, from the hour I was born. Perhaps from the time I was seven years old I knew I was ridiculous. Afterwards I went to school, studied at the university, and, do you know, the more I learned, the more thoroughly I understood that I was ridiculous. So that it seemed in the end as though all the sciences I studied at the university existed only to prove and make evident to me as I went more deeply into them that I was ridiculous. It was the same with life as it was with science. With every year the same consciousness of the ridiculous figure I cut in every relation grew and strengthened. Every one always laughed at me. But not one of them knew or guessed that if there were one man on earth who knew better than anybody else that I was absurd, it was myself, and what I resented most of all was that they did not know that. But that was my own fault; I was so proud that nothing would have ever induced me to tell it to any one. This pride grew in me with the years; and if it had happened that I allowed myself to confess to any one that I was ridiculous, I believe that I should have blown out my brains the same evening. Oh, how I suffered in my early youth from the fear that I might give way and confess it to my schoolfellows. But since I grew to manhood, I have for some unknown reason become calmer, though I realised my awful characteristic more fully every year. I say "unknown," for to this day I cannot tell why it was. Perhaps it was owing to the terrible misery that was growing in my soul through something which was of more consequence than anything else about me: that something was the conviction that had come upon me that *nothing in the world mattered.* I had long had an inkling of it, but the full realisation came last year almost suddenly. I suddenly felt that it was all the same to me whether the world existed or whether there had never been anything at all: I began to feel with all my being that there was *nothing existing.* At first I fancied that many things had existed in the past, but afterwards I guessed that there never had been anything in the past either, but that it had only seemed so for some reason. Little by little I guessed that there would be nothing in the future either. Then I left off being angry with people and almost ceased to notice them. Indeed this showed itself even in the pettiest trifles: I used, for instance, to knock against people in the street. And not so much from being lost in thought: what had I to think about? I had almost given up thinking by that time; nothing mattered to me. If at least I had solved my problems! Oh, I had not settled one of them, and how many they were! But I gave up caring about anything, and all the problems disappeared.

And it was after that that I found out the truth. I learnt the truth last November—on the third of November, to be precise —and I remember every instant since. It was a gloomy evening, one of the gloomiest possible evenings. I was going home at about eleven o'clock, and I remember that I thought that the evening could not be gloomier. Even physically. Rain had been falling all day, and it had been a cold, gloomy, almost menacing rain, with, I remember, an unmistakable spite against mankind. Suddenly between ten and eleven it had stopped, and was followed by a horrible dampness, colder and damper than the rain, and a sort of steam was rising from everything, from every stone in the street, and from every by-lane if one looked down it as far as one could. A thought suddenly occurred to me, that if all the street lamps had been put out it would have been less cheerless, that the gas made one's heart sadder because it lighted it all up. I had had scarcely any dinner that day, and had been spending the evening with an engineer, and two other friends had been there also. I sat silent—I fancy I bored them. They talked of something rousing and suddenly they got excited over it. But they did not really care, I could see that, and only made a show of being excited. I suddenly said as much to them. "My friends," I said, "you really do not care one way or the other." They were not offended, but they all laughed at me. That was because I spoke without any note of reproach, simply because it did not matter to me. They saw it did not, and it amused them.

As I was thinking about the gas lamps in the street I looked up at the sky. The sky was horribly dark, but one could distinctly see tattered clouds, and between them fathomless black patches. Suddenly I noticed in one of these patches a star, and began watching it intently. That was because that star gave me an idea: I decided to kill myself that night. I had firmly determined to do so two months before, and poor as I was, I bought a splendid revolver that very day, and loaded it. But two months had passed and it was still lying in my drawer; I was so utterly indifferent that I wanted to seize a moment when I would not be so indifferent—why, I don't know. And so for two months every night that I came home I thought I would shoot myself. I kept waiting for the right moment. And so now this star gave me a thought. I made up my mind that it should certainly be that night. And why the star gave me the thought I don't know.

And just as I was looking at the sky, this little girl took me by the elbow. The street was empty, and there was scarcely any one to be seen. A cabman was sleeping in the distance in his cab. It was a child of eight with a kerchief on her head, wearing nothing but a wretched little dress all soaked with rain, but I noticed particularly her wet broken shoes and I recall them now. They caught my eye particularly. She suddenly pulled me by the elbow and called me. She was not weeping, but was spasmodically crying out some words which she could not utter properly, because she was shivering and shuddering all over. She was in terror about something, and kept crying, "Mammy, mammy!" I turned facing her, I did not say a word and went on; but she ran, pulling at me, and there was that note in her voice which in frightened children means despair. I know that sound. Though she did not articulate the words, I understood that her mother was dying, or that something of the sort was happening to them, and that she had run out to call some one, to find something to help her mother. I did not go with her; on the contrary, I had an impulse to drive her away. I told her first to

go to a policeman. But clasping her hands, she ran beside me
sobbing and gasping, and would not leave me. Then I stamped
my foot, and shouted at her. She called out "Sir! sir! . . ." but
suddenly abandoned me and rushed headlong across the road.
Some other passer-by appeared there, and she evidently flew
from me to him.

I mounted up to my fifth storey. I have a room in a flat
where there are other lodgers. My room is small and poor, with
a garret window in the shape of a semicircle. I have a sofa
covered with American leather, a table with books on it, two
chairs and a comfortable arm-chair, as old as old can be, but of
the good old-fashioned shape. I sat down, lighted the candle,
and began thinking. In the room next to mine, through the
partition wall, a perfect Bedlam was going on. It had been
going on for the last three days. A retired captain lived there,
and he had half a dozen visitors, gentlemen of doubtful reputation, drinking vodka and playing *stoss* with old cards. The night
before there had been a fight, and I know that two of them
had been for a long time engaged in dragging each other about
by the hair. The landlady wanted to complain, but she was in
abject terror of the captain. There was only one other lodger
in the flat, a thin little regimental lady, on a visit to Petersburg,
with three little children who had been taken ill since they
came into the lodgings. Both she and her children were in mortal
fear of the captain, and lay trembling and crossing themselves
all night, and the youngest child had a sort of fit from fright.
That captain, I know for a fact, sometimes stops people in
the Nevsky Prospect and begs. They won't take him into the
service, but strange to say (that's why I am telling this), all
this month that the captain has been here his behaviour has
caused me no annoyance. I have, of course, tried to avoid his
acquaintance from the very beginning, and he, too, was bored
with me from the first; but I never care how much they shout
the other side of the partition nor how many of them there

are in there: I sit up all night and forget them so completely that I do not even hear them. I stay awake till daybreak, and have been going on like that for the last year. I sit up all night in my arm-chair at the table, doing nothing. I only read by day. I sit—don't even think; ideas of a sort wander through my mind and I let them come and go as they will. A whole candle is burnt every night. I sat down quietly at the table, took out the revolver and put it down before me. When I had put it down I asked myself, I remember, "Is that so?" and answered with complete conviction, "It is." That is, I shall shoot myself. I knew that I should shoot myself that night for certain, but how much longer I should go on sitting at the table I did not know. And no doubt I should have shot myself if it had not been for that little girl.

II

You see, though nothing mattered to me, I could feel pain, for instance. If any one had struck me it would have hurt me. It was the same morally: if anything very pathetic happened, I should have felt pity just as I used to do in old days when there were things in life that did matter to me. I had felt pity that evening. I should have certainly helped a child. Why, then, had I not helped the little girl? Because of an idea that occurred to me at the time: when she was calling and pulling at me, a question suddenly arose before me and I could not settle it. The question was an idle one, but I was vexed. I was vexed at the reflection that if I were going to make an end of myself that night, nothing in life ought to have mattered to me. Why was it that all at once I did not feel that nothing mattered and was sorry for the little girl? I remember that I was very sorry for her, so much so that I felt a strange pang, quite incongruous in my position. Really I do not know better how to convey my fleeting sensation at the moment, but the sensation persisted at home when I was sitting at the table, and I was very much irritated as I had not been for a long time past. One reflection followed another. I saw clearly that so long as I was still a human being and not nothingness, I was alive and so could suffer, be angry and feel shame at my actions. So be it. But if I am going to kill myself, in two hours, say, what is the little girl to me and what have I to do with shame or with anything else in the world? I shall turn into nothing, absolutely nothing. And can it really be true that the consciousness that I shall *completely* cease to exist immediately and so everything else will cease to exist, does not in the least affect my feeling of pity for the child nor the feeling of shame after a contemptible action? I stamped and shouted at the unhappy child as though to say—not only I feel no pity, but even if I behave inhumanly and contemptibly, I am free to, for in another two hours everything will be extinguished. Do you believe that that was why I shouted that? I am almost convinced of it now. It seemed clear to me that life and the world somehow depended upon me now. I may almost say that the world now seemed created for me alone: if I shot myself the world would cease to be at least for me. I say nothing of its being likely that nothing will exist for any one when I am gone, and that as soon as my consciousness is extinguished the whole world will vanish too and become void like a phantom, as a mere appurtenance of my consciousness, for possibly all this world and all these people are only me myself. I remember that as I sat and reflected, I turned all these new questions that swarmed one after another quite the other way, and thought of something quite new. For instance, a strange reflection suddenly occurred to me, that if I had lived before on the moon or on Mars and there had committed the most disgraceful and dishonourable action and had there been put to such shame and ignominy as one can only conceive and realise in dreams, in nightmares, and if, finding myself afterwards on earth, I were able to retain the memory of what I had done on the other planet and at the same time knew that I should never, under any circumstances, return there, then looking from the earth to the moon—*should I care or not?* Should I feel shame for that action or not? These were idle and superfluous questions for the revolver was already lying before me, and I knew in every fibre of my being that *it* would happen for certain, but they excited me and I raged. I could not die now without having first settled something. In short, the child had saved me, for I put off my pistol shot for the sake of these questions. Meanwhile the clamour had begun to subside in the captain's room: they had finished their game, were settling down to sleep, and meanwhile were grumbling and languidly winding up their quarrels. At that point I suddenly fell asleep in my chair at the table—a thing which had never happened to me before. I dropped asleep quite unawares.

Dreams, as we all know, are very queer things: some parts are presented with appalling vividness, with details worked up with the elaborate finish of jewellery, while others one gallops through, as it were, without noticing them at all, as, for instance, through space and time. Dreams seem to be spurred on not by reason but by desire, not by the head but by the heart, and yet what complicated tricks my reason has played sometimes in dreams, what utterly incomprehensible things happen to it! My brother died five years ago, for instance. I sometimes dream of him; he takes part in my affairs, we are very much interested, and yet all through my dream I quite know and remember that my brother is dead and buried. How is it that I am not surprised that, though he is dead, he is here beside me and working with me? Why is it that my reason fully accepts it? But enough. I will begin about my dream. Yes, I dreamed a dream, my dream of the third of November. They tease me now, telling me it was only a dream. But does it matter whether it was a dream or reality, if the dream made known to me the truth? If once one has recognised the truth and seen it, you know that it is the truth and that there is no other and there cannot be, whether you are asleep or awake. Let it be a dream, so be it, but that real life of which you make so much I had meant to extinguish by suicide, and my dream, my dream —oh, it revealed to me a different life, renewed, grand and full of power!

Listen.

III

I have mentioned that I dropped asleep unawares and even seemed to be still reflecting on the same subjects. I suddenly dreamt that I picked up the revolver and aimed it straight at my heart—my heart, and not my head; and I had determined beforehand to fire at my head, at my right temple. After aiming at my chest I waited a second or two, and suddenly my candle, my table, and the wall in front of me began moving and heaving. I made haste to pull the trigger.

In dreams you sometimes fall from a height, or are stabbed, or beaten, but you never feel pain unless, perhaps, you really bruise yourself against the bedstead, then you feel pain and almost always wake up from it. It was the same in my dream. I did not feel any pain, but it seemed as though with my shot everything within me was shaken and everything was suddenly dimmed, and it grew horribly black around me. I seemed to be blinded and benumbed, and I was lying on something hard, stretched on my back; I saw nothing, and could not make the slightest movement. People were walking and shouting around me, the captain bawled, the landlady shrieked—and suddenly another break and I was being carried in a closed coffin. And I felt how the coffin was shaking and reflected upon it, and for the first time the idea struck me that I was dead, utterly dead, I knew it and had no doubt of it, I could neither see nor move and yet I was feeling and reflecting. But I was soon reconciled to the position, and as one usually does in a dream, accepted the facts without disputing them.

And now I was buried in the earth. They all went away, I was left alone, utterly alone. I did not move. Whenever before I had imagined being buried the one sensation I associated with the grave was that of damp and cold. So now I felt that I was very cold, especially the tips of my toes, but I felt nothing else.

I lay still, strange to say I expected nothing, accepting without dispute that a dead man had nothing to expect. But it was damp. I don't know how long a time passed—whether an hour, or several days, or many days. But all at once a drop of water fell on my closed left eye, making its way through a coffin lid; it was followed a minute later by a second, then a minute later by a third—and so on, regularly every minute. There was a sudden glow of profound indignation in my heart, and I suddenly felt in it a pang of physical pain. "That's my wound," I thought; "that's the bullet. . . ." And drop after drop every minute kept falling on my closed eyelid. And all at once, not with my voice, but with my whole being, I called upon the power that was responsible for all that was happening to me:

"Whoever you may be, if you exist, and if anything more rational than what is happening here is possible, suffer it to be here now. But if you are revenging yourself upon me for my senseless suicide by the hideousness and absurdity of this subsequent existence, then let me tell you that no torture could ever equal the contempt which I shall go on dumbly feeling, though my martyrdom may last a million years!"

I made this appeal and held my peace. There was a full minute of unbroken silence and again another drop fell, but I knew with infinite unshakable certainty that everything would change immediately. And behold my grave suddenly was rent asunder, that is, I don't know whether it was opened or dug up, but I was caught up by some dark and unknown being and we found ourselves in space. I suddenly regained my sight. It was the dead of night, and never, never had there been such darkness. We were flying through space far away from the earth. I did not question the being who was taking me; I was proud and waited. I assured myself that I was not afraid, and was thrilled with ecstasy at the thought that I was not afraid. I do not know how long we were flying, I cannot imagine; it happened as it always does in dreams when you skip over space and time, and the laws of thought and existence, and only pause upon the points for which the heart yearns. I remember that I suddenly saw in the darkness a star. "Is that Sirius?" I asked impulsively, though I had not meant to ask any questions.

"No, that is the star you saw between the clouds when you were coming home," the being who was carrying me replied.

I knew that it had something like a human face. Strange to say, I did not like that being, in fact I felt an intense aversion for it. I had expected complete non-existence, and that was why I had put a bullet through my heart. And here I was in the hands of a creature not human, of course, but yet living, existing. "And so there is life beyond the grave," I thought with the strange frivolity one has in dreams. But in its inmost depth my heart remained unchanged. "And if I have got to exist again," I thought, "and live once more under the control of some irresistible power, I won't be vanquished and humiliated."

"You know that I am afraid of you and despise me for that," I said suddenly to my companion, unable to refrain from the humiliating question which implied a confession, and feeling my humiliation stab my heart as with a pin. He did not answer my question, but all at once I felt that he was not even despising me, but was laughing at me and had no compassion for me, and that our journey had an unknown and mysterious object that concerned me only. Fear was growing in my heart. Something was mutely and painfully communicated to me from my silent companion, and permeated my whole being. We were flying through dark, unknown space. I had for some time lost sight of the constellations familiar to my eyes. I knew that there were stars in the heavenly spaces the light of which took thousands or millions of years to reach the earth. Perhaps we were already flying through those spaces. I expected something with a terrible anguish that tortured my heart. And suddenly I was thrilled by a familiar feeling that stirred me to the depths: I suddenly caught sight of our sun! I knew that it could not be *our* sun, that gave life to *our* earth, and that we were an infinite distance from our sun, but for some reason I knew in my whole being that it was a sun exactly like ours, a duplicate of it. A sweet, thrilling feeling resounded with ecstasy in my heart: the kindred power of the same light which had given me light stirred an echo in my heart and awakened it, and I had a sensation of life, the old life of the past for the first time since I had been in the grave.

"But if that is the sun, if that is exactly the same as our sun," I cried, "where is the earth?"

And my companion pointed to a star twinkling in the distance with an emerald light. We were flying straight towards it.

"And are such repetitions possible in the universe? Can that be the law of Nature? . . . And if that is an earth there, can it be just the same earth as ours . . . just the same, as poor, as unhappy, but precious and beloved for ever, arousing in the most ungrateful of her children the same poignant love for her that we feel for our earth?" I cried out, shaken by irresistible, ecstatic love for the old familiar earth which I had left. The image of the poor child whom I had repulsed flashed through my mind.

"You shall see it all," answered my companion, and there was a note of sorrow in his voice.

But we were rapidly approaching the planet. It was growing before my eyes; I could already distinguish the ocean, the outline of Europe; and suddenly a feeling of a great and holy jealousy glowed in my heart.

"How can it be repeated and what for? I love and can love only that earth which I have left, stained with my blood, when, in my ingratitude, I quenched my life with a bullet in my heart. But I have never, never ceased to love that earth, and perhaps on the very night I parted from it I loved it more than ever. Is there suffering upon this new earth? On our earth we can only love with suffering and through suffering. We cannot love otherwise, and we know of no other sort of love. I want suffering in order to love. I long, I thirst, this very instant, to kiss with tears the earth that I have left, and I don't want, I won't accept life on any other!"

But my companion had already left me. I suddenly, quite without noticing how, found myself on this other earth, in the bright light of a sunny day, fair as paradise. I believe I was standing on one of the islands that make up on our globe the Greek archipelago, or on the coast of the mainland facing that archipelago. Oh, everything was exactly as it is with us, only everything seemed to have a festive radiance, the splendour of some great, holy triumph attained at last. The caressing sea, green as emerald, splashed softly upon the shore and kissed it with manifest, almost conscious love. The tall, lovely trees stood in all the glory of their blossom, and their innumerable leaves greeted me, I am certain, with their soft, caressing rustle and seemed to articulate words of love. The grass glowed with bright and fragrant flowers. Birds were flying in flocks in the air, and perched fearlessly on my shoulders and arms and joyfully struck me with their darling, fluttering wings. And at last I saw and knew the people of this happy land. They came to me of themselves, they surrounded me, kissed me. The children of the sun, the children of their sun—oh, how beautiful they were! Never had I seen on our own earth such beauty in mankind. Only perhaps in our children, in their earliest years, one might find some remote, faint reflection of this beauty. The eyes of these happy people shone with a clear brightness. Their faces were radiant with the light of reason and fulness of a serenity that comes of perfect understanding, but those faces were gay; in their words and voices there was a note of childlike joy. Oh, from the first moment, from the first glance at them, I understood it all! It was the earth untarnished by the Fall; on it lived people who had not sinned. They lived just in such a paradise as that in which, according to all the legends of mankind, our first parents lived before they sinned; the only difference was that all this earth was the same paradise. These people, laughing joyfully, thronged round me and caressed me; they took me home with them, and each of them tried to reassure me. Oh, they asked me no questions, but they seemed, I fancied, to know everything without asking, and they wanted to make haste and smooth away the signs of suffering from my face.

IV

And do you know what? Well, granted that it was only a dream, yet the sensation of the love of those innocent and beautiful people has remained with me for ever, and I feel as though their love is still flowing out to me from over there. I have seen them myself, have known them and been convinced; I loved them, I suffered for them afterwards. Oh, I understood at once even at the time that in many things I could not understand them at all; as an up-to-date Russian progressive and contemptible Petersburger, it struck me as inexplicable that, knowing so much, they had, for instance, no science like ours. But I soon realised that their knowledge was gained and fostered by intuitions different from those of us on earth, and that their aspirations, too, were quite different. They desired nothing and were at peace; they did not aspire to knowledge of life as we aspire to understand it, because their lives were full. But their knowledge was higher and deeper than ours; for our science seeks to explain what life is, aspires to understand it in order to teach others how to live, while they without science knew how to live; and that I understood, but I could not understand their knowledge. They showed me their trees, and I could not understand the intense love with which they looked at them; it was as though they were talking with creatures like themselves. And perhaps I shall not be mistaken if I say that they conversed with them. Yes, they had found their language, and I am convinced that the trees understood them. They looked at all Nature like that—at the animals who lived in peace with them and did not attack them, but loved them, conquered by their love. They pointed to the stars and told me something about them which I could not understand, but I am convinced that they were somehow in touch with the stars, not only in thought, but by some living channel. Oh, these people did not persist in trying to make me understand them, they loved me without that, but I knew that they would never understand me, and so I hardly spoke to them about our earth. I only kissed in their presence the earth on which they lived and mutely worshipped them themselves. And they saw that and let me worship them without being abashed at my adoration, for they themselves loved much. They were not unhappy on my account when at times I kissed their feet with tears, joyfully conscious of the love with which they would respond to mine. At times I asked myself with wonder how it was they were able never to offend a creature like me, and never once to arouse a feeling of jealousy or envy in me? Often I wondered how it could be that, boastful and untruthful as I was, I never talked to them of what I knew—of which, of course, they had no notion—that I was never tempted to do so by a desire to astonish or even to benefit them.

They were as gay and sportive as children. They wandered about their lovely woods and copses, they sang their lovely songs; their fare was light—the fruits of their trees, the honey from their woods, and the milk of the animals who loved them. The work they did for food and raiment was brief and not laborious. They loved and begot children, but I never noticed in them the impulse of that *cruel* sensuality which overcomes almost every man on this earth, all and each, and is the source of almost every sin of mankind on earth. They rejoiced at the arrival of children as new beings to share their happiness. There was no quarrelling, no jealousy among them, and they did not even know what the words meant. Their children were the children of all, for they all made up one family. There was scarcely any illness among them, though there was death; but their old people died peacefully, as though falling asleep, giving blessings and smiles to those who surrounded them to take their last farewell with bright and loving smiles. I never saw grief or tears on those occasions, but only love, which reached the point of ecstasy, but a calm ecstasy, made perfect and contemplative. One might think that they were still in contact with the departed after death, and that their earthly union was not cut short by death. They scarcely understood me when I questioned them about immortality, but evidently they were so convinced of it without reasoning that it was not for them a question at all. They had no temples, but they had a real living and uninterrupted sense of oneness with the whole of the universe; they had no creed, but they had a certain knowledge that when their earthly joy had reached the limits of earthly nature, then there would come for them, for the living and for the dead, a still greater fulness of contact with the whole of the universe. They looked forward to that moment with joy, but without haste, not pining for it, but seeming to have a foretaste of it in their hearts, of which they talked to one another.

In the evening before going to sleep they liked singing in musical and harmonious chorus. In those songs they expressed all the sensations that the parting day had given them, sang its glories and took leave of it. They sang the praises of nature, of the sea, of the woods. They liked making songs about one another, and praised each other like children; they were the simplest songs, but they sprang from their hearts and went to one's heart. And not only in their songs but in all their lives they seemed to do nothing but admire one another. It was like being in love with each other, but an all-embracing, universal feeling.

Some of their songs, solemn and rapturous, I scarcely understood at all. Though I understood the words I could never fathom their full significance. It remained, as it were, beyond the grasp of my mind, yet my heart unconsciously absorbed it more and more. I often told them that I had had a presentiment of it long before, that this joy and glory had come to me on our earth in the form of a yearning melancholy that at times approached insufferable sorrow; that I had had a foreknowledge of them all and of their glory in the dreams of my heart and the visions of my mind; that often on our earth I could not look at the setting sun without tears . . . that in my hatred for the men of our earth there was always a yearning anguish: why could I not hate them without loving them? why could I not help forgiving them? and in my love for them there was a yearning grief: why could I not love them without hating them? They listened to me, and I saw they could not conceive what I was saying, but I did not regret that I had spoken to them of it: I knew that they understood the intensity of my yearning anguish over those whom I had left. But when they looked at me with their sweet eyes full of love, when I felt that in their presence my heart, too, became as innocent and just as theirs, the feeling of the fulness of life took my breath away, and I worshipped them in silence.

Oh, every one laughs in my face now, and assures me that one cannot dream of such details as I am telling now, that I only dreamed or felt one sensation that arose in my heart in delirium and made up the details myself when I woke up. And when I told them that perhaps it really was so, my God, how they shouted with laughter in my face, and what mirth I caused! Oh, yes, of course I was overcome by the mere sensation of my dream, and that was all that was preserved in my cruelly wounded heart; but the actual forms and images of my dream, that is, the very ones I really saw at the very time of my dream, were filled with such harmony, were so lovely and enchanting and were so actual, that on awakening I was, of course, incapable of clothing them in our poor language, so that they were bound to become blurred in my mind; and so perhaps I really was forced afterwards to make up the details, and so of course to distort them in my passionate desire to convey some at least of them as quickly as I could. But on the other hand, how can I help believing that it was all true? It was perhaps a thousand times brighter, happier and more joyful than I describe it. Granted that I dreamed it, yet it must have been real. You know, I will tell you a secret: perhaps it was not a dream at all! For then something happened so awful, something so horribly true, that it could not have been imagined in a dream. My heart may have originated the dream, but would my heart alone have been capable of originating the awful event which happened to me afterwards? How could I alone have invented it or imagined it in my dream? Could my petty heart and my fickle, trivial mind have risen to such a revelation of truth? Oh, judge for yourselves: hitherto I have concealed it, but now I will tell the truth. The fact is that I . . . corrupted them all!

V

Yes, yes, it ended in my corrupting them all! How it could come to pass I do not know, but I remember it clearly. The dream embraced thousands of years and left in me only a sense of the whole. I only know that I was the cause of their sin and downfall. Like a vile trichina, like a germ of the plague infecting whole kingdoms, so I contaminated all this earth, so happy and sinless before my coming. They learnt to lie, grew fond of lying, and discovered the charm of falsehood. Oh, at first perhaps it began innocently, with a jest, coquetry, with amorous play, perhaps indeed with a germ, but that germ of falsity made its way into their hearts and pleased them. Then sensuality was soon begotten, sensuality begot jealousy, jealousy—cruelty. . . . Oh, I don't know, I don't remember; but soon, very soon the first blood was shed. They marvelled and were horrified, and began to be split up and divided. They formed into unions, but it was against one another. Reproaches, upbraidings followed. They came to know shame, and shame brought them to virtue. The conception of honour sprang up, and every union began waving its flags. They began torturing animals, and the animals withdrew from them into the forests and became hostile to them. They began to struggle for separation, for isolation, for individuality, for mine and thine. They began to talk in different languages. They became acquainted with sorrow and loved sorrow; they thirsted for suffering, and said that truth could only be attained through suffering. Then science appeared. As they became wicked they began talking of brotherhood and humanitarianism, and understood those ideas. As they became criminal, they invented justice and drew up whole legal codes in order to observe it, and to ensure their being kept, set up a guillotine. They hardly remembered what they had lost, in fact refused to believe that they had ever been happy and innocent. They even laughed at the possibility of this happiness in the past, and called it a dream. They could not even imagine it in definite form and shape, but, strange and wonderful to relate, though they lost all faith in their past happiness and called it a legend, they so longed to be happy and innocent once more that they succumbed to this desire like children, made an idol of it, set up temples and worshipped their own idea, their own desire; though at the same time they fully believed that it was unattainable and could not be realised, yet they bowed down to it and adored it with tears! Nevertheless, if it could have happened that they had returned to the innocent and happy condition which they had lost, and if some one had shown it to them again and had asked them whether they wanted to go back to it, they would certainly have refused. They answered me:

"We may be deceitful, wicked and unjust, we *know* it and weep over it, we grieve over it; we torment and punish ourselves more perhaps than that merciful Judge Who will judge us and whose Name we know not. But we have science, and by means of it we shall find the truth and we shall arrive at it consciously. Knowledge is higher than feeling, the consciousness of life is higher than life. Science will give us wisdom, wisdom will reveal the laws, and the knowledge of the laws of happiness is higher than happiness."

That is what they said, and after saying such things every one began to love himself better than any one else, and indeed they could not do otherwise. All became so jealous of the rights of their own personality that they did their very utmost to curtail and destroy them in others, and made that the chief thing in their lives. Slavery followed, even voluntary slavery; the weak eagerly submitted to the strong, on condition that the latter aided them to subdue the still weaker. Then there were saints who came to these people, weeping, and talked to them of their pride, of their loss of harmony and due proportion, of their loss of shame. They were laughed at or pelted with stones. Holy blood was shed on the threshold of the temples. Then there arose men who began to think how to bring all people together again, so that everybody, while still loving himself best of all, might not interfere with others, and all might live together in something like a harmonious society. Regular wars sprang up over this idea. All the combatants at the same time firmly believed that science, wisdom and the instinct of self-preservation would force men at last to unite into a harmonious and rational society; and so, meanwhile, to hasten matters, "the wise" endeavoured to exterminate as rapidly as possible all who were "not wise" and did not understand their idea, that the latter might not hinder its triumph. But the instinct of self-preservation grew rapidly weaker; there arose men, haughty and sensual, who demanded all or nothing. In order to obtain everything they resorted to crime, and if they did not succeed—to suicide. There arose religions with a cult of non-existence and self-destruction for the sake of the everlasting peace of annihilation. At last these people grew weary of their meaningless toil, and signs of suffering came into their faces, and then they proclaimed that suffering was a beauty, for in suffering alone was there meaning. They glorified suffering in their songs. I moved about among them, wringing my hands and weeping over them, but I loved them perhaps more than in old days when there was no suffering in their faces and when they were innocent and so lovely. I loved the earth they had polluted even more than when it had been a paradise, if only because sorrow had come to it. Alas! I always loved sorrow and tribulation, but only for myself, for myself; but I wept over them, pitying them. I stretched out my hands to them in despair, blaming, cursing and despising myself. I told them that all this was my doing, mine alone; that it was I had brought them corruption, contamination and falsity. I besought them to crucify me, I taught them how to make a cross. I could not kill myself, I had not the strength, but I wanted to suffer at their hands. I yearned for suffering, I longed that my blood should be drained to the last drop in these agonies. But they only laughed at me, and began at last to look upon me as crazy. They justified me, they declared that they had only got what they wanted themselves, and that all that now was could not have been otherwise. At last they declared to me that I was becoming dangerous and that they should lock me up in a madhouse if I did not hold my tongue. Then such grief took possession of my soul that my heart was wrung, and I felt as though I were dying; and then . . . then I awoke.

It was morning, that is, it was not yet daylight, but about six o'clock. I woke up in the same arm-chair; my candle had burnt out; every one was asleep in the captain's room, and there was a stillness all round, rare in our flat. First of all I leapt up in great amazement: nothing like this had ever happened to me before, not even in the most trivial detail; I had never, for instance, fallen asleep like this in my arm-chair. While I was standing and coming to myself I suddenly caught sight of my revolver lying loaded, ready—but instantly I thrust it away! Oh, now, life, life! I lifted up my hands and called upon eternal truth, not with words but with tears; ecstasy, immeasurable ecstasy flooded my soul. Yes, life and spreading the good tidings! Oh, I at that moment resolved to spread the tidings, and resolved it, of course, for my whole life. I go to spread the tidings, I want to spread the tidings—of what? Of the truth, for I have seen it, have seen it with my own eyes, have seen it in all its glory.

And since then I have been preaching! Moreover I love all those who laugh at me more than any of the rest. Why that is so I do not know and cannot explain, but so be it. I am told that I am vague and confused, and if I am vague and confused now, what shall I be later on? It is true indeed: I am vague and confused, and perhaps as time goes on I shall be more so. And of course I shall make many blunders before I find out how to preach, that is, find out what words to say, what things to do, for it is a very difficult task. I see all that as clear as daylight, but, listen, who does not make mistakes? And yet, you know, all are making for the same goal, all are striving in the same direction anyway, from the sage to the lowest robber, only by different roads. It is an old truth, but this is what is new: I cannot go far wrong. For I have seen the truth; I have seen and I know that people can be beautiful and happy without losing the power of living on earth. I will not and cannot believe that evil is the normal condition of mankind. And it is just this faith of mine that they laugh at. But how can I help believing it? I have seen the truth—it is not as though I had invented it with my mind, I have seen it, seen it, and the *living image* of it has filled my soul for ever. I have seen it in such full perfection that I cannot believe that it is impossible for people to have it. And so how can I go wrong? I shall make some slips no doubt, and shall perhaps talk in second-hand language, but not for long: the living image of what I saw will always be with me and will always correct and guide me. Oh, I am full of courage and freshness, and I will go on and on if it were for a thousand years! Do you know, at first I meant to conceal the fact that I corrupted them, but that was a mistake—that was my first mistake! But truth whispered to me that I was *lying*, and preserved me and corrected me. But how establish paradise—I don't know, because I do not know how to put it into words. After my dream I lost command of words. All the chief words, anyway, the most necessary ones. But never mind, I shall go and I shall keep talking, I won't leave off, for anyway I have seen it with my own eyes, though I cannot describe what I saw. But the scoffers do not understand that. It was a dream, they say, delirium, hallucination. Oh! As though that meant so much! And they are so proud! A dream! What is a dream? And is not our life a dream? I will say more. Suppose that this paradise will never come to pass (that I understand), yet I shall go on preaching it. And yet how simple it is: in one day, *in one hour* everything could be arranged at once! The chief thing is to love others like yourself, that's the great thing, and that's everything; nothing else is wanted—you will find out at once how to arrange it all. And yet it's an old truth which has been told and retold a billion times—but it has not formed part of our lives! The consciousness of life is higher than life, the knowledge of the laws of happiness is higher than happiness—that is what one must contend against. And I shall. If only every one wants it, it can all be arranged at once.

And I tracked out that little girl . . . and I shall go on and on!

The Brushwood Boy

RUDYARD KIPLING

~~~~~~

Girls and boys, come out to play:
The moon is shining as bright as day!
Leave your supper and leave your sleep,
And come with your playfellows out in the street!
Up the ladder and down the wall—

A child of three sat up in his crib and screamed at the top of his voice, his fists clinched and his eyes full of terror. At first no one heard, for his nursery was in the west wing, and the nurse was talking to a gardener among the laurels. Then the house-keeper passed that way, and hurried to soothe him. He was her special pet, and she disapproved of the nurse.

"What was it, then? What was it, then? There's nothing to frighten him, Georgie dear."

"It was—it was a policeman! He was on the Down—I saw him! He came in. Jane *said* he would."

"Policemen don't come into houses, dearie. Turn over, and take my hand."

"I saw him—on the Down. He came here. Where is your hand, Harper?"

The housekeeper waited till the sobs changed to the regular breathing of sleep before she stole out.

"Jane, what nonsense have you been telling Master Georgie about policemen?"

"I haven't told him anything."

"You have. He's been dreaming about them."

"We met Tisdall on Dowhead when we were in the donkey-cart this morning. P'r'aps that's what put it into his head."

"Oh! Now you aren't going to frighten the child into fits with your silly tales, and the master know nothing about it. If ever I catch you again," etc.

A child of six was telling himself stories as he lay in bed. It was a new power, and he kept it a secret. A month before it had occurred to him to carry on a nursery tale left unfinished by his mother, and he was delighted to find the tale as it came out of his own head just as surprising as though he were listening to it "all new from the beginning." There was a prince in that tale, and he killed dragons, but only for one night. Ever afterwards Georgie dubbed himself prince, pasha, giant-killer, and all the rest (you see, he could not tell any one, for fear of being laughed at), and his tales faded gradually into dreamland, where adventures were so many that he could not recall the half of them. They all began in the same way, or, as Georgie explained to the shadows of the night-light, there was "the same starting-off place"—a pile of brushwood stacked somewhere near a beach; and round this pile Georgie found himself running races with little boys and girls. These ended, ships ran high up the dry land and opened into cardboard boxes; or gilt-and-green iron railings that surrounded beautiful gardens turned all soft and could be walked through and overthrown so long as he remembered it was only a dream. He could never hold that knowledge more than a few seconds ere things became real, and instead of pushing down houses full of grown-up people (a just revenge), he sat miserably upon gigantic door-steps try-ing to sing the multiplication-table up to four times six.

The princess of his tales was a person of wonderful beauty (she came from the old illustrated edition of Grimm, now out of print), and as she always applauded Georgie's valour among the dragons and buffaloes, he gave her the two finest names he had ever heard in his life—Annie and Louise, pronounced "Annie*an*louise." When the dreams swamped the stories, she would change into one of the little girls round the brushwood-pile, still keeping her title and crown. She saw Georgie drown once in a dream-sea by the beach (it was the day after he had been taken to bathe in a real sea by his nurse); and he said as he sank: "Poor Annie*an*louise! She'll be sorry for me now!" But "Annie*an*louise," walking slowly on the beach, called, "'Ha! ha!' said the duck, laughing," which to a waking mind might not seem to bear on the situation. It consoled Georgie at once, and must have been some kind of spell, for it raised the bottom of the deep, and he waded out with a twelve-inch flower-pot on each foot. As he was strictly forbidden to meddle with flower-pots in real life, he felt triumphantly wicked.

The movements of the grown-ups, whom Georgie tolerated, but did not pretend to understand, removed his world, when he was seven years old, to a place called "Oxford-on-a-visit." Here were huge buildings surrounded by vast prairies, with streets of infinite length, and, above all, something called the "buttery," which Georgie was dying to see, because he knew it must be greasy, and therefore delightful. He perceived how correct were his judgments when his nurse led him through a stone arch into the presence of an enormously fat man, who asked him if he would like some bread and cheese. Georgie was used to eat all round the clock, so he took what "buttery" gave him, and would have taken some brown liquid called "auditale" but that his nurse led him away to an afternoon performance of a thing called "Pepper's Ghost." This was intensely thrilling. People's heads came off and flew all over the stage, and skeletons danced bone by bone, while Mr. Pepper himself, beyond question a man of the worst, waved his arms and flapped a long gown, and in a deep bass voice (Georgie had never heard a man sing before) told of his sorrows unspeakable. Some grown-up or other tried to explain that the illusion was made with mirrors, and that there was no need to be frightened. Georgie did not know what illusions were, but he did know that a mirror was the looking-glass with the ivory handle on his mother's dressing-table. Therefore the "grown-up" was "just saying things" after the distressing custom of "grown-ups," and Georgie cast about for amusement between scenes. Next to him sat a little girl dressed all in black, her hair combed off her forehead exactly like the girl in the book called "Alice in Wonderland," which had been given him on his last birthday. The little girl looked at Georgie, and Georgie looked at her. There seemed to be no need of any further introduction.

"I've got a cut on my thumb," said he. It was the first work of his first real knife, a savage triangular hack, and he esteemed it a most valuable possession.

"I'm tho thorry!" she lisped. "Let me look—pleathe."

"There's a di-ack-lum plaster on, but it's all raw under," Georgie answered, complying.

"Dothent it hurt?"—her grey eyes were full of pity and interest.

"Awf'ly. Perhaps it will give me lockjaw."

"It lookth very horrid. I'm tho thorry!" She put a forefinger to his hand, and held her head sidewise for a better view.

Here the nurse turned, and shook him severely.

"You mustn't talk to strange little girls, Master Georgie."

"She isn't strange. She's very nice. I like her, an' I've showed her my new cut."

"The idea! You change places with me."

She moved him over, and shut out the little girl from his view, while the grown-up behind renewed the futile explanations.

"I am *not* afraid, truly," said the boy, wriggling in despair; "but why don't you go to sleep in the afternoons, same as Provost of Oriel?"

Georgie had been introduced to a grown-up of that name, who slept in his presence without apology. Georgie understood that he was the most important grown-up in Oxford; hence he strove to gild his rebuke with flatteries. This grown-up did not seem to like it, but he collapsed, and Georgie lay back in his seat, silent and enraptured. Mr. Pepper was singing again, and the deep, ringing voice, the red fire, and the misty, waving gown all seemed to be mixed up with the little girl who had been so kind about his cut. When the performance was ended she nodded to Georgie, and Georgie nodded in return. He spoke no more than was necessary till bedtime, but meditated on new colors and sounds and lights and music and things as far as he understood them; the deep-mouthed agony of Mr. Pepper mingling with the little girl's lisp. That night he made a new tale, from which he shamelessly removed the Rapunzel-Rapunzel-let-down-your-hair princess, gold crown, Grimm edition, and all, and put a new Annie*an*louise in her place. So it was perfectly right and natural that when he came to the brushwood-pile he should find her waiting for him, her hair combed off her forehead more like Alice in Wonderland than ever, and the races and adventures began.

Ten years at an English public school do not encourage dreaming. Georgie won his growth and chest measurement, and a few other things which did not appear in the bills, under a system of cricket, foot-ball, and paper-chases, from four to five days a week, which provided for three lawful cuts of a ground-ash if any boy absented himself from these entertainments. He became a rumple-collared, dusty-hatted fag of the Lower Third, and a light half-back at Little Side foot-ball; was pushed and prodded through the slack back-waters of the Lower Fourth, where the raffle of a school generally accumulates; won his "second-fifteen" cap at foot-ball, enjoyed the dignity of a study with two companions in it, and began to look forward to office as a sub-prefect. At last he blossomed into full glory as head of the school, ex-officio captain of the games; head of his house, where he and his lieutenants preserved discipline and decency among seventy boys from twelve to seventeen; general arbiter in the quarrels that spring up among the touchy Sixth— and intimate friend and ally of the Head himself. When he stepped forth in the black jersey, white knickers, and black stockings of the First Fifteen, the new match-ball under his arm, and his old and frayed cap at the back of his head, the small fry of the lower forms stood apart and worshipped, and the "new caps" of the team talked to him ostentatiously, that the world might see. And so, in summer, when he came back to the pavilion after a slow but eminently safe game, it mattered not whether he had made nothing or, as once happened, a hundred and three, the school shouted just the same, and women-folk who had come to look at the match looked at Cottar—Cottar, *major*; "that's Cottar!" Above all, he was responsible for that thing called the tone of the school, and few realise with what passionate devotion a certain type of boy throws himself into this work. Home was a far-away country, full of ponies and fishing and shooting, and men-visitors who interfered with one's plans; but school was the real world, where things of vital importance happened, and crises arose that must be dealt with promptly and quietly. Not for nothing was it written, "Let the Consuls look to it that the Republic takes no harm," and Georgie was glad to be back in authority when the holidays ended. Behind him, but not too near, was the wise and temperate Head, now suggesting the wisdom of the serpent, now counselling the mildness of the dove; leading him on to see, more by half-hints than by any direct word, how boys and men are all of a piece, and how he who can handle the one will assuredly in time control the other.

For the rest, the school was not encouraged to dwell on its emotions, but rather to keep in hard condition, to avoid false quantities, and to enter the army direct, without the help of the expensive London crammer, under whose roof young blood learns too much. Cottar, *major*, went the way of hundreds before him. The Head gave him six months' final polish, taught him what kind of answers best please a certain kind of examiners, and handed him over to the properly constituted authorities, who passed him into Sandhurst. Here he had sense enough to see that he was in the Lower Third once more, and behaved with respect toward his seniors, till they in turn respected him, and he was promoted to the rank of corporal, and sat in authority over mixed peoples with all the vices of men and boys combined. His reward was another string of athletic cups, a good-conduct sword, and, at last, Her Majesty's commission as a subaltern in a first-class line regiment. He did not know that he bore with him from school and college a character worth much fine gold, but was pleased to find his mess so kindly. He had plenty of money of his own; his training had set the public-school mask upon his face, and had taught him how many were the "things no fellow can do." By virtue of the same training he kept his pores open and his mouth shut.

The regular working of the Empire shifted his world to India, where he tasted utter loneliness in subaltern's quarters, —one room and one bullock-trunk,—and, with his mess, learned the new life from the beginning. But there were horses in the land—ponies at reasonable price; there was polo for such as could afford it; there were the disreputable remnants of a pack of hounds; and Cottar worried his way along without too much despair. It dawned on him that a regiment in India was nearer the chance of active service than he had conceived, and that a man might as well study his profession. A major of the new school backed this idea with enthusiasm, and he and Cottar accumulated a library of military works, and read and argued and disputed far into the nights. But the adjutant said the old thing: "Get to know your men, young un, and they'll follow you anywhere. That's all you want—know your men." Cottar thought he knew them fairly well at cricket and the regimental sports, but he never realised the true inwardness of them till he was sent off with a detachment of twenty to sit down in a mud fort near a rushing river which was spanned by a bridge of boats. When the floods came they went forth and hunted strayed pontoons along the banks. Otherwise there was nothing to do, and the men got drunk, gambled, and quarrelled. They were a sickly crew, for a junior subaltern is by custom saddled with the worst men. Cottar endured their rioting as long as he could, and then sent down-country for a dozen pairs of boxing-gloves.

"I wouldn't blame you for fightin'," said he, "if you only knew how to use your hands; but you don't. Take these things, and I'll show you." The men appreciated his efforts. Now, instead of blaspheming and swearing at a comrade, and threatening to shoot him, they could take him apart, and soothe themselves to exhaustion. As one explained whom Cottar found with a shut eye and a diamond-shaped mouth spitting blood through an embrasure: "We tried it with the gloves, sir, for twenty minutes, and *that* done us no good, sir. Then we took off the gloves and tried it that way for another twenty minutes, same as you showed us, sir, an' that done us a world o' good. 'T wasn't fightin', sir; there was a bet on."

Cottar dared not laugh, but he invited his men to other sports, such as racing across country in shirt and trousers after

a trail of torn paper, and to single-stick in the evenings, till the
native population, who had a lust for sport in every form,
wished to know whether the white men understood wrestling.
They sent in an ambassador, who took the soldiers by the neck
and threw them about the dust; and the entire command were
all for this new game. They spent money on learning new falls
and holds, which was better than buying other doubtful com-
modities; and the peasantry grinned five deep round the tourna-
ments.

That detachment, who had gone up in bullock-carts, returned
to headquarters at an average rate of thirty miles a day, fair heel-
and-toe; no sick, no prisoners, and no court martials pending.
They scattered themselves among their friends, singing the
praises of their lieutenant and looking for causes of offense.

"How did you do it, young un?" the adjutant asked.

"Oh, I sweated the beef off 'em, and then I sweated some
muscle on to 'em. It was rather a lark."

"If that's your way of lookin' at it, we can give you all the
larks you want. Young Davies isn't feelin' quite fit, and he's
next for detachment duty. Care to go for him?"

"Sure he wouldn't mind? I don't want to shove myself forward, you know."

"You needn't bother on Davies's account. We'll give you the
sweepin's of the corps, and you can see what you can make of
'em."

"All right," said Cottar. "It's better fun than loafin' about
cantonments."

"Rummy thing," said the adjutant, after Cottar had returned
to his wilderness with twenty other devils worse than the first.
"If Cottar only knew it, half the women in the station would
give their eyes—confound 'em!—to have the young un in tow."

"That accounts for Mrs. Elery sayin' I was workin' my nice
new boy too hard," said a wing commander.

"Oh, yes; and 'Why doesn't he come to the bandstand in

the evenings?' and 'Can't I get him to make up a four at tennis with the Hammon girls?'" the adjutant snorted. "Look at young Davies makin' an ass of himself over mutton-dressed-as-lamb old enough to be his mother!"

"No one can accuse young Cottar of runnin' after women, white or black," the major replied thoughtfully. "But, then, that's the kind that generally goes the worst mucker in the end."

"Not Cottar. I've only run across one of his muster before—a fellow called Ingles, in South Africa. He was just the same hard-trained, athletic-sports build of animal. Always kept himself in the pink of condition. Didn't do him much good, though. Shot at Wesselstroom the week before Majuba. Wonder how the young un will lick his detachment into shape."

Cottar turned up six weeks later, on foot, with his pupils. He never told his experiences, but the men spoke enthusiastically, and fragments of it leaked back to the colonel through sergeants, bâtmen, and the like.

There was great jealousy between the first and second detachments, but the men united in adoring Cottar, and their way of showing it was by sparing him all the trouble that men know how to make for an unloved officer. He sought popularity as little as he had sought it at school, and therefore it came to him. He favoured no one—not even when the company sloven pulled the company cricket-match out of the fire with an unexpected forty-three at the last moment. There was very little getting round him, for he seemed to know by instinct exactly when and where to head off a malingerer; but he did not forget that the difference between a dazed and sulky junior of the upper school and a bewildered, browbeaten lump of a private fresh from the depot was very small indeed. The sergeants, seeing these things, told him secrets generally hid from young officers. His words were quoted as barrack authority on bets in canteen and at tea; and the veriest shrew of the corps, bursting with charges against other women who had used the cooking-ranges out of turn, forbore to speak when Cottar, as the regulations ordained, asked of a morning if there were "any complaints."

"I'm full o' complaints," said Mrs. Corporal Morrison, "an' I'd kill O'Halloran's fat sow of a wife any day, but ye know how it is. 'E puts 'is head just inside the door, an' looks down 'is blessed nose so bashful, an' 'e whispers, 'Any complaints?' Ye can't complain after that. I want to kiss him. Some day I think I will. Heigh-ho! she'll be a lucky woman that gets Young Innocence. See 'im now, girls. Do ye blame me?"

Cottar was cantering across to polo, and he looked a very satisfactory figure of a man as he gave easily to the first excited bucks of his pony, and slipped over a low mud wall to the practice-ground. There were more than Mrs. Corporal Morrison who felt as she did. But Cottar was busy for eleven hours of the day. He did not care to have his tennis spoiled by petticoats in the court; and after one long afternoon at a garden-party, he explained to his major that this sort of thing was "futile piffle," and the major laughed. Theirs was not a married mess, except for the colonel's wife, and Cottar stood in awe of the good lady. She said "my regiment," and the world knows what that means. None the less, when they wanted her to give away the prizes after a shooting-match, and she refused because one of the prize-winners was married to a girl who had made a jest of her behind her broad back, the mess ordered Cottar to "tackle her," in his best calling-kit. This he did, simply and laboriously, and she gave way altogether.

"She only wanted to know the facts of the case," he explained. "I just told her, and she saw at once."

"Ye-es," said the adjutant. "I expect that's what she did. Comin' to the Fusiliers' dance to-night, Galahad?"

"No, thanks. I've got a fight on with the major." The virtuous apprentice sat up till midnight in the major's quarters, with a stop-watch and a pair of compasses, shifting little painted lead-blocks about a four-inch map.

Then he turned in and slept the sleep of innocence, which is full of healthy dreams. One peculiarity of his dreams he noticed at the beginning of his second hot weather. Two or three times a month they duplicated or ran in series. He would find himself sliding into dreamland by the same road—a road that ran along a beach near a pile of brushwood. To the right lay the sea, sometimes at full tide, sometimes withdrawn to the very horizon; but he knew it for the same sea. By that road he would travel over a swell of rising ground covered with short, withered grass, into valleys of wonder and unreason. Beyond the ridge, which was crowned with some sort of street-lamp, anything was possible; but up to the lamp it seemed to him that he knew the road as well as he knew the parade-ground. He learned to look forward to the place; for, once there, he was sure of a good night's rest, and Indian hot weather can be rather trying. First, shadowy under closing eyelids, would come the outline of the brushwood-pile, next the white sand of the beach-road, almost overhanging the black, changeful sea; then the turn inland and uphill to the single light. When he was unrestful for any reason, he would tell himself how he was sure to get there—sure to get there—if he shut his eyes and surrendered to the drift of things. But one night after a foolishly hard hour's polo (the thermometer was 94° in his quarters at ten o'clock), sleep stood away from him altogether, though he did his best to find the well-known road, the point where true sleep began. At last he saw the brushwood-pile, and hurried along to the ridge, for behind him he felt was the wide-awake, sultry world. He reached the lamp in safety, tingling with drowsiness, when a policeman—a common country policeman—sprang up before him and touched him on the shoulder ere he could dive into the dim valley below. He was filled with terror,—the hopeless terror of dreams,—for the policeman said, in the awful, distinct voice of dream-people, "I am Policeman Day coming back from the City of Sleep. You come with me." Georgie knew it was true—that just beyond him in the valley lay the lights of the City of Sleep, where he would have been sheltered, and that this Policeman-Thing had full power and authority to head him back to miserable wakefulness. He found himself looking at the moonlight on the wall, dripping with fright; and he never overcame that horror, though he met the Policeman several times that hot weather, and his coming was the forerunner of a bad night.

But other dreams—perfectly absurd ones—filled him with an incommunicable delight. All those that he remembered began by the brushwood-pile. For instance, he found a small clock-work steamer (he had noticed it many nights before) lying by the sea-road, and stepped into it, whereupon it moved with surpassing swiftness over an absolutely level sea. This was glorious, for he felt he was exploring great matters; and it stopped by a lily carved in stone, which, most naturally, floated on the water. Seeing the lily was labelled "Hong-Kong," Georgie said: "Of course. This is precisely what I expected Hong-Kong would be like. How magnificent!" Thousands of miles farther on it halted at yet another stone lily, labelled "Java"; and this, again, delighted him hugely, because he knew that now he was at the world's end. But the little boat ran on and on till it lay in a deep fresh-water lock, the sides of which were carven marble, green with moss. Lily-pads lay on the water, and reeds arched above. Some one moved among the reeds—some one whom Georgie knew he had travelled to this world's end to reach. Therefore everything was entirely well with him. He was unspeakably happy, and vaulted over the ship's side to find this person. When his feet touched that still water, it changed, with the rustle of unrolling maps, to nothing less than a sixth quarter of the globe, beyond the most remote imagining of man—a place where islands were coloured yellow and blue, their lettering strung across their faces. They gave on unknown seas, and Georgie's urgent desire was to return swiftly across this floating atlas to known bearings. He told himself repeatedly that it was no good to hurry; but still he hurried desperately, and the islands slipped and slid under his feet, the straits yawned and widened, till he found himself utterly lost in the world's fourth dimension, with no hope of return. Yet only a little distance away he could see the old world with the rivers and mountain-chains marked according to the Sandhurst rules of map-making. Then that person for whom he had come to the Lily Lock (that was its name) ran up across unexplored territories, and showed him a way. They fled hand in hand till they reached a road that spanned ravines, and ran along the edge of precipices, and was tunnelled through mountains. "This goes to our brushwood-pile," said his companion; and all his trouble was at an end. He took a pony, because he understood that this was the Thirty-Mile Ride and he must ride swiftly, and raced through the clattering tunnels and round the curves, always downhill, till he heard the sea to his left, and saw it raging under a full moon, against sandy cliffs. It was heavy going, but he recognised the nature of the country, the dark-purple downs inland, and the bents that whistled in the wind. The road was eaten away in places, and the sea lashed at him—black, foamless tongues of smooth and glossy rollers; but he was sure that there was less danger from the sea than from "Them," whoever "They" were, inland to his right. He knew, too, that he would be safe if he could reach the down with the lamp on it. This came as he expected: he saw the one light a mile ahead along the beach, dismounted, turned to the right, walked quietly over to the brushwood-pile, found the little steamer had returned to the beach whence he had unmoored it, and—must have fallen asleep, for he could remember no more. "I'm gettin' the hang of the geography of that place," he said to himself, as he shaved next morning. "I must have made some sort of circle. Let's see.

The Thirty-Mile Ride (now how the deuce did I know it was called the Thirty-Mile Ride?) joins the sea-road beyond the first down where the lamp is. And that atlas-country lies at the back of the Thirty-Mile Ride, somewhere out to the right beyond the hills and tunnels. Rummy things, dreams. Wonder what makes mine fit into each other so?"

He continued on his solid way through the recurring duties of the seasons. The regiment was shifted to another station, and he enjoyed road-marching for two months, with a good deal of mixed shooting thrown in, and when they reached their new cantonments he became a member of the local Tent Club, and chased the mighty boar on horseback with a short stabbing-spear. There he met the *mahseer* of the Poonch, beside whom the tarpon is as a herring, and he who lands him can say that he is a fisherman. This was as new and as fascinating as the big-game shooting that fell to his portion, when he had himself photographed for the mother's benefit, sitting on the flank of his first tiger.

Then the adjutant was promoted, and Cottar rejoiced with him, for he admired the adjutant greatly, and marvelled who might be big enough to fill his place; so that he nearly collapsed when the mantle fell on his own shoulders, and the colonel said a few sweet things that made him blush. An adjutant's position does not differ materially from that of head of the school, and Cottar stood in the same relation to the colonel as he had to his old Head in England. Only, tempers wear out in hot weather, and things were said and done that tried him sorely, and he made glorious blunders, from which the regimental sergeant-major pulled him with a loyal soul and a shut mouth. Slovens and incompetents raged against him; the weak-minded strove to lure him from the ways of justice; the small-minded —yea, men who Cottar believed would never do "things no fellow can do"—imputed motives mean and circuitous to actions that he had not spent a thought upon; and he tasted in-

justice, and it made him very sick. But his consolation came on
parade, when he looked down the full companies, and reflected
how few were in hospital or cells, and wondered when the time
would come to try the machine of his love and labour.

But they needed and expected the whole of a man's working-
day, and maybe three or four hours of the night. Curiously
enough, he never dreamed about the regiment as he was
popularly supposed to. The mind, set free from the day's do-
ings, generally ceased working altogether, or, if it moved at all,
carried him along the old beach-road to the downs, the lamp-
post, and, once in a while, to terrible Policeman Day. The
second time that he returned to the world's lost continent (this
was a dream that repeated itself again and again, with varia-
tions, on the same ground) he knew that if he only sat still
the person from the Lily Lock would help him, and he was not
disappointed. Sometimes he was trapped in mines of vast depth
hollowed out of the heart of the world, where men in torment
chanted echoing songs; and he heard this person coming along
through the galleries, and everything was made safe and delightful. They met again in low-roofed Indian railway-carriages that
halted in a garden surrounded by gilt-and-green railings, where
a mob of stony white people, all unfriendly, sat at breakfast-
tables covered with roses, and separated Georgie from his companion, while underground voices sang deep-voiced songs. Georgie was filled with enormous despair till they two met again.
They foregathered in the middle of an endless, hot tropic night,
and crept into a huge house that stood, he knew, somewhere
north of the railway-station where the people ate among the
roses. It was surrounded with gardens, all moist and dripping;
and in one room, reached through leagues of whitewashed pas-
sages, a Sick Thing lay in bed. Now the least noise, Georgie
knew, would unchain some waiting horror, and his companion
knew it, too; but when their eyes met across the bed, Georgie

was disgusted to see that she was a child—a little girl in strapped shoes, with her black hair combed back from her forehead.

"What disgraceful folly!" he thought. "Now she could do nothing whatever if Its head came off."

Then the Thing coughed, and the ceiling shattered down in plaster on the mosquito-netting, and "They" rushed in from all quarters. He dragged the child through the stifling garden, voices chanting behind them, and they rode the Thirty-Mile Ride under whip and spur along the sandy beach by the booming sea, till they came to the downs, the lamp-post, and the brushwood-pile, which was safety. Very often dreams would break up about them in this fashion, and they would be separated, to endure awful adventures alone. But the most amusing times were when he and she had a clear understanding that it was all make-believe, and walked through mile-wide roaring rivers without even taking off their shoes, or set light to populous cities to see how they would burn, and were rude as any children to the vague shadows met in their rambles. Later in the night they were sure to suffer for this, either at the hands of the Railway People eating among the roses, or in the tropic uplands at the far end of the Thirty-Mile Ride. Together, this did not much affright them; but often Georgie would hear her shrill cry of "Boy! Boy!" half a world away, and hurry to her rescue before "They" maltreated her.

He and she explored the dark-purple downs as far inland from the brushwood-pile as they dared, but that was always a dangerous matter. The interior was filled with "Them," and "They" went about singing in the hollows, and Georgie and she felt safer on or near the seaboard. So thoroughly had he come to know the place of his dreams that even waking he accepted it as a real country, and made a rough sketch of it. He kept his own counsel, of course; but the permanence of the land puzzled him. His ordinary dreams were as formless and as fleeting as any healthy dreams could be, but once at the brushwood-pile he moved within known limits and could see where he was going. There were months at a time when nothing notable crossed his sleep. Then the dreams would come in a batch of five or six, and next morning the map that he kept in his writing case would be written up to date, for Georgie was a most methodical person. There was, indeed, a danger—his seniors said so—of his developing into a regular "Auntie Fuss" of an adjutant, and

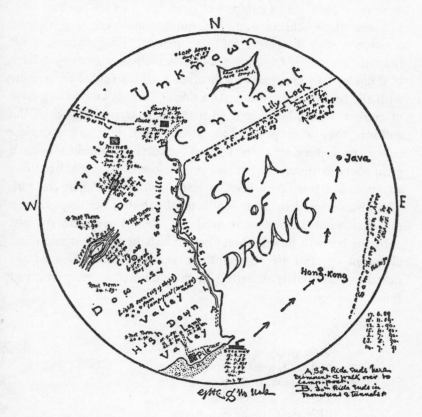

when an officer once takes to old-maidism there is more hope for the virgin of seventy than for him.

But fate sent the change that was needed, in the shape of a little winter campaign on the Border, which, after the manner of little campaigns, flashed out into a very ugly war; and Cottar's regiment was chosen among the first.

"Now," said a major, "this'll shake the cobwebs out of us all—especially you, Galahad; and we can see what your hen-with-one-chick attitude has done for the regiment."

Cottar nearly wept with joy as the campaign went forward. They were fit—physically fit beyond the other troops; they were good children in camp, wet or dry, fed or unfed; and they followed their officers with the quick suppleness and trained obedience of a first-class foot-ball fifteen. They were cut off from their apology for a base, and cheerfully cut their way back to it again; they crowned and cleaned out hills full of the enemy with the precision of well-broken dogs of chase; and in the hour of retreat, when, hampered with the sick and wounded of the column, they were persecuted down eleven miles of waterless valley, they, serving as rear-guard, covered themselves with a great glory in the eyes of fellow-professionals. Any regiment can advance, but few know how to retreat with a sting in the tail. Then they turned to made roads, most often under fire, and dismantled some inconvenient mud redoubts. They were the last corps to be withdrawn when the rubbish of the campaign was all swept up; and after a month in standing camp, which tries morals severely, they departed to their own place in column of fours, singing:

> "'E's goin' to do without 'em—
> Don't want 'em any more;
> 'E's goin' to do without 'em,
> As 'e 's often done before.
> 'E's goin' to be a martyr
> On a 'ighly novel plan,
> An' all the boys and girls will say,
> 'Ow! what a nice young man—man—man!
> Ow! what a nice young man!'"

There came out a "Gazette" in which Cottar found that he had been behaving with "courage and coolness and discretion" in all his capacities; that he had assisted the wounded under fire, and blown in a gate, also under fire. Net result, his captaincy and a brevet majority, coupled with the Distinguished Service Order.

As to his wounded, he explained that they were both heavy men, whom he could lift more easily than any one else. "Otherwise, of course, I should have sent out one of my men; and, of course, about that gate business, we were safe the minute we were well under the walls." But this did not prevent his men from cheering him furiously whenever they saw him, or the mess from giving him a dinner on the eve of his departure to England. (A year's leave was among the things he had "snaffled out of the campaign," to use his own words.) The doctor, who had taken quite as much as was good for him, quoted poetry about "a good blade carving the casques of men," and so on, and everybody told Cottar that he was an excellent person; but when he rose to make his maiden speech they shouted so that he was understood to say, "It isn't any use tryin' to speak with you chaps rottin' me like this. Let's have some pool."

It is not unpleasant to spend eight-and-twenty days in an easy-going steamer on warm waters, in the company of a woman who lets you see that you are head and shoulders superior to the rest of the world, even though that woman may be, and most often is, ten counted years your senior. P.O. boats are not lighted with the disgustful particularity of Atlantic liners. There is more phosphorescence at the bows, and greater silence and darkness by the hand-steering gear aft.

Awful things might have happened to Georgie but for the little fact that he had never studied the first principles of the game he was expected to play. So when Mrs. Zuleika, at Aden, told him how motherly an interest she felt in his welfare, medals, brevet, and all, Georgie took her at the foot of the letter, and promptly talked of his own mother, three hundred miles nearer each day, of his home, and so forth, all the way up the Red Sea. It was much easier than he had supposed to converse with a woman for an hour at a time. Then Mrs. Zuleika, turning from parental affection, spoke of love in the abstract as a thing not unworthy of study, and in discreet twilights after dinner demanded confidences. Georgie would have been delighted to supply them, but he had none, and did not know it was his duty to manufacture them. Mrs. Zuleika expressed surprise and unbelief, and asked those questions which deep asks of deep. She learned all that was necessary to conviction, and, being very much a woman, resumed (Georgie never knew that she had abandoned) the motherly attitude.

"Do you know," she said, somewhere in the Mediterranean, "I think you're the very dearest boy I have ever met in my life, and I'd like you to remember me a little. You will when you are older, but I want you to remember me now. You'll make some girl very happy."

"Oh! Hope so," said Georgie, gravely; "but there's heaps of time for marryin' an' all that sort of thing, ain't there?"

"That depends. Here are your bean-bags for the Ladies' Competition. I think I'm growing too old to care for those *tamashas.*"

They were getting up sports, and Georgie was on the committee. He never noticed how perfectly the bags were sewn, but another woman did, and smiled—once. He liked Mrs. Zuleika greatly. She was a bit old, of course, but uncommonly nice. There was no nonsense about her.

A few nights after they passed Gibraltar his dream returned to him. She who waited by the brushwood-pile was no longer a little girl, but a woman with black hair that grew into a "widow's peak," combed back from her forehead. He knew her for the child in black, the companion of the last six years, and, as it had been in the time of the meetings on the Lost Continent, he was filled with delight unspeakable. "They," for some dream-land reason, were friendly or had gone away that night, and the two flitted together over all their country, from the brush-wood-pile up the Thirty-Mile Ride, till they saw the House of the Sick Thing, a pin-point in the distance to the left; stamped through the Railway Waiting-room where the roses lay on the spread breakfast-tables; and returned, by the ford and the city they had once burned for sport, to the great swells of the downs under the lamp-post. Wherever they moved a strong sing-ing followed them underground, but this night there was no panic. All the land was empty except for themselves, and at the last (they were sitting by the lamp-post hand in hand) she turned and kissed him. He woke with a start, staring at the waving curtain of the cabin door; he could almost have sworn that the kiss was real.

Next morning the ship was rolling in a Biscay sea, and people were not happy; but as Georgie came to breakfast, shaven, tubbed, and smelling of soap, several turned to look at him be-cause of the light in his eyes and the splendour of his counte-nance.

"Well, you look beastly fit," snapped a neighbour. "Any one left you a legacy in the middle of the Bay?"

Georgie reached for the curry, with a seraphic grin. "I sup-pose it's the gettin' so near home, and all that. I do feel rather festive this mornin'. Rolls a bit, doesn't she?"

Mrs. Zuleika stayed in her cabin till the end of the voyage, when she left without bidding him farewell, and wept pas-sionately on the dock-head for pure joy of meeting her children, who, she had often said, were so like their father.

Georgie headed for his own country, wild with delight of his first long furlough after the lean seasons. Nothing was changed in that orderly life, from the coachman who met him at the station to the white peacock that stormed at the car-riage from the stone wall above the shaven lawns. The house took toll of him with due regard to precedence—first the mother; then the father; then the housekeeper, who wept and praised God; then the butler, and so on down to the under-keeper, who had been dog-boy in Georgie's youth, and called him "Master Georgie," and was reproved by the groom who had taught Georgie to ride.

"Not a thing changed," he sighed contentedly, when the three of them sat down to dinner in the late sunlight, while the rabbits crept out upon the lawn below the cedars, and the big trout in the ponds by the home paddock rose for their evening meal.

"*Our* changes are all over, dear," cooed the mother; "and now I am getting used to your size and your tan (you're very brown, Georgie), I see you haven't changed in the least. You're exactly like the pater."

The father beamed on this man after his own heart,— "youngest major in the army, and should have had the V.C., sir,"—and the butler listened with his professional mask off when Master Georgie spoke of war as it is waged to-day, and his father cross-questioned.

They went out on the terrace to smoke among the roses, and the shadow of the old house lay long across the wonderful English foliage, which is the only living green in the world.

"Perfect! By Jove, it's perfect!" Georgie was looking at the round-bosomed woods beyond the home paddock, where the white pheasant boxes were ranged; and the golden air was full of a hundred sacred scents and sounds. Georgie felt his father's arm tighten in his.

"It's not half bad—but *hodie mihi, cras tibi*, isn't it? I suppose you'll be turning up some fine day with a girl under your arm, if you haven't one now, eh?"

"You can make your mind easy, sir. I haven't one."

"Not in all these years?" said the mother.

"I hadn't time, mummy. They keep a man pretty busy, these days, in the service, and most of our mess are unmarried, too."

"But you must have met hundreds in society—at balls, and so on?"

"I'm like the Tenth, mummy: I don't dance."

"Don't dance! What have you been doing with yourself, then —backing other men's bills?" said the father.

"Oh, yes; I've done a little of that too; but you see, as things are now, a man has all his work cut out for him to keep abreast of his profession, and my days were always too full to let me lark about half the night."

"Hmm!"—suspiciously.

"It's never too late to learn. We ought to give some kind of housewarming for the people about, now you've come back. Unless you want to go straight up to town, dear?"

"No. I don't want anything better than this. Let's sit still and enjoy ourselves. I suppose there will be something for me to ride if I look for it?"

"Seeing I've been kept down to the old brown pair for the last six weeks because all the others were being got ready for Master Georgie, I should say there might be," the father chuckled. "They're reminding me in a hundred ways that I must take the second place now."

"Brutes!"

"The pater doesn't mean it, dear; but every one has been trying to make your home-coming a success; and you *do* like it, don't you?"

"Perfect! Perfect! There's no place like England—when you've done your work."

"That's the proper way to look at it, my son."

And so up and down the flagged walk till their shadows grew long in the moonlight, and the mother went indoors and played such songs as a small boy once clamoured for, and the squat silver candlesticks were brought in, and Georgie climbed to the two rooms in the west wing that had been his nursery and his playroom in the beginning. Then who should come to tuck him up for the night but the mother? And she sat down on the bed, and they talked for a long hour, as mother and son should, if there is to be any future for the Empire. With a simple woman's deep guile she asked questions and suggested answers that should have waked some sign in the face on the pillow, and there was neither quiver of eyelid nor quickening of breath, neither evasion nor delay in reply. So she blessed him and kissed him on the mouth, which is not always a mother's property, and said something to her husband later, at which he laughed profane and incredulous laughs.

All the establishment waited on Georgie next morning, from the tallest six-year-old, "with a mouth like a kid glove, Master Georgie," to the under-keeper strolling carelessly along the horizon, Georgie's pet rod in his hand, and "There's a four-pounder risin' below the lasher. You don't 'ave 'em in Injia, Mast—Major Georgie." It was all beautiful beyond telling, even though the mother insisted on taking him out in the landau (the leather had the hot Sunday smell of his youth) and showing him off to her friends at all the houses for six miles round; and the pater bore him up to town and a lunch at the club, where he introduced him, quite carelessly, to not less than thirty ancient warriors whose sons were not the youngest majors in the army and had not the D.S.O. After that it was Georgie's turn; and remembering his friends, he filled up the house with that kind of officer who live in cheap lodgings at Southsea or Montpelier Square, Brompton—good men all, but not well off. The mother perceived that they needed girls to play with; and as there was no scarcity of girls, the house hummed like a dovecote in spring. They tore up the place for amateur theatricals; they disappeared in the gardens when they ought to have been rehearsing; they swept off every available horse and vehicle, especially the governess-cart and the fat pony; they fell into the trout-ponds; they picnicked and they tennised; and they sat on gates in the twilight, two by two, and Georgie found that he was not in the least necessary to their entertainment.

"My word!" said he, when he saw the last of their dear backs. "They told me they've enjoyed 'emselves, but they haven't done half the things they said they would."

"I know they've enjoyed themselves—immensely," said the mother. "You're a public benefactor, dear."

"Now we can be quiet again, can't we?"

"Oh, quite. I've a very dear friend of mine that I want you to know. She couldn't come with the house so full, because she's an invalid, and she was away when you first came. She's a Mrs. Lacy."

"Lacy! I don't remember the name about here."

"No; they came after you went to India—from Oxford. Her husband died there, and she lost some money, I believe. They bought The Firs on the Bassett Road. She's a very sweet woman, and we're very fond of them both."

"She's a widow, didn't you say?"

"She has a daughter. Surely I said so, dear?"

"Does she fall into trout-ponds, and gas and giggle, and 'Oh, Major Cottah!' and all that sort of thing?"

"No, indeed. She's a very quiet girl, and very musical. She always came over here with her music books—composing, you know; and she generally works all day, so you won't—"

"Talking about Miriam?" said the pater, coming up. The mother edged toward him within elbow-reach. There was no finesse about Georgie's father. "Oh, Miriam's a dear girl. Plays beautifully. Rides beautifully, too. She's a regular pet of the household. Used to call me—" The elbow went home, and ignorant but obedient always, the pater shut himself off.

"What used she to call you, sir?"

"All sorts of pet names. I'm very fond of Miriam."

"Sounds Jewish—Miriam."

"Jew! You'll be calling yourself a Jew next. She's one of the Herefordshire Lacys. When her aunt dies—" Again the elbow.

"Oh, you won't see anything of her, Georgie. She's busy with her music or her mother all day. Besides, you're going up to town to-morrow, aren't you? I thought you said something about an Institute meeting?" The mother spoke.

"Go up to town *now!* What nonsense!" Once more the pater was shut off.

"I had some idea of it, but I'm not quite sure," said the son of the house. Why did the mother try to get him away because a musical girl and her invalid parent were expected? He did not approve of unknown females calling his father pet names. He would observe these pushing persons who had been only seven years in the county.

All of which the delighted mother read in his countenance, herself keeping an air of sweet disinterestedness.

"They'll be here this evening for dinner. I'm sending the carriage over for them, and they won't stay more than a week."

"Perhaps I shall go up to town. I don't quite know yet." Georgie moved away irresolutely. There was a lecture at the United Services Institute on the supply of ammunition in the field, and the one man whose theories most irritated Major Cottar would deliver it. A heated discussion was sure to follow, and perhaps he might find himself moved to speak. He took his rod that afternoon and went down to thrash it out among the trout.

"Good sport, dear!" said the mother, from the terrace.

"'Fraid it won't be, mummy. All those men from town, and the girls particularly, have put every trout off his feed for weeks. There isn't one of 'em that cares for fishin'—really. Fancy stampin' and shoutin' on the bank, and tellin' every fish for half a mile exactly what you're goin' to do, and then chuckin' a brute of a fly at him! By Jove, it would scare *me* if I was a trout!"

But things were not as bad as he had expected. The black gnat was on the water, and the water was strictly preserved. A three-quarter-pounder at the second cast set him for the campaign, and he worked down-stream, crouching behind the reed and meadow-sweet; creeping between a hornbeam hedge and a foot-wide strip of bank, where he could see the trout, but where they could not distinguish him from the background; lying almost on his stomach to switch the blue-upright side-wise through the checkered shadows of a gravelly ripple under overarching trees. But he had known every inch of the water since he was four feet high. The aged and astute between sunk roots, with the large and fat that lay in the frothy scum below some strong rush of water, sucking as lazily as carp, came to trouble in their turn, at the hand that imitated so delicately the flicker and wimple of an egg-dropping fly. Consequently, Georgie found himself five miles from home when he ought to have been dressing for dinner. The housekeeper had taken good care that her boy should not go empty, and before he changed to the white moth he sat down to excellent claret with sandwiches of potted egg and things that adoring women make and men never notice. Then back, to surprise the otter grubbing for fresh-water mussels, the rabbits on the edge of the beechwoods foraging in the clover, and the policeman-like white owl stooping to the little field-mice, till the moon was strong, and he took his rod apart, and went home through well-remembered gaps in the hedges. He fetched a compass round the house, for, though he might have broken every law of the establishment every hour, the law of his boyhood was unbreakable: after fishing you went in by the south garden back-door, cleaned up in the outer scullery, and did not present yourself to your elders and your betters till you had washed and changed.

"Half-past ten, by Jove! Well, we'll make the sport an excuse. They wouldn't want to see me the first evening, at any rate. Gone to bed, probably." He skirted by the open French windows of the drawing-room. "No, they haven't. They look very comfy in there."

He could see his father in his own particular chair, the mother in hers, and the back of a girl at the piano by the big potpourri-jar. The gardens looked half divine in the moonlight, and he turned down through the roses to finish his pipe.

A prelude ended, and there floated out a voice of the kind that in his childhood he used to call "creamy"—a full, true contralto; and this is the song that he heard, every syllable of it:

Over the edge of the purple down,
  Where the single lamplight gleams,
Know ye the road to the Merciful Town
  That is hard by the Sea of Dreams—
Where the poor may lay their wrongs away,
  And the sick may forget to weep?
But we—pity us! Oh, pity us!
  We wakeful; ah, pity us!—
We must go back with Policeman Day—
  Back from the City of Sleep!

Weary they turn from the scroll and crown,
  Fetter and prayer and plough—
They that go up to the Merciful Town,
  For her gates are closing now.
It is their right in the Baths of Night
  Body and soul to steep:
But we—pity us! ah, pity us!
  We wakeful; oh, pity us!—
We must go back with Policeman Day—
  Back from the City of Sleep!

Over the edge of the purple down,
  Ere the tender dreams begin,
Look—we may look—at the Merciful Town,
  But we may not enter in!

Outcasts all, from her guarded wall
Back to our watch we creep:
We—pity us! ah, pity us!—
We wakeful; oh, pity us!—
We that go back with Policeman Day—
Back from the City of Sleep!

At the last echo he was aware that his mouth was dry and unknown pulses were beating in the roof of it. The housekeeper, who would have it that he must have fallen in and caught a chill, was waiting to catch him on the stairs, and, since he neither saw nor answered her, carried a wild tale abroad that brought his mother knocking at the door.

"Anything happened, dear? Harper said she thought you weren't—"

"No; it's nothing. I'm all right, mummy. *Please* don't bother."

He did not recognise his own voice, but that was a small matter beside what he was considering. Obviously, most obviously, the whole coincidence was crazy lunacy. He proved it to the satisfaction of Major George Cottar, who was going up to town to-morrow to hear a lecture on the supply of ammunition in the field; and having so proved it, the soul and brain and heart and body of Georgie cried joyously: "That's the Lily Lock girl—the Lost Continent girl—the Thirty-Mile Ride girl —the Brushwood girl! *I* know her!"

He waked, stiff and cramped in his chair, to reconsider the situation by sunlight, when it did not appear normal. But a man must eat, and he went to breakfast, his heart between his teeth, holding himself severely in hand.

"Late, as usual," said the mother. "My boy, Miss Lacy."

A tall girl in black raised her eyes to his, and Georgie's life training deserted him—just as soon as he realised that she did not know. He stared coolly and critically. There was the abundant black hair, growing in a widow's peak, turned back from the forehead, with that peculiar ripple over the right ear; there were the grey eyes set a little close together; the short upper lip, resolute chin, and the known poise of the head. There was also the small well-cut mouth that had kissed him.

"Georgie—*dear!*" said the mother, amazedly, for Miriam was flushing under the stare.

"I—I beg your pardon!" he gulped. "I don't know whether the mother has told you, but I'm rather an idiot at times, specially before I've had my breakfast. It's—it's a family failing."

He turned to explore among the hot-water dishes on the sideboard, rejoicing that she did not know—she did not know.

His conversation for the rest of the meal was mildly insane, though the mother thought she had never seen her boy look half so handsome. How could any girl, least of all one of Miriam's discernment, forbear to fall down and worship? But deeply Miriam was displeased. She had never been stared at in that fashion before, and promptly retired into her shell when Georgie announced that he had changed his mind about going to town, and would stay to play with Miss Lacy if she had nothing better to do.

"Oh, but don't let me throw you out. I'm at work. I've things to do all the morning."

"What possessed Georgie to behave so oddly?" the mother sighed to herself. "Miriam's a bundle of feelings—like her mother."

"You compose—don't you? Must be a fine thing to be able to do that. ["Pig—oh, pig!" thought Miriam.] I think I heard you singin' when I came in last night after fishin'. All about a Sea of Dreams, wasn't it? [Miriam shuddered to the core of the soul that afflicted her.] Awfully pretty song. How d'you think of such things?"

"You only composed the music, dear, didn't you?"

"The words too. I'm sure of it," said Georgie, with a sparkling eye. No; she did not know.

"Yeth; I wrote the words too." Miriam spoke slowly, for she
knew she lisped when she was nervous.

"Now how *could* you tell, Georgie?" said the mother, as delighted as though the youngest major in the army were ten
years old, showing off before company.

"I was sure of it, somehow. Oh, there are heaps of things
about me, mummy, that you don't understand. Looks as if it
were goin' to be a hot day—for England. Would you care for
a ride this afternoon, Miss Lacy? We can start out after tea, if
you'd like it."

Miriam could not in decency refuse, but any woman might
see she was not filled with delight.

"That will be very nice, if you take the Bassett Road. It
will save me sending Martin down to the village," said the
mother, filling in gaps.

Like all good managers, the mother had her one weakness
—a mania for little strategies that should economise horses and
vehicles. Her men-folk complained that she turned them into
common carriers, and there was a legend in the family that she
had once said to the pater on the morning of a meet: "If you
should kill near Bassett, dear, and if it isn't too late, would
you mind just popping over and matching me this?"

"I knew that was coming. You'd never miss a chance, mother.
If it's a fish or a trunk I won't." Georgie laughed.

"It's only a duck. They can do it up very neatly at Mallett's,"
said the mother, simply. "You won't mind, will you? We'll have
a scratch dinner at nine, because it's so hot."

The long summer day dragged itself out for centuries; but
at last there was tea on the lawn, and Miriam appeared.

She was in the saddle before he could offer to help, with
the clean spring of the child who mounted the pony for the
Thirty-Mile Ride. The day held mercilessly, though Georgie

got down thrice to look for imaginary stones in Rufus's foot. One cannot say even simple things in broad light, and this that Georgie meditated was not simple. So he spoke seldom, and Miriam was divided between relief and scorn. It annoyed her that the great hulking thing should know she had written the words of the song overnight; for though a maiden may sing her most secret fancies aloud, she does not care to have them trampled over by the male Philistine. They rode into the little red-brick street of Bassett, and Georgie made untold fuss over the disposition of that duck. It must go in just such a package, and be fastened to the saddle in just such a manner, though eight o'clock had struck and they were miles from dinner.

"We must be quick!" said Miriam, bored and angry.

"There's no great hurry; but we can cut over Dowhead Down, and let 'em out on the grass. That will save us half an hour."

The horses capered on the short, sweet-smelling turf, and the delaying shadows gathered in the valley as they cantered over the great dun down that overhangs Bassett and the Western coaching-road. Insensibly the pace quickened without thought of mole-hills; Rufus, gentleman that he was, waiting on Miriam's Dandy till they should have cleared the rise. Then down the two-mile slope they raced together, the wind whistling in their ears, to the steady throb of eight hoofs and the light click-click of the shifting bits.

"Oh, that was glorious!" Miriam cried, reining in. "Dandy and I are old friends, but I don't think we've ever gone better together."

"No; but you've gone quicker, once or twice."

"Really? When?"

Georgie moistened his lips. "Don't you remember the Thirty-Mile Ride—with me—when 'They' were after us—on the beach-road, with the sea to the left—going toward the lamp-post on the downs?"

The girl gasped. "What—what do you mean?" she said hysterically.

"The Thirty-Mile Ride, and—and all the rest of it."

"You mean—? I didn't sing anything about the Thirty-Mile Ride. I know I didn't. I have never told a living soul."

"You told about Policeman Day, and the lamp at the top of the downs, and the City of Sleep. It all joins on, you know—it's the same country—and it was easy enough to see where you had been."

"Good God!—It joins on—of course it does; but—I have been—you have been— Oh, let's walk, please, or I shall fall off!"

Georgie ranged alongside, and laid a hand that shook below her bridle-hand, pulling Dandy into a walk. Miriam was sobbing as he had seen a man sob under the touch of the bullet.

"It's all right—it's all right," he whispered feebly. "Only—only it's true, you know."

"True! Am I mad?"

"Not unless I'm mad as well. Do try to think a minute quietly. How could any one conceivably know anything about the Thirty-Mile Ride having anything to do with you, unless he had been there?"

"But where? But *where?* Tell me!"

"There—wherever it may be—in our country, I suppose. Do you remember the first time you rode it—the Thirty-Mile Ride, I mean? You must."

"It was all dreams—all dreams!"

"Yes, but tell, please; because I know."

"Let me think. I—we were on no account to make any noise—on no account to make any noise." She was staring between Dandy's ears, with eyes that did not see, and a suffocating heart.

"Because 'It' was dying in the big house?" Georgie went on, reining in again.

"There was a garden with green-and-gilt railings—all hot. Do *you* remember?"

"I ought to. I was sitting on the other side of the bed before 'It' coughed and 'They' came in."

"You!"—the deep voice was unnaturally full and strong, and the girl's wide-opened eyes burned in the dusk as she stared him through and through. "Then you're the Boy—my Brushwood Boy, and I've known you all my life!"

She fell forward on Dandy's neck. Georgie forced himself out of the weakness that was overmastering his limbs, and slid an arm round her waist. The head dropped on his shoulder, and he found himself with parched lips saying things that up till then he believed existed only in printed works of fiction. Mercifully the horses were quiet. She made no attempt to draw herself away when she recovered, but lay still, whispering, "Of course you're the Boy, and I didn't know—I didn't know."

"I knew last night; and when I saw you at breakfast—"

"Oh, *that* was why! I wondered at the time. You would, of course."

"I couldn't speak before this. Keep your head where it is, dear. It's all right now—all right now, isn't it?"

"But how was it *I* didn't know—after all these years and years? I remember—oh, what lots of things I remember!"

"Tell me some. I'll look after the horses."

"I remember waiting for you when the steamer came in. Do you?"

"At the Lily Lock, beyond Hong-Kong and Java?"

"Do *you* call it that, too?"

"You told me it was when I was lost in the continent. That was you that showed me the way through the mountains?"

"When the islands slid? It must have been, because you're the only one I remember. All the others were 'Them.'"

"Awful brutes they were, too."

"I remember showing you the Thirty-Mile Ride the first time. You ride just as you used to—then. You *are* you!"

"That's odd. I thought that of you this afternoon. Isn't it wonderful?"

"What does it all mean? Why should you and I of the millions of people in the world have this—this thing between us? What does it mean? I'm frightened."

"This!" said Georgie. The horses quickened their pace. They thought they had heard an order. "Perhaps when we die we may find out more, but it means this now."

There was no answer. What could she say? As the world went, they had known each other rather less than eight and a half hours, but the matter was one that did not concern the world. There was a very long silence, while the breath in their nostrils drew cold and sharp as it might have been a fume of ether.

"That's the second," Georgie whispered. "You remember, don't you?"

"It's not!"—furiously. "It's not!"

"On the downs the other night—months ago. You were just as you are now, and we went over the country for miles and miles."

"It was all empty, too. They had gone away. Nobody frightened us. I wonder why, Boy?"

"Oh, if you remember *that*, you must remember the rest. Confess!"

"I remember lots of things, but I *know* I didn't. I never have—till just now."

"You *did*, dear."

"I know I didn't, because—oh, it's no use keeping anything back!—because I truthfully meant to."

"And truthfully did."

"No; meant to; but some one else came by."

"There wasn't any one else. There never has been."

"There was—there always is. It was another woman—out there on the sea. I saw her. It was the 26th of May. I've got it written down somewhere."

"Oh, *you've* kept a record of your dreams, too? That's odd about the other woman, because I happened to be on the sea just then."

"I was right. How do I know what you've done when you were awake—and I thought it was only *you!*"

"You never were more wrong in your life. What a little temper you've got! Listen to me a minute, dear." And Georgie, though he knew it not, committed black perjury. "It—it isn't the kind of thing one says to any one, because they'd laugh; but on my word and honour, darling, I've never been kissed by a living soul outside my own people in all my life. Don't laugh, dear. I wouldn't tell any one but you, but it's the solemn truth."

"I knew! You are you. Oh, I *knew* you'd come some day; but I didn't know you were you in the least till you spoke."

"Then give me another."

"And you never cared or looked anywhere? Why, all the round world must have loved you from the very minute they saw you, Boy."

"They kept it to themselves if they did. No; I never cared."

"And we shall be late for dinner—horribly late. Oh, how can I look at you in the light before your mother—and mine!"

"We'll play you're Miss Lacy till the proper time comes. What's the shortest limit for people to get engaged? S'pose we have got to go through all the fuss of an engagement, haven't we?"

"Oh, I don't want to talk about that. It's so commonplace. I've thought of something that you don't know. I'm sure of it. What's my name?"

"Miri—no, it isn't, by Jove! Wait half a second, and it'll come back to me. You aren't—you can't? Why, *those* old tales—before I went to school! I've never thought of 'em from that day to this. Are you the original, only Anni*ean*louise?"

"It was what you always called me ever since the beginning. Oh! We've turned into the avenue, and we must be an hour late."

"What does it matter? The chain goes as far back as those days? It must, of course—of course it must. I've got to ride round with this pestilent old bird—confound him!"

" ' "Ha! ha!" said the duck, laughing'—do you remember *that?*"

"Yes, I do—flower-pots on my feet, and all. We've been together all this while; and I've got to say good-bye to you till dinner. *Sure* I'll see you at dinner-time? *Sure* you won't sneak up to your room, darling, and leave me all the evening? Good-bye, dear—good-bye."

"Good-bye, Boy, good-bye. Mind the arch! Don't let Rufus bolt into his stables. Good-bye. Yes, I'll come down to dinner; but—what shall I do when I see you in the light!"

Lord Mountdrago

W. SOMERSET MAUGHAM

Dr. Audlin looked at the clock on his desk. It was twenty minutes to six. He was surprised that his patient was late, for Lord Mountdrago prided himself on his punctuality; he had a sententious way of expressing himself which gave the air of an epigram to a commonplace remark, and he was in the habit of saying that punctuality is a compliment you pay to the intelligent and a rebuke you administer to the stupid. Lord Mountdrago's appointment was for five-thirty.

There was in Dr. Audlin's appearance nothing to attract attention. He was tall and spare, with narrow shoulders and something of a stoop; his hair was grey and thin; his long, sallow face deeply lined. He was not more than fifty, but he looked older. His eyes, pale blue and rather large, were weary. When you had been with him for a while you noticed that they moved very little; they remained fixed on your face, but so empty of expression were they that it was no discomfort. They seldom lit up. They gave no clue to his thoughts nor changed with the words he spoke. If you were of an observant turn it might have struck you that he blinked much less often than most of us. His hands were on the large side, with long, tapering fingers; they were soft but firm, cool but not clammy. You could never have said what Dr. Audlin wore unless you had made a point of looking. His clothes were dark. His tie was black. His dress made his sallow lined face paler and his pale eyes more wan. He gave you the impression of a very sick man.

Dr. Audlin was a psychoanalyst. He had adopted the profession by accident and practised it with misgiving. When the war broke out he had not been long qualified and was getting experience at various hospitals; he offered his services to the authorities, and after a time was sent out to France. It was then that he discovered his singular gift. He could allay certain pains by the touch of his cool, firm hands, and by talking to them often induce sleep in men who were suffering from sleeplessness. He spoke slowly. His voice had no particular colour, and its tone did not alter with the words he uttered, but it was musical, soft and lulling. He told the men that they must rest, that they mustn't worry, that they must sleep; and rest stole into their jaded bones, tranquillity pushed their anxieties away, like a man finding a place for himself on a crowded bench, and slumber fell on their tired eyelids like the light rain of spring upon the fresh-turned earth. Dr. Audlin found that by speaking to men with that low, monotonous voice of his, by looking at them with his pale, quiet eyes, by stroking their weary foreheads with his long firm hands, he could soothe their perturbations, resolve the conflicts that distracted them and banish the phobias that made their lives a torment. Sometimes he effected cures that seemed miraculous. He restored speech to a man who, after being buried under the earth by a bursting shell, had been struck dumb, and he gave back the use of his limbs to another who had been paralyzed after a crash in a plane. He could not understand his powers; he was of a sceptical turn, and though they say that in circumstances of this kind the first thing is to believe in yourself, he never quite succeeded in doing that; and it was only the outcome of his activities, patent to the most incredulous observer, that obliged him to admit that he had some faculty, coming from he knew not where, obscure and uncertain, that enabled him to do things for which he could offer no explanation. When the war was over he went to Vienna and studied there, and afterwards to Zurich; and then settled down in London to practise the art he had so strangely acquired. He had been practising now for fifteen years, and had attained, in the speciality he followed, a distinguished reputation. People told one another of the amazing things he had done, and though his fees were high, he had as many patients as he had time to see. Dr. Audlin knew that he had achieved some very extraordinary results; he had saved men from suicide, others from the lunatic asylum, he had assuaged griefs that embittered useful lives, he had turned unhappy marriages into happy ones, he had eradicated abnormal instincts and thus delivered not a few from a hateful bondage, he had given health to the sick in spirit; he had done all this, and yet at the back of his mind remained the suspicion that he was little more than a quack.

It went against his grain to exercise a power that he could not understand, and it offended his honesty to trade on the faith of the people he treated when he had no faith in himself. He was rich enough now to live without working, and the work exhausted him; a dozen times he had been on the point of giving up practice. He knew all that Freud and Jung and the rest of them had written. He was not satisfied; he had an intimate conviction that all their theory was hocus-pocus, and yet there the results were, incomprehensible, but manifest. And what had he not seen of human nature during the fifteen years that patients had been coming to his dingy back room in Wimpole Street? The revelations that had been poured into his ears, sometimes only too willingly, sometimes with shame, with reservations, with anger, had long ceased to surprise him. Nothing could shock him any longer. He knew by now that men were liars, he knew how extravagant was their vanity; he knew far worse than that about them; but he knew that it was not for him to judge or to condemn. But year by year as these terrible confidences were imparted to him his face grew a little greyer, its lines a little more marked and his pale eyes more weary. He seldom laughed, but now and again when for relaxation he read a novel he smiled. Did their authors really think the men and women they wrote of were like that? If they only knew how much more complicated they were, how much more unexpected, what irreconcilable elements coexisted within their souls and what dark and sinister contentions afflicted them!

It was a quarter to six. Of all the strange cases he had been called upon to deal with, Dr. Audlin could remember none stranger than that of Lord Mountdrago. For one thing the personality of his patient made it singular. Lord Mountdrago was an able and a distinguished man. Appointed Secretary for Foreign Affairs when still under forty, now after three years in office he had seen his policy prevail. It was generally acknowledged that he was the ablest politician in the Conservative Party, and only the fact that his father was a peer, on whose death he would no longer be able to sit in the House of Commons, made it impossible for him to aim at the premiership. But if in these democratic times it is out of the question for a Prime Minister of England to be in the House of Lords, there was nothing to prevent Lord Mountdrago from continuing to be Secretary for Foreign Affairs in successive Conservative administrations and so for long directing the foreign policy of his country.

Lord Mountdrago had many good qualities. He had intelligence and industry. He was widely travelled and spoke several languages fluently. From early youth he had specialized in for-

eign affairs and had conscientiously made himself acquainted
with the political and economic circumstances of other countries. He had courage, insight and determination. He was a
good speaker, both on the platform and in the House, clear,
precise and often witty. He was a brilliant debater and his gift
of repartee was celebrated. He had a fine presence: he was a
tall, handsome man, rather bald and somewhat too stout, but
this gave him solidity and an air of maturity that were of service to him. As a young man he had been something of an
athlete and had rowed in the Oxford boat, and he was known
to be one of the best shots in England. At twenty-four he had
married a girl of eighteen whose father was a duke and her
mother a great American heiress, so that she had both position and wealth, and by her he had two sons. For several years
they had lived privately apart, but in public united, so that
appearances were saved, and no other attachment on either
side had given the gossips occasion to whisper. Lord Mountdrago indeed was too ambitious, too hard-working, and it must
be added too patriotic, to be tempted by any pleasures that
might interfere with his career. He had in short a great deal
to make him a popular and successful figure. He had unfor-
tunately great defects.

He was a fearful snob. You would not have been surprised
at this if his father had been the first holder of the title. That
the son of an ennobled lawyer, manufacturer or distiller should
attach an inordinate importance to his rank is understandable. The earldom held by Lord Mountdrago's father was created
by Charles II, and the barony held by the first earl dated from
the Wars of the Roses. For three hundred years the successive
holders of the title had allied themselves with the noblest fami-
lies of England. But Lord Mountdrago was as conscious of his
birth as a *nouveau riche* is conscious of his money. He never
missed an opportunity of impressing it upon others. He had
beautiful manners when he chose to display them, but this

he did only with people whom he regarded as his equals. He was coldly insolent to those whom he looked upon as his social inferiors. He was rude to his servants and insulting to his secretaries. The subordinate officials in the government offices to which he had been successively attached feared and hated him. His arrogance was horrible. He knew that he was a great deal cleverer than most of the persons he had to do with, and never hesitated to apprise them of the fact. He had no patience with the infirmities of human nature. He felt himself born to command and was irritated with people who expected him to listen to their arguments or wished to hear the reasons for his decisions. He was immeasurably selfish. He looked upon any service that was rendered him as a right due to his rank and intelligence and therefore deserving of no gratitude. It never entered his head that he was called upon to do anything for others. He had many enemies: he despised them. He knew no one who merited his assistance, his sympathy or his compassion. He had no friends. He was distrusted by his chiefs, because they doubted his loyalty; he was unpopular with his party, because he was overbearing and discourteous; and yet his merit was so great, his patriotism so evident, his intelligence so solid and his management of affairs so brilliant, that they had to put up with him. And what made it possible to do this was that on occasion he could be enchanting: when he was with persons whom he considered his equals, or whom he wished to captivate, in the company of foreign dignitaries or women of distinction, he could be gay, witty and debonair; his manners then reminded you that in his veins ran the same blood as had run in the veins of Lord Chesterfield; he could tell a story with point, he could be natural, sensible and even profound. You were surprised at the extent of his knowledge and the sensitiveness of his taste. You thought him the best company in the world; you forgot that he had insulted you the day before and was quite capable of cutting you dead the next.

Lord Mountdrago almost failed to become Dr. Audlin's patient. A secretary rang up the doctor and told him that his lordship, wishing to consult him, would be glad if he would come to his house at ten o'clock on the following morning. Dr. Audlin answered that he was unable to go to Lord Mountdrago's house, but would be pleased to give him an appointment at his consulting room at five o'clock on the next day but one. The secretary took the message and presently rang back to say that Lord Mountdrago insisted on seeing Dr. Audlin in his own house and the doctor could fix his own fee. Dr. Audlin replied that he saw patients only in his consulting room and expressed his regret that unless Lord Mountdrago was prepared to come to him he could not give him his attention. In a quarter of an hour a brief message was delivered to him that his lordship would come not next day but one, but next day, at five.

When Lord Mountdrago was then shown in he did not come forward, but stood at the door and insolently looked the doctor up and down. Dr. Audlin perceived that he was in a rage; he gazed at him, silently, with still eyes. He saw a big heavy man, with greying hair, receding on the forehead so that it gave nobility to his brow, a puffy face with bold regular features and an expression of haughtiness. He had somewhat the look of one of the Bourbon sovereigns of the eighteenth century.

"It seems that it is as difficult to see you as a Prime Minister, Dr. Audlin. I'm an extremely busy man."

"Won't you sit down?" said the doctor.

His face showed no sign that Lord Mountdrago's speech in any way affected him. Dr. Audlin sat in his chair at the desk. Lord Mountdrago still stood, and his frown darkened.

"I think I should tell you that I am His Majesty's Secretary for Foreign Affairs," he said acidly.

"Won't you sit down?" the doctor repeated.

Lord Mountdrago made a gesture, which might have suggested that he was about to turn on his heel and stalk out of the room; but if that was his intention he apparently thought better of it. He seated himself. Dr. Audlin opened a large book and took up his pen. He wrote without looking at his patient.

"How old are you?"

"Forty-two."

"Are you married?"

"Yes."

"How long have you been married?"

"Eighteen years."

"Have you any children?"

"I have two sons."

Dr. Audlin noted down the facts as Lord Mountdrago abruptly answered his questions. Then he leaned back in his chair and looked at him. He did not speak; he just looked, gravely, with pale eyes that did not move.

"Why have you come to see me?" he asked at length.

"I've heard about you. Lady Canute is a patient of yours, I understand. She tells me you've done her a certain amount of good."

Dr. Audlin did not reply. His eyes remained fixed on the other's face, but they were so empty of expression that you might have thought he did not even see him.

"I can't do miracles," he said at length. Not a smile, but the shadow of a smile flickered in his eyes. "The Royal College of Physicians would not approve of it if I did."

Lord Mountdrago gave a brief chuckle. It seemed to lessen his hostility. He spoke more amiably.

"You have a very remarkable reputation. People seem to believe in you."

"Why have you come to me?" repeated Dr. Audlin.

Now it was Lord Mountdrago's turn to be silent. It looked as though he found it hard to answer. Dr. Audlin waited. At last Lord Mountdrago seemed to make an effort. He spoke.

"I'm in perfect health. Just as a matter of routine I had myself examined by my own doctor the other day, Sir Augustus Fitzherbert, I daresay you've heard of him, and he tells me I have the physique of a man of thirty. I work hard, but I'm never tired, and I enjoy my work. I smoke very little and I'm an extremely moderate drinker. I take a sufficiency of exercise and I lead a regular life. I am a perfectly sound, normal, healthy man. I quite expect you to think it very silly and childish of me to consult you."

Dr. Audlin saw that he must help him.

"I don't know if I can do anything to help you. I'll try. You're distressed?"

Lord Mountdrago frowned.

"The work that I'm engaged in is important. The decisions I am called upon to make can easily affect the welfare of the country and even the peace of the world. It is essential that my judgment should be balanced and my brain clear. I look upon it as my duty to eliminate any cause of worry that may interfere with my usefulness."

Dr. Audlin had never taken his eyes off him. He saw a great deal. He saw behind his patient's pompous manner and arrogant pride an anxiety that he could not dispel.

"I asked you to be good enough to come here because I know by experience that it's easier for someone to speak openly in the dingy surroundings of a doctor's consulting room than in his accustomed environment."

"They're certainly dingy," said Lord Mountdrago acidly. He paused. It was evident that this man who had so much self-assurance, so quick and decided a mind that he was never at a loss, at this moment was embarrassed. He smiled in order to show the doctor that he was at his ease, but his eyes betrayed his disquiet. When he spoke again it was with unnatural heartiness.

"The whole thing's so trivial that I can hardly bring myself to bother you with it. I'm afraid you'll just tell me not to be a fool and waste your valuable time."

"Even things that seem very trivial may have their importance. They can be a symptom of a deep-seated derangement. And my time is entirely at your disposal."

Dr. Audlin's voice was low and grave. The monotone in which he spoke was strangely soothing. Lord Mountdrago at length made up his mind to be frank.

"The fact is I've been having some very tiresome dreams lately. I know it's silly to pay any attention to them, but—well, the honest truth is that I'm afraid they've got on my nerves."

"Can you describe any of them to me?"

Lord Mountdrago smiled, but the smile that tried to be careless was only rueful.

"They're so idiotic, I can hardly bring myself to narrate them."

"Never mind."

"Well, the first I had was about a month ago. I dreamt that I was at a party at Connemara House. It was an official party. The King and Queen were to be there, and of course decorations were worn. I was wearing my ribbon and my star. I went into a sort of cloakroom they have to take off my coat. There was a little man there called Owen Griffiths, who's a Welsh member of Parliament, and to tell you the truth, I was surprised to see him. He's very common, and I said to myself: 'Really, Lydia Connemara is going too far, whom will she ask next?' I thought he looked at me rather curiously, but I didn't take any notice of him; in fact I cut the little bounder and walked upstairs. I suppose you've never been there?"

"Never."

"No, it's not the sort of house you'd ever be likely to go to.

It's a rather vulgar house, but it's got a very fine marble stair-case, and the Connemaras were at the top receiving their guests. Lady Connemara gave me a look of surprise when I shook hands with her, and began to giggle; I didn't pay much attention—she's a very silly, ill-bred woman, and her manners are no better than those of her ancestress whom King Charles II made a duchess. I must say the reception rooms at Connemara House are stately. I walked through, nodding to a number of people and shaking hands; then I saw the German Ambassador talking with one of the Austrian archdukes. I particularly wanted to have a word with him, so I went up and held out my hand. The moment the Archduke saw me he burst into a roar of laughter. I was deeply affronted. I looked him up and down sternly, but he only laughed the more. I was about to speak to him rather sharply, when there was a sudden hush, and I realized that the King and Queen had come. Turning my back on the Archduke, I stepped forward, and then, quite suddenly, I noticed that I hadn't got any trousers on. I was in short silk drawers, and I wore scarlet sock suspenders. No wonder Lady Connemara had giggled; no wonder the Archduke had laughed! I can't tell you what that moment was. An agony of shame. I awoke in a cold sweat. Oh, you don't know the relief I felt to find it was only a dream."

"It's the kind of dream that's not so very uncommon," said Dr. Audlin.

"I daresay not. But an odd thing happened next day. I was in the lobby of the House of Commons, when that fellow Griffiths walked slowly past me. He deliberately looked down at my legs, and then he looked me full in the face, and I was almost certain he winked. A ridiculous thought came to me. He'd been there the night before and seen me make that ghastly exhibition of myself and was enjoying the joke. But of course I knew that was impossible because it was only a dream. I gave him an icy glare, and he walked on. But he was grinning his head off."

Lord Mountdrago took his handkerchief out of his pocket and wiped the palms of his hands. He was making no attempt now to conceal his perturbation. Dr. Audlin never took his eyes off him.

"Tell me another dream."

"It was the night after, and it was even more absurd than the first one. I dreamt that I was in the House. There was a debate on foreign affairs which not only the country, but the world, had been looking forward to with the gravest concern. The government had decided on a change in their policy which vitally affected the future of the Empire. The occasion was historic. Of course the House was crowded. All the ambassadors were there. The galleries were packed. It fell to me to make the important speech of the evening. I had prepared it carefully. A man like me has enemies—there are a lot of people who resent my having achieved the position I have at an age when even the cleverest men are content with situations of relative obscurity—and I was determined that my speech should not only be worthy of the occasion, but should silence my detractors. It excited me to think that the whole world was hanging on my lips. I rose to my feet. If you've ever been in the House you'll know how members chat to one another during a debate, rustle papers and turn over reports. The silence was the silence of the grave when I began to speak. Suddenly I caught sight of that odious little bounder on one of the benches opposite, Griffiths, the Welsh member; he put out his tongue at me. I don't know if you've ever heard a vulgar music-hall song called 'A Bicycle Made for Two.' It was very popular a great many years ago. To show Griffiths how completely I despised him I began to sing it. I sang the first verse right through. There was a moment's surprise, and when I finished they cried 'Hear, hear,' on the opposite benches. I put up my hand to silence them and sang the second verse. The House listened to me in stony silence and I felt the song wasn't going down very well. I was vexed, for I have a good baritone voice, and I was determined that they should do me justice. When I started the third verse the members began to laugh; in an instant the laughter spread; the ambassadors, the strangers in the Distinguished Strangers' Gallery, the ladies in the Ladies' Gallery, the reporters, they shook, they bellowed, they held their sides, they rolled in their seats; everyone was overcome with laughter except the ministers on the Front Bench immediately behind me. In that incredible, in that unprecedented, uproar they sat petrified. I gave them a glance, and suddenly the enormity of what I had done fell upon me. I had made myself the laughing-stock of the whole world. With misery I realized that I should have to resign. I woke and knew it was only a dream."

Lord Mountdrago's grand manner had deserted him as he narrated this, and now having finished he was pale and trembling. But with an effort he pulled himself together. He forced a laugh to his shaking lips.

"The whole thing was so fantastic that I couldn't help being amused. I didn't give it another thought, and when I went into the House on the following afternoon I was feeling in very good form. The debate was dull, but I had to be there, and I read some documents that required my attention. For some reason I chanced to look up, and I saw that Griffiths was speaking. He had an unpleasant Welsh accent and an unprepossessing appearance. I couldn't imagine that he had anything to say that it was worth my while to listen to, and I was about to return to my papers when he quoted two lines from 'A Bicycle Made for Two.' I couldn't help glancing at him, and I saw that his eyes were fixed on me with a grin of bitter mockery. I faintly shrugged my shoulders. It was comic

that a scrubby little Welsh member should look at me like
that. It was an odd coincidence that he should quote two lines
from that disastrous song that I'd sung all through in my
dream. I began to read my papers again, but I don't mind
telling you that I found it difficult to concentrate on them. I
was a little puzzled. Owen Griffiths had been in my first dream,
the one at Connemara House, and I'd received a very definite
impression afterwards that he knew the sorry figure I'd cut.
Was it a mere coincidence that he had just quoted those two
lines? I asked myself if it was possible that he was dreaming
the same dreams as I was. But of course the idea was preposterous, and I determined not to give it a second thought."

There was a silence. Dr. Audlin looked at Lord Mountdrago
and Lord Mountdrago looked at Dr. Audlin.

"Other people's dreams are very boring. My wife used to
dream occasionally and insist on telling me her dreams next
day with circumstantial detail. I found it maddening."

Dr. Audlin faintly smiled.

"You're not boring me."

"I'll tell you one more dream I had a few days later. I
dreamt that I went into a public house at Limehouse. I've
never been to Limehouse in my life and I don't think I've ever
been in a public house since I was at Oxford, and yet I saw
the street and the place I went into as exactly as if I were at
home there. I went into a room—I don't know whether they
call it the saloon bar or the private bar; there was a fireplace
and a large leather armchair on one side of it, and on the other
a small sofa; a bar ran the whole length of the room, and over
it you could see into the public bar. Near the door was a round
marble-topped table and two armchairs beside it. It was a
Saturday night, and the place was packed. It was brightly lit,
but the smoke was so thick that it made my eyes smart. I was
dressed like a rough, with a cap on my head and a handkerchief
round my neck. It seemed to me that most of the people

there were drunk. I thought it rather amusing. There was a
gramophone going, or the radio, I don't know which, and in
front of the fireplace two women were doing a grotesque dance.
There was a little crowd round them, laughing, cheering and
singing. I went up to have a look, and some man said to me:
''Ave a drink, Bill.' There were glasses on the table full of a
dark liquid which I understand is called brown ale. He gave
me a glass, and not wishing to be conspicuous, I drank it. One
of the women who were dancing broke away from the other
and took hold of the glass. ''Ere, what's the idea?' she said.
'That's my beer you're putting away.' 'Oh, I'm so sorry,' I
said, 'this gentleman offered it to me, and I very naturally
thought it was his to offer.' 'All right, mate,' she said, 'I don't
mind. You come an' 'ave a dance with me.' Before I could
protest she'd caught hold of me and we were dancing together.
And then I found myself sitting in the armchair with the
woman on my lap and we were sharing a glass of beer. I
should tell you that sex has never played any great part in my
life. I married young because in my position it was desirable
that I should marry, but also in order to settle once for all
the question of sex. I had the two sons I had made up my
mind to have, and then I put the whole matter on one side.
I've always been too busy to give much thought to that kind
of thing, and living so much in the public eye as I do, it
would have been madness to do anything that might give rise
to scandal. The greatest asset a politician can have is a blame-
less record as far as women are concerned. I have no patience
with the men who smash up their careers for women. I only
despise them. The woman I had on my knees was drunk; she
wasn't pretty and she wasn't young: in fact, she was just a
blowsy old prostitute. She filled me with disgust, and yet when
she put her mouth to mine and kissed me, though her breath
stank of beer and her teeth were decayed, though I loathed
myself, I wanted her—I wanted her with all my soul. Suddenly

I heard a voice: 'That's right, old boy, have a good time.' I looked up, and there was Owen Griffiths. I tried to spring out of the chair, but that horrible woman wouldn't let me. 'Don't pay no attention to 'im,' she said, ''e's only one of them nosy parkers.' 'You go to it,' he said. 'I know Moll. She'll give you your money's worth all right.' You know, I wasn't so much annoyed at his seeing me in that absurd situation as angry that he should address me as old boy. I pushed the woman aside and stood up and faced him. 'I don't know you, and I don't want to know you,' I said. 'I know you all right,' he said. 'And my advice to you, Molly, is, see that you get your money, he'll bilk you if he can.' There was a bottle of beer standing on the table close by. Without a word I seized it by the neck and hit him over the head with it as hard as I could. I made such a violent gesture that it woke me up."

"A dream of that sort is not incomprehensible," said Dr. Audlin. "It is the revenge nature takes on persons of unimpeachable character."

"The story's idiotic. I haven't told it you for its own sake. I've told it you for what happened next day. I wanted to look up something in a hurry, and I went into the library of the House. I got the book and began reading. I hadn't noticed when I sat down that Griffiths was sitting in a chair close by me. Another of the Labour Members came in and went up to him. 'Hullo, Owen,' he said to him, 'you're looking pretty dicky today.' 'I've got an awful headache,' he answered, 'I feel as if I'd been cracked over the head with a bottle.'"

Now Lord Mountdrago's face was grey with anguish.

"I knew then that the idea I'd had and dismissed as preposterous was true. I know that Griffiths was dreaming my dreams and that he remembered them as well as I did."

"It may also have been a coincidence."

"When he spoke he didn't speak to his friend, he deliberately spoke to me. He looked at me with sullen resentment."

"Can you offer any suggestion why this same man should come into your dreams?"

"None."

Dr. Audlin's eyes had not left his patient's face and he saw that he lied. He had a pencil in his hand, and he drew a straggling line or two on his blotting paper. It often took a long time to get people to tell the truth, and yet they knew that unless they told it he could do nothing for them.

"The dream you've just described to me took place just over three weeks ago. Have you had any since?"

"Every night."

"And does this man Griffiths come into them all?"

"Yes."

The doctor drew more lines on his blotting paper. He wanted the silence, the drabness, the dull light of that little room to have its effect on Lord Mountdrago's sensibility. Lord Mountdrago threw himself back in his chair and turned his head away so that he should not see the other's grave eyes.

"Dr. Audlin, you must do something for me. I'm at the end of my tether. I shall go mad if this goes on. I'm afraid to go to sleep. Two or three nights I haven't. I've sat up reading and when I felt drowsy put on my coat and walked till I was exhausted. But I must have sleep. With all the work I have to do I must be at concert pitch; I must be in complete control of all my faculties. I need rest; sleep brings me none. I no sooner fall asleep than my dreams begin, and he's always there, that vulgar little cad, grinning at me, mocking me, despising me. It's a monstrous persecution. I tell you, Doctor, I'm not the man of my dreams; it's not fair to judge me by them. Ask anyone you like. I'm an honest, upright, decent man. No one can say anything against my moral character either private or public. My whole ambition is to serve my country and maintain its greatness. I have money, I have rank, I'm not exposed to many of the temptations of lesser men, so that it's no credit to me to be incorruptible; but this I can claim, that no honour, no personal advantage, no thought of self would induce me to swerve by a hair's breadth from my duty. I've sacrificed everything to become the man I am. Greatness is my aim. Greatness is within my reach, and I'm losing my nerve. I'm not that mean, despicable, cowardly, lewd creature that horrible little man sees. I've told you three of my dreams; they're nothing; that man has seen me do things that are so beastly, so horrible, so shameful, that even if my life depended on it I wouldn't tell them. And he remembers them. I can hardly meet the derision and disgust I see in his eyes, and I even hesitate to speak because I know my words can seem to him nothing but utter humbug. He's seen me do things that no man with any self-respect would do, things for which men are driven out of the society of their fellows and sentenced to long terms of imprisonment; he's heard the foulness of my speech; he's seen me not only ridiculous, but revolting. He despises me and he no longer pretends to conceal it. I tell you that if you can't do something to help me I shall either kill myself or kill him."

"I wouldn't kill him if I were you," said Dr. Audlin coolly, in that soothing voice of his. "In this country the consequences of killing a fellow creature are awkward."

"I shouldn't be hanged for it, if that's what you mean. Who would know that I'd killed him? That dream of mine has shown me how. I told you, the day after I'd hit him over the head with a beer bottle he had such a headache that he couldn't see straight. He said so himself. That shows that he can feel with his waking body what happens to his body asleep. It's not with a bottle I shall hit him next time. One night, when I'm dreaming, I shall find myself with a knife in my hand or a revolver in my pocket—I must because I want to so intensely

—and then I shall seize my opportunity. I'll stick him like a pig; I'll shoot him like a dog. In the heart. And then I shall be free of this fiendish persecution."

Some people might have thought that Lord Mountdrago was mad; after all the years during which Dr. Audlin had been treating the diseased souls of men he knew how thin a line divides those whom we call sane from those whom we call insane. He knew how often in men who to all appearance were healthy and normal, who were seemingly devoid of imagination, and who fulfilled the duties of common life with credit to themselves and with benefit to their fellows, when you gained their confidence, when you tore away the mask they wore to the world, you found not only hideous abnormality, but kinks so strange, mental extravagances so fantastic, that in that respect you could only call them lunatic. If you put them in an asylum, not all the asylums in the world would be large enough. Anyhow, a man was not certifiable because he had strange dreams and they had shattered his nerve. The case was singular, but it was only an exaggeration of others that had come under Dr. Audlin's observation; he was doubtful, however, whether the methods of treatment that he had so often found efficacious would here avail.

"Have you consulted any other member of my profession?" he asked.

"Only Sir Augustus. I merely told him that I suffered from nightmares. He said I was overworked and recommended me to go for a cruise. That's absurd. I can't leave the Foreign Office just now when the international stituation needs constant attention. I'm indispensable, and I know it. On my conduct at the present juncture my whole future depends. He gave me sedatives. They had no effect. He gave me tonics. They were worse than useless. He's an old fool."

"Can you give any reason why it should be this particular man who persists in coming into your dreams?"

"You asked me that question before. I answered it."

That was true. But Dr. Audlin had not been satisfied with the answer.

"Just now you talked of persecution. Why should Owen Griffiths want to persecute you?"

"I don't know."

Lord Mountdrago's eyes shifted a little. Dr. Audlin was sure that he was not speaking the truth.

"Have you ever done him an injury?"

"Never."

Lord Mountdrago made no movement, but Dr. Audlin had a queer feeling that he shrank into his skin. He saw before him a large, proud man who gave the impression that the questions put to him were an insolence, and yet for all that, behind that façade, was something shifty and startled that made you think of a frightened animal in a trap. Dr. Audlin leaned forward and by the power of his eyes forced Lord Mountdrago to meet them.

"Are you quite sure?"

"Quite sure. You don't seem to understand that our ways lead along different paths. I don't wish to harp on it, but I must remind you that I am a Minister of the Crown and Griffiths is an obscure member of the Labour Party. Naturally there's no social connection between us; he's a man of very humble origin, he's not the sort of person I should be likely to meet at any of the houses I go to; and politically our respective stations are so far separated that we could not possibly have anything in common."

"I can do nothing for you unless you tell me the complete truth."

Lord Mountdrago raised his eyebrows. His voice was rasping.

"I'm not accustomed to having my word doubted, Dr. Audlin. If you're going to do that, I think to take up any more of your time can only be a waste of mine. If you will kindly let my secretary know what your fee is, he will see that a cheque is sent to you."

For all the expression that was to be seen on Dr. Audlin's face you might have thought that he simply had not heard what Lord Mountdrago said. He continued to look steadily into his eyes, and his voice was grave and low.

"Have you done anything to this man that *he* might look upon as an injury?"

Lord Mountdrago hesitated. He looked away, and then, as though there were in Dr. Audlin's eyes a compelling force that he could not resist, looked back. He answered sulkily:

"Only if he was a dirty, second-rate little cad."

"But that is exactly what you've described him to be."

Lord Mountdrago sighed. He was beaten. Dr. Audlin knew that the sigh meant he was going at last to say what he had till then held back. Now he had no longer to insist. He dropped his eyes and began again drawing vague geometrical figures on his blotting paper. The silence lasted two or three minutes.

"I'm anxious to tell you everything that can be of any use to you. If I didn't mention this before, it's only because it was so unimportant that I didn't see how it could possibly have anything to do with the case. Griffiths won a seat at the last election, and he began to make a nuisance of himself almost at once. His father's a miner, and he worked in a mine himself when he was a boy; he's been a schoolmaster in the board schools and a journalist. He's that half-baked, conceited intellectual, with inadequate knowledge, ill-considered ideas and impractical plans, that compulsory education has brought forth from the working classes. He's a scrawny, grey-faced man who looks half starved, and he's always very slovenly in appearance; heaven knows members nowadays don't bother much about their dress, but his clothes are an outrage to the dignity of the House. They're ostentatiously shabby, his collar's never clean, and his tie's never tied properly; he looks as if he hadn't had a bath for a month, and his hands are filthy. The Labour Party have two or three fellows on the Front Bench who've got a certain ability, but the rest of them don't amount to much. In the kingdom of the blind the one-eyed man is king: because Griffiths is glib and has a lot of superficial information on a number of subjects, the Whips on his side began to put him up to speak whenever there was a chance. It appeared that he fancied himself on foreign affairs, and he was continually asking me silly, tiresome questions. I don't mind telling you that I made a point of snubbing him as soundly as I thought he deserved. From the beginning I hated the way he talked, his whining voice and his vulgar accent; he had nervous mannerisms that intensely irritated me. He talked rather shyly, hesitatingly, as though it were torture for him to speak and yet he was forced to by some inner passion, and often he used to say some very disconcerting things. I'll admit that now and again he had a sort of tub-thumping eloquence. It had a certain influence over the ill-regulated minds of the members of his party. They were impressed by his earnestness, and they weren't, as I was, nauseated by his sentimentality. A certain sentimentality is the common coin of political debate. Nations are governed by self-interest, but they prefer to believe that their aims are altruistic, and the politician is justified if with fair words and fine phrases he can persuade the electorate that the hard bargain he is driving for his country's advantage tends to the good of humanity. The mistake people like Griffiths make is to take these fair words and fine phrases at their face value. He's a crank, and a noxious crank. He calls himself an idealist. He has at his tongue's end all the tedious blather that the intelligentsia have been boring us with for years. Nonresistance. The brotherhood of man. You know the hopeless rubbish. The worst of it was that it impressed not only his own party, it even shook some of the sillier, more sloppy-minded members of ours. I heard rumours that Griffiths was likely to get office when a Labour Government came in; I even heard it suggested that he might get the Foreign Office. The notion was grotesque but not impossible. One day I had occasion to wind up a debate on foreign affairs which Griffiths had opened. He'd spoken for an hour. I thought it a very good opportunity to cook his goose, and by God, sir, I cooked it. I tore his speech to pieces. I pointed out the faultiness of his reasoning and emphasized the deficiency of his knowledge. In the House of Commons the most devastating weapon is ridicule: I mocked him; I bantered him; I was in good form that day and the House rocked with laughter. Their laughter excited me, and I excelled myself. The Opposition sat glum and silent, but even some of them couldn't help laughing once or twice; it's not intolerable, you know, to see a colleague, perhaps a rival, made a fool of. And if ever a man was made a fool of, I made a fool of Griffiths. He shrank down in his seat; I saw his face go white, and presently he buried it in his hands. When I sat down I'd killed him. I'd destroyed his prestige for ever; he had no more chance of getting office when a Labour Government came in than the policeman at the door. I heard afterwards that his father, the old miner, and his mother had come up from Wales, with various supporters of his in the constituency, to watch the triumph they expected him to have. They had seen only his utter humiliation. He'd won the constituency by the narrowest margin. An incident like that might very easily lose him his seat. But that was no business of mine."

"Should I be putting it too strongly if I said you had ruined his career?" asked Dr. Audlin.

"I don't suppose you would."

"That is a very serious injury you've done him."

"He brought it on himself."

"Have you never felt any qualms about it?"

"I think perhaps if I'd known that his father and mother were there I might have let him down a little more gently."

There was nothing further for Dr. Audlin to say, and he set about treating his patient in such a manner as he thought might avail. He sought by suggestion to make him forget his dreams when he awoke; he sought to make him sleep so deeply that he would not dream. He found Lord Mountdrago's resistance impossible to break down. At the end of an hour he dismissed him.

Since then he had seen Lord Mountdrago half a dozen times. He had done him no good. The frightful dreams continued every night to harass the unfortunate man, and it was clear that his general condition was growing rapidly worse. He was worn out. His irritability was uncontrollable. Lord Mountdrago was angry because he received no benefit from his treatment, and yet continued it, not only because it seemed his only hope, but because it was a relief to him to have someone with whom he could talk openly. Dr. Audlin came to the conclusion at last that there was only one way in which Lord Mountdrago could achieve deliverance, but he knew him well enough to be assured that of his own free will he would never, never take it. If Lord Mountdrago was to be saved from the breakdown that was threatening, he must be induced to take a step that must be abhorrent to his pride of birth and his self-complacency. Dr. Audlin was convinced that to delay was impossible. He was treating his patient by suggestion, and after several visits found him more susceptible to it. At length he managed to get him into a condition of somnolence. With his low, soft, monotonous voice he soothed his tortured nerves. He repeated the same words over and over again. Lord Mountdrago lay quite still, his eyes closed; his breathing was regular, and his limbs were relaxed. Then Dr. Audlin in the same quiet tone spoke the words he had prepared.

"You will go to Owen Griffiths and say that you are sorry

that you caused him that great injury. You will say that you will do whatever lies in your power to undo the harm that you have done him."

The words acted on Lord Mountdrago like the blow of a whip across his face. He shook himself out of his hypnotic state and sprang to his feet. His eyes blazed with passion, and he poured forth upon Dr. Audlin a stream of angry vituperation such as even he had never heard. He swore at him. He cursed him. He used language of such obscenity that Dr. Audlin, who had heard every sort of foul word, sometimes from the lips of chaste and distinguished women, was surprised that he knew it.

"Apologize to that filthy little Welshman? I'd rather kill myself."

"I believe it to be the only way in which you can regain your balance."

Dr. Audlin had not often seen a man presumably sane in such a condition of uncontrollable fury. Lord Mountdrago grew red in the face, and his eyes bulged out of his head. He did really foam at the mouth. Dr. Audlin watched him coolly, waiting for the storm to wear itself out, and presently he saw that Lord Mountdrago, weakened by the strain to which he had been subjected for so many weeks, was exhausted.

"Sit down," he said then, sharply.

Lord Mountdrago crumpled up into a chair.

"Christ, I feel all in. I must rest a minute and then I'll go."

For five minutes perhaps they sat in complete silence. Lord Mountdrago was a gross, blustering bully, but he was also a gentleman. When he broke the silence he had recovered his self-control.

"I'm afraid I've been very rude to you. I'm ashamed of the things I've said to you, and I can only say you'd be justified if you refused to have anything more to do with me. I hope you won't do that. I feel that my visits to you do help me. I think you're my only chance."

"You mustn't give another thought to what you said. It was of no consequence."

"But there's one thing you mustn't ask me to do, and that is to make excuses to Griffiths."

"I've thought a great deal about your case. I don't pretend to understand it, but I believe that your only chance of release is to do what I proposed. I have a notion that we're none of us one self, but many, and one of the selves in you has risen up against the injury you did Griffiths and has taken on the form of Griffiths in your mind and is punishing you for what you cruelly did. If I were a priest I should tell you that it is your conscience that has adopted the shape and lineaments of this man to scourge you to repentance and persuade you to reparation."

"My conscience is clear. It's not my fault if I smashed the man's career. I crushed him like a slug in my garden. I regret nothing."

It was on these words that Lord Mountdrago had left him. Reading through his notes, while he waited, Dr. Audlin considered how best he could bring his patient to the state of mind that, now that his usual methods of treatment had failed, he thought alone could help him. He glanced at his clock. It was six. It was strange that Lord Mountdrago did not come. He knew he had intended to because a secretary had rung up that morning to say that he would be with him at the usual hour. He must have been detained by pressing work. This notion gave Dr. Audlin something else to think of: Lord Mountdrago was quite unfit to work and in no condition to deal with important matters of state. Dr. Audlin wondered whether it behooved him to get in touch with someone in authority, the Prime Minister or the Permanent Under Secretary for Foreign Affairs, and impart to him his conviction that Lord Mountdrago's mind was so unbalanced that it was dangerous to leave affairs of moment in his hands. It was a ticklish thing to do. He might cause needless trouble and get roundly snubbed for his pains. He shrugged his shoulders.

"After all," he reflected, "the politicians have made such a mess of the world during the last five-and-twenty years, I don't suppose it makes much odds if they're mad or sane."

He rang the bell.

"If Lord Mountdrago comes now, will you tell him that I have another appointment at six-fifteen and so I'm afraid I can't see him."

"Very good, sir."

"Has the evening paper come yet?"

"I'll go and see."

In a moment the servant brought it in. A huge headline ran across the front page: Tragic Death of Foreign Minister.

"My God!" cried Dr. Audlin.

For once he was wrenched out of his wonted calm. He was shocked, horribly shocked, and yet he was not altogether surprised. The possibility that Lord Mountdrago might commit suicide had occurred to him several times, for that it was suicide he could not doubt. The paper said that Lord Mountdrago had been waiting in a tube station, standing on the edge of the platform, and as the train came in was seen to fall on the rail. It was supposed that he had had a sudden attack of faintness. The paper went on to say that Lord Mountdrago had been suffering for some weeks from the effects of overwork, but had felt it impossible to absent himself while the foreign situation demanded his unremitting attention. Lord Mountdrago was another victim of the strain that modern politics placed upon those who played the more important parts in it. There was a neat little piece about the talents and industry, the patriotism and vision, of the deceased statesman, followed by various surmises upon the Prime Minister's choice of his successor. Dr. Audlin read all this. He had not liked Lord Mountdrago. The chief emotion that his death caused in him was dissatisfaction with himself because he had been able to do nothing for him.

Perhaps he had done wrong in not getting into touch with

Lord Mountdrago's doctor. He was discouraged, as always when failure frustrated his conscientious efforts, and repulsion seized him for the theory and practice of this empiric doctrine by which he earned his living. He was dealing with dark and mysterious forces that it was perhaps beyond the powers of the human mind to understand. He was like a man blindfold trying to feel his way to he knew not whither. Listlessly he turned the pages of the paper. Suddenly he gave a great start, and an exclamation once more was forced from his lips. His eyes had fallen on a small paragraph near the bottom of a column. Sudden Death of an M.P., he read. Mr. Owen Griffiths, member for so-and-so, had been taken ill in Fleet Street that afternoon and when he was brought to Charing Cross Hospital life was found to be extinct. It was supposed that death was due to natural causes, but an inquest would be held. Dr. Audlin could hardly believe his eyes. Was it possible that the night before Lord Mountdrago had at last in his dream found himself possessed of the weapon, knife or gun, that he had wanted, and had killed his tormentor, and had that ghostly murder, in the same way as the blow with the bottle had given him a racking headache on the following day, taken effect a certain number of hours later on the waking man? Or was it, more mysterious and more frightful, that when Lord Mountdrago sought relief in death, the enemy he had so cruelly wronged, unappeased, escaping from his own mortality, had pursued him to some other sphere, there to torment him still? It was strange. The sensible thing was to look upon it merely as an odd coincidence. Dr. Audlin rang the bell.

"Tell Mrs. Milton that I'm sorry I can't see her this evening, I'm not well."

It was true; he shivered as though of an ague. With some kind of spiritual sense he seemed to envisage a bleak, a horrible void. The dark night of the soul engulfed him, and he felt a strange, primeval terror of he knew not what.

Mr. Arcularis

CONRAD AIKEN

Mr. Arcularis stood at the window of his room in the hospital and looked down at the street. There had been a light shower, which had patterned the sidewalks with large drops, but now again the sun was out, blue sky was showing here and there between the swift white clouds, a cold wind was blowing the poplar trees. An itinerant band had stopped before the building and was playing, with violin, harp, and flute, the finale of *Cavalleria Rusticana.* Leaning against the window-sill—for he felt extraordinarily weak after his operation—Mr. Arcularis suddenly, listening to the wretched music, felt like crying. He rested the palm of one hand against a cold window-pane and stared down at the old man who was blowing the flute, and blinked his eyes. It seemed absurd that he should be so weak, so emotional, so like a child—and especially now that everything was over at last. In spite of all their predictions, in spite, too, of his own dreadful certainty that he was going to die, here he was, as fit as a fiddle—but what a fiddle it was, so out of tune!—with a long life before him. And to begin with, a voyage to England ordered by the doctor. What could be more delightful? Why should he feel sad about it and want to cry like a baby? In a few minutes Harry would arrive with his car to take him to the wharf; in an hour he would be on the sea, in two hours he would see the sunset behind him, where Boston had been, and his new life would be opening before him. It was many years since he had been abroad. June, the best of the year to come—England, France, the Rhine—how ridiculous that he should already be homesick!

There was a light footstep outside the door, a knock, the door opened, and Harry came in.

"Well, old man, I've come to get you. The old bus actually got here. Are you ready? Here, let me take your arm. You're tottering like an octogenarian!"

Mr. Arcularis submitted gratefully, laughing, and they made the journey slowly along the bleak corridor and down the stairs to the entrance hall. Miss Hoyle, his nurse, was there, and the Matron, and the charming little assistant with freckles who had helped to prepare him for the operation. Miss Hoyle put out her hand.

"Good-bye, Mr. Arcularis," she said, "and *bon voyage.*"

"Good-bye, Miss Hoyle, and thank you for everything. You were very kind to me. And I fear I was a nuisance."

The girl with the freckles, too, gave him her hand, smiling. She was very pretty, and it would have been easy to fall in love with her. She reminded him of someone. Who was it? He tried in vain to remember while he said good-bye to her and turned to the Matron.

"And not too many latitudes with the young ladies, Mr. Arcularis!" she was saying.

Mr. Arcularis was pleased, flattered, by all this attention to a middle-aged invalid, and felt a joke taking shape in his mind, and no sooner in his mind than on his tongue.

"Oh, no latitudes," he said, laughing. "I'll leave the latitudes to the ship!"

"Oh, come now," said the Matron, "we don't seem to have hurt him much, do we?"

"I think we'll have to operate on him again and *really* cure him," said Miss Hoyle.

He was going down the front steps, between the potted palmettos, and they all laughed and waved. The wind was cold, very cold for June, and he was glad he had put on his coat. He shivered.

"Damned cold for June!" he said. "Why should it be so cold?"

"East wind," Harry said, arranging the rug over his knees. "Sorry it's an open car, but I believe in fresh air and all that sort of thing. I'll drive slowly. We've got plenty of time."

They coasted gently down the long hill towards Beacon Street, but the road was badly surfaced, and despite Harry's care Mr. Arcularis felt his pain again. He found that he could alleviate it a little by leaning to the right, against the arm-rest, and not breathing too deeply. But how glorious to be out again! How strange and vivid the world looked! The trees had innumerable green fresh leaves—they were all blowing and shifting and turning and flashing in the wind; drops of rainwater fell downward sparkling; the robins were singing their absurd, delicious little four-noted songs; even the street cars looked unusually bright and beautiful, just as they used to look when he was a child and had wanted above all things to be a motorman. He found himself smiling foolishly at everything, foolishly and weakly, and wanted to say something about it to Harry. It was no use, though—he had no strength, and the mere finding of words would be almost more than he could manage. And even if he should succeed in saying it, he would then most likely burst into tears. He shook his head slowly from side to side.

"Ain't it grand?" he said.

"I'll bet it looks good," said Harry.

"Words fail me."

"You wait till you get out to sea. You'll have a swell time."

"Oh, swell! . . . I hope not. I hope it'll be calm."

"Tut tut."

When they passed the Harvard Club Mr. Arcularis made a slow and somewhat painful effort to turn in his seat and look at it. It might be the last chance to see it for a long time. Why this sentimental longing to stare at it, though? There it was, with the great flag blowing in the wind, the Harvard seal now concealed by the swift folds and now revealed, and there were the windows in the library, where he had spent so many delightful hours reading—Plato, and Kipling, and the Lord knows what—and the balconies from which for so many years he had watched the finish of the Marathon. Old Talbot might be in there now, sleeping with a book on his knee, hoping forlornly to be interrupted by anyone, for anything.

"Good-bye to the old club," he said.

"The bar will miss you," said Harry, smiling with friendly irony and looking straight ahead.

"But let there be no moaning," said Mr. Arcularis.

"What's *that* a quotation from?"

" 'The Odyssey.' "

In spite of the cold, he was glad of the wind on his face, for it helped to dissipate the feeling of vagueness and dizziness that came over him in a sickening wave from time to time. All of a sudden everything would begin to swim and dissolve, the houses would lean their heads together, he had to close his eyes, and there would be a curious and dreadful humming noise, which at regular intervals rose to a crescendo and then drawlingly subsided again. It was disconcerting. Perhaps he still had a trace of fever. When he got on the ship he would have a glass of whisky. . . . From one of these spells he opened his eyes and found that they were on the ferry, crossing to East Boston. It must have been the ferry's engines that he had heard. From another spell he woke to find himself on the wharf, the car at a standstill beside a pile of yellow packing-cases.

"We're here because we're here because we're here," said Harry.

"Because we're here," added Mr. Arcularis.

He dozed in the car while Harry—and what a good friend Harry was!—attended to all the details. He went and came with tickets and passports and baggage checks and porters. And at last he unwrapped Mr. Arcularis from the rugs and led him up the steep gangplank to the deck, and thence by devious windings to a small cold stateroom with a solitary porthole like the eye of a cyclops.

"Here you are," he said, "and now I've got to go. Did you hear the whistle?"

"No."

"Well, you're half asleep. It's sounded the all-ashore. Goodbye, old fellow, and take care of yourself. Bring me back a spray of edelweiss. And send me a picture post card from the Absolute."

"Will you have it finite or infinite?"

"Oh, infinite. But with your signature on it. Now you'd better turn in for a while and have a nap. Cheerio!"

Mr. Arcularis took his hand and pressed it hard, and once more felt like crying. Absurd! Had he become a child again?

"Good-bye," he said.

He sat down in the little wicker chair, with his overcoat still on, closed his eyes, and listened to the humming of the air in the ventilator. Hurried footsteps ran up and down the corridor. The chair was not too comfortable, and his pain began to bother him again, so he moved, with his coat still on, to the narrow berth and fell asleep. When he woke up, it was dark, and the porthole had been partly opened. He groped for the switch and turned on the light. Then he rang for the steward.

"It's cold in here," he said. "Would you mind closing the port?"

The girl who sat opposite him at dinner was charming. Who was it she reminded him of? Why, of course, the girl at the hospital, the girl with the freckles. Her hair was beautiful, not quite red, not quite gold, nor had it been bobbed; arranged with a sort of graceful untidiness, it made him think of a Melozzo da Forli angel. Her face was freckled, she had a mouth which was both humorous and voluptuous. And she seemed to be alone.

He frowned at the bill of fare and ordered the thick soup.

"No hors d'oeuvres?" asked the steward.

"I think not," said Mr. Arcularis. "They might kill me."

The steward permitted himself to be amused and deposited the menu card on the table against the water-bottle. His eyebrows were lifted. As he moved away, the girl followed him with her eyes and smiled.

"I'm afraid you shocked him," she said.

"Impossible," said Mr. Arcularis. "These stewards, they're dead souls. How could they be stewards otherwise? And they think they've seen and known everything. They suffer terribly from the *déjà vu*. Personally, I don't blame them."

"It must be a dreadful sort of life."

"It's because they're dead that they accept it."

"Do you think so?"

"I'm sure of it. I'm enough of a dead soul myself to know the signs!"

"Well, I don't know what you mean by that!"

"But nothing mysterious! I'm just out of hospital, after an operation. I was given up for dead. For six months I had given *myself* up for dead. If you've ever been seriously ill you know the feeling. You have a posthumous feeling—a mild, cynical tolerance for everything and everyone. What is there you haven't seen or done or understood? Nothing."

Mr. Arcularis waved his hands and smiled.

"I wish I could understand you," said the girl, "but I've never been ill in my life."

"Never?"

"Never."

"Good God!"

The torrent of the unexpressed and inexpressible paralyzed him and rendered him speechless. He stared at the girl, wondering who she was and then, realizing that he had perhaps stared too fixedly, averted his gaze, gave a little laugh, rolled a pill of bread between his fingers. After a second or two he allowed himself to look at her again and found her smiling.

"Never pay any attention to invalids," he said, "or they'll drag you to the hospital."

She examined him critically, with her head tilted a little to one side, but with friendliness.

"You don't *look* like an invalid," she said.

Mr. Arcularis thought her charming. His pain ceased to bother him, the disagreeable humming disappeared, or rather, it was dissociated from himself and became merely, as it should be, the sound of the ship's engines, and he began to think the voyage was going to be really delightful. The parson on his right passed him the salt.

"I fear you will need this in your soup," he said.

"Thank you. Is it as bad as that?"

The steward, overhearing, was immediately apologetic and solicitous. He explained that on the first day everything was at sixes and sevens. The girl looked up at him and asked him a question.

"Do you think we'll have a good voyage?" she said.

He was passing the hot rolls to the parson, removing the napkins from them with a deprecatory finger.

"Well, madam, I don't like to be a Jeremiah, but——"

"Oh, come," said the parson, "I hope we have no Jeremiahs."

"What do you mean?" said the girl.

Mr. Arcularis ate his soup with gusto—it was nice and hot.

"Well, maybe I shouldn't say it, but there's a corpse on board, going to Ireland; and I never yet knew a voyage with a corpse on board that we didn't have bad weather."

"Why, steward, you're just superstitious! What nonsense."

"That's a very ancient superstition," said Mr. Arcularis. "I've heard it many times. Maybe it's true. Maybe we'll be wrecked. And what does it matter, after all?" He was very bland.

"Then let's be wrecked," said the parson coldly.

Nevertheless, Mr. Arcularis felt a shudder go through him on hearing the steward's remark. A corpse in the hold—a coffin? Perhaps it was true. Perhaps some disaster would befall them. There might be fogs. There might be icebergs. He thought of all the wrecks of which he had read. There was the *Titanic*, which he had read about in the warm newspaper room at the Harvard Club—it had seemed dreadfully real, even there. That band, playing "Nearer My God to Thee" on the after-deck while the ship sank! It was one of the darkest of his memories. And the *Empress of Ireland*—all those poor people trapped in the smoking-room, with only one door between them and life, and that door locked for the night by the deck-steward, and the deck-steward nowhere to be found! He shivered, feeling a draft, and turned to the parson.

"How do these strange delusions arise?" he said.

The parson looked at him searchingly, appraisingly—from chin to forehead, from forehead to chin—and Mr. Arcularis, feeling uncomfortable, straightened his tie.

"From nothing but fear," said the parson. "Nothing on earth but fear."

"How strange!" said the girl.

Mr. Arcularis again looked at her—she had lowered her face

—and again tried to think of whom she reminded him. It wasn't only the little freckle-faced girl at the hospital—both of them had reminded him of someone else. Someone far back in his life: remote, beautiful, lovely. But he couldn't think. The meal came to an end, they all rose, the ship's orchestra played a feeble fox-trot, and Mr. Arcularis, once more alone, went to the bar to have his whisky. The room was stuffy, and the ship's engines were both audible and palpable. The humming and throbbing oppressed him, the rhythm seemed to be the rhythm of his own pain, and after a short time he found his way, with slow steps, holding on to the walls in his moments of weakness and dizziness, to his forlorn and white little room. The port had been—thank God!—closed for the night: it was cold enough anyway. The white and blue ribbons fluttered from the ventilator, the bottle and glasses clicked and clucked as the ship swayed gently to the long, slow motion of the sea. It was all very peculiar—it was all like something he had experienced somewhere before. What was it? Where was it? . . . He untied his tie, looking at his face in the glass, and wondered, and from time to time put his hand to his side to hold in the pain. It wasn't at Portsmouth, in his childhood, nor at Salem, nor in the rose-garden at his Aunt Julia's, nor in the school-room at Cambridge. It was something very queer, very intimate, very precious. The jackstones, the Sunday-School cards which he had loved when he was a child. . . . He fell asleep.

The sense of time was already hopelessly confused. One hour was like another, the sea looked always the same, morning was indistinguishable from afternoon—and was it Tuesday or Wednesday? Mr. Arcularis was sitting in the smoking-room, in his favorite corner, watching the parson teach Miss Dean to play chess. On the deck outside he could see the people passing and repassing in their restless round of the ship. The red jacket went by, then the black hat with the white feather, then the purple scarf, the brown tweed coat, the Bulgarian mustache, the monocle, the Scotch cap with fluttering ribbons, and in no time at all the red jacket again, dipping past the windows with its own peculiar rhythm, followed once more by the black hat and the purple scarf. How odd to reflect on the fixed little orbits of these things—as definite and profound, perhaps, as the orbits of the stars, and as important to God or the Absolute. There was a kind of tyranny in this fixedness, too—to think of it too much made one uncomfortable. He closed his eyes for a moment, to avoid seeing for the fortieth time the Bulgarian mustache and the pursuing monocle. The parson was explaining the movements of knights. Two forward and one to the side. Eight possible moves, always to the opposite color from that on which the piece stands. Two forward and one to the side: Miss Dean repeated the words several times with reflective emphasis. Here, too, was the terrifying fixed curve of the infinite, the creeping curve of logic which at last must become the final signpost at the edge of nothing. After that—the deluge. The great white light of annihilation. The bright flash of death. . . . Was it merely the sea which made these abstractions so insistent, so intrusive? The mere notion of *orbit* had somehow become extraordinarily naked; and to rid himself of the discomfort and also to forget a little the pain which bothered his side whenever he sat down, he walked slowly and carefully into the writing-room, and examined a pile of superannuated magazines and catalogues of travel. The bright colors amused him, the photographs of remote islands and mountains, savages in sampans or sarongs or both—it was all very far off and delightful, like something in a dream or a fever. But he found that he was too tired to read and was incapable of concentration. Dreams! Yes, that reminded him. That rather alarming business—sleep-walking!

Later in the evening—at what hour he didn't know—he was

telling Miss Dean about it, as he had intended to do. They were sitting in deck-chairs on the sheltered side. The sea was black, and there was a cold wind. He wished they had chosen to sit in the lounge.

Miss Dean was extremely pretty—no, beautiful. She looked at him, too, in a very strange and lovely way, with something of inquiry, something of sympathy, something of affection. It seemed as if, between the question and the answer, they had sat thus for a very long time, exchanging an unspoken secret, simply looking at each other quietly and kindly. Had an hour or two passed? And was it at all necessary to speak?

"No," she said, "I never have."

She breathed into the low words a note of interrogation and gave him a slow smile.

"That's the funny part of it. I never had either until last night. Never in my life. I hardly ever even dream. And it really rather frightens me."

"Tell me about it, Mr. Arcularis."

"I dreamed at first that I was walking, alone, in a wide plain covered with snow. It was growing dark, I was very cold, my feet were frozen and numb, and I was lost. I came then to a signpost—at first it seemed to me there was nothing on it. Nothing but ice. Just before it grew finally dark, however, I made out on it the one word 'Polaris.'"

"The Pole Star."

"Yes—and you see, I didn't myself know that. I looked it up only this morning. I suppose I must have seen it somewhere? And of course it rhymes with my name."

"Why, so it does!"

"Anyway, it gave me—in the dream—an awful feeling of despair, and the dream changed. This time, I dreamed I was standing *outside* my stateroom in the little dark corridor, or *cul-de-sac*, and trying to find the door-handle to let myself in. I was in my pajamas, and again I was very cold. And at this point

I woke up. . . . The extraordinary thing is that's exactly where I was!"

"Good heavens. How strange!"

"Yes. And now the question is, *where had I been?* I was frightened, when I came to—not unnaturally. For among other things I *did* have, quite definitely, the feeling that I *had been* somewhere. Somewhere where it was very cold. It doesn't sound very proper. Suppose I had been seen!"

"That might have been awkward," said Miss Dean.

"Awkward! It might indeed. It's very singular. I've never done such a thing before. It's this sort of thing that reminds one —rather wholesomely, perhaps, don't you think?"—and Mr. Arcularis gave a nervous little laugh—"how extraordinarily little we know about the workings of our own minds or souls. After all, what *do* we know?"

"Nothing—nothing—nothing—nothing," said Miss Dean slowly.

"*Absolutely* nothing."

Their voices had dropped, and again they were silent; and again they looked at each other gently and sympathetically, as if for the exchange of something unspoken and perhaps unspeakable. Time ceased. The orbit—so it seemed to Mr. Arcularis—once more became pure, became absolute. And once more he found himself wondering who it was that Miss Dean —Clarice Dean—reminded him of. Long ago and far away. Like those pictures of the islands and mountains. The little freckle-faced girl at the hospital was merely, as it were, the stepping-stone, the signpost, or, as in algebra, the "equals" sign. But what was it they both "equalled"? The jackstones came again into his mind and his Aunt Julia's rose-garden—at sunset; but this was ridiculous. It couldn't be simply that they reminded him of his childhood! And yet why not? And yet why not? And yet why not?

They went into the lounge. The ship's orchestra, in the oval-shaped balcony among faded palms, was playing the finale of *Cavalleria Rusticana*, playing it badly.

"Good God!" said Mr. Arcularis, "can't I ever escape from that damned sentimental tune? It's the last thing I heard in America, and the last thing I *want* to hear."

"But don't you like it?"

"As music? No! It moves me too much, but in the wrong way."

"What, exactly, do you mean?"

"Exactly? Nothing. When I heard it at the hospital—when was it?—it made me feel like crying. Three old Italians tootling it in the rain. I suppose, like most people, I'm afraid of my feelings."

"Are they so dangerous?"

"Now then, young woman! Are you pulling my leg?"

The stewards had rolled away the carpets, and the passengers were beginning to dance. Miss Dean accepted the invitation of a young officer, and Mr. Arcularis watched them with envy. Odd, that last exchange of remarks—very odd; in fact, everything was odd. Was it possible that they were falling in love? Was that what it was all about—all these concealed references and recollections? He had read of such things. But at his age! And with a girl of twenty-two!

After an amused look at his old friend Polaris from the open door on the sheltered side, he went to bed.

The rhythm of the ship's engines was positively a persecution. It gave one no rest, it followed one like the Hound of Heaven, it drove one out into space and across the Milky Way and then back home by way of Betelgeuse. It was cold there, too. Mr. Arcularis, making the round trip by way of Betelgeuse and Polaris, sparkled with frost. He felt like a Christmas tree. Icicles on his fingers and icicles on his toes. He tinkled and spangled in the void, hallooed to the waste echoes, rounded the buoy on the verge of the Unknown, and tacked glittering homeward. The wind whistled. He was barefooted. Snowflakes and tinsel blew past him. Next time, by George, he would go farther still—for altogether it was rather a lark. Forward into the untrodden! as somebody said. Some intrepid explorer of his own backyard, probably, some middle-aged professor with an umbrella: those were the fellows for courage! But give us time, thought Mr. Arcularis, give us time, and we will bring back with us the night-rime of the Absolute. Or was it Absolete? If only there weren't this perpetual throbbing, this iteration of sound, like a pain, these circles and repetitions of light—the feeling as of everything coiling inward to a center of misery . . .

Suddenly it was dark, and he was lost. He was groping, he touched the cold, white, slippery woodwork with his fingernails, looking for an electric switch. The throbbing, of course, was the throbbing of the ship. But he was almost home—almost home. Another corner to round, a door to be opened, and there he would be. Safe and sound. Safe in his father's home.

It was at this point that he woke up: in the corridor that led to the dining saloon. Such pure terror, such horror, seized him as he had never known. His heart felt as if it would stop beating. His back was towards the dining saloon; apparently he had just come from it. He was in his pajamas. The corridor was dim, all but two lights having been turned out for the night, and—thank God!—deserted. Not a soul, not a sound. He was perhaps fifty yards from his room. With luck he could get to it unseen. Holding tremulously to the rail that ran along the wall, a brown, greasy rail, he began to creep his way forward. He felt very weak, very dizzy, and his thoughts refused to concentrate. Vaguely he remembered Miss Dean—Clarice—and the freckled girl, as if they were one and the same person. But he wasn't in the hospital, he was on the ship. Of course. How absurd. The Great Circle. Here we are, old fellow . . . steady round the corner . . . hold hard to your umbrella . . .

In his room, with the door safely shut behind him, Mr.

Arcularis broke into a cold sweat. He had no sooner got into his bunk, shivering, than he heard the night watchman pass.

"But where"—he thought, closing his eyes in agony—"have I been? . . ."

A dreadful idea had occurred to him.

"It's nothing serious—how could it be anything serious? Of course it's nothing serious," said Mr. Arcularis.

"No, it's nothing serious," said the ship's doctor urbanely.

"I knew you'd think so. But just the same——"

"Such a condition is the result of worry," said the doctor. "Are you worried—do you mind telling me—about something? Just try to think."

"Worried?"

Mr. Arcularis knitted his brows. *Was* there something? Some little mosquito of a cloud disappearing into the southwest, the northeast? Some little gnat-song of despair? But no, that was all over. All over.

"Nothing," he said, "nothing whatever."

"It's very strange," said the doctor.

"Strange! I should say so. I've come to sea for a rest, not for a nightmare! What about a bromide?"

"Well, I can give you a bromide, Mr. Arcularis——"

"Then, please, if you don't mind, give me a bromide."

He carried the little phial hopefully to his stateroom, and took a dose at once. He could see the sun through his porthole. It looked northern and pale and small, like a little peppermint, which was only natural enough, for the latitude was changing with every hour. But why was it that doctors were all alike? and all, for that matter, like his father, or that other fellow at the hospital? Smythe, his name was. Doctor Smythe. A nice, dry little fellow, and they said he was a writer. Wrote poetry, or something like that. Poor fellow—disappointed. Like everybody else. Crouched in there, in his cabin, night after night, writing blank verse or something—all about the stars and flowers and love and death; ice and the sea and the infinite; time and tide—well, every man to his own taste.

"But it's nothing serious," said Mr. Arcularis, later, to the parson. "How could it be?"

"Why of course not, my dear fellow," said the parson, patting his back. "How could it be?"

"I know it isn't and yet I worry about it."

"It would be ridiculous to think it serious," said the parson.

Mr. Arcularis shivered: it was colder than ever. It was said that they were near icebergs. For a few hours in the morning there had been a fog, and the siren had blown—devastatingly—at three-minute intervals. Icebergs caused fog—he knew that.

"These things always come," said the parson, "from a sense of guilt. You feel guilty about something. I won't be so rude as to inquire what it is. But if you could rid yourself of the sense of guilt——"

And later still, when the sky was pink:

"But is it anything to worry about?" said Miss Dean. "Really?"

"No, I suppose not."

"Then don't worry. We aren't children any longer!"

"Aren't we? I wonder!"

They leaned, shoulders touching, on the deck-rail, and looked at the sea, which was multitudinously incarnadined. Mr. Arcularis scanned the horizon in vain for an iceberg.

"Anyway," he said, "the colder we are the less we feel!"

"I hope that's no reflection on *you*," said Miss Dean.

"Here . . . feel my hand," said Mr. Arcularis.

"Heaven knows it's cold!"

"It's been to Polaris and back! No wonder."

"Poor thing, poor thing!"

"Warm it."

"May I?"

"You can."

"I'll try."

Laughing, she took his hand between both of hers, one palm under and one palm over, and began rubbing it briskly. The decks were deserted, no one was near them, everyone was dressing for dinner. The sea grew darker, the wind blew colder.

"I wish I could remember who you are," he said.

"And you—who are you?"

"Myself."

"Then perhaps I am yourself."

"Don't be metaphysical!"

"But I *am* metaphysical!"

She laughed, withdrew, pulled the light coat about her shoulders.

The bugle blew the summons for dinner—"The Roast Beef of Old England"—and they walked together along the darkening deck toward the door, from which a shaft of soft light fell across the deck-rail. As they stepped over the brass door-sill Mr. Arcularis felt the throb of the engines again; he put his hand quickly to his side.

"*Auf wiedersehen,*" he said. "*Tomorrow and tomorrow and tomorrow.*"

Mr. Arcularis was finding it impossible, absolutely impossible, to keep warm. A cold fog surrounded the ship, had done so, it seemed, for days. The sun had all but disappeared, the transition from day to night was almost unnoticeable. The ship, too, seemed scarcely to be moving—it was as if anchored among walls of ice and rime. Monstrous, that merely because it was June, and supposed, therefore, to be warm, the ship's authorities should consider it unnecessary to turn on the heat! By day, he wore his heavy coat and sat shivering in the corner of the smoking-room. His teeth chattered, his hands were blue. By night, he heaped blankets on his bed, closed the porthole's black eye against the sea, and drew the yellow curtains across it, but in vain. Somehow, despite everything, the fog crept in, and the icy fingers touched his throat. The steward, questioned about it, merely said, "Icebergs." Of course—any fool knew that. But how long, in God's name, was it going to last? They surely ought to be past the Grand Banks by this time! And surely it wasn't necessary to sail to England by way of Greenland and Iceland!

Miss Dean—Clarice—was sympathetic.

"It's simply because," she said, "your vitality has been lowered by your illness. You can't expect to be your normal self so soon after an operation! When *was* your operation, by the way?"

Mr. Arcularis considered. Strange—he couldn't be quite sure. It was all a little vague—his sense of time had disappeared.

"Heaven knows!" he said. "Centuries ago. When I was a tadpole and you were a fish. I should think it must have been at about the time of the Battle of Teutoburg Forest. Or perhaps when I was a Neanderthal man with a club!"

"Are you sure it wasn't farther back still?"

What did she mean by that?

"Not at all. Obviously, we've been on this damned ship for ages—for eras—for aeons. And even on this ship, you must remember, I've had plenty of time, in my nocturnal wanderings, to go several times to Orion and back. I'm thinking, by the way, of going farther still. There's a nice little star off to the left, as you round Betelgeuse, which looks as if it might be right at the edge. The last outpost of the finite. I think I'll have a look at it and bring you back a frozen rime-feather."

"It would melt when you got it back."

"Oh, no, it wouldn't—not on *this* ship!"

Clarice laughed.

"I wish I could go with you," she said.

"If only you would! If only——"

He broke off his sentence and looked hard at her—how lovely she was, and how desirable! No such woman had ever before come into his life; there had been no one with whom he had at once felt so profound a sympathy and understanding. It was a miracle, simply—a miracle. No need to put his arm around her or to kiss her—delightful as such small vulgarities would be. He had only to look at her, and to feel, gazing into those extraordinary eyes, that she knew him, had always known him. It was as if, indeed, she might be his own soul.

But as he looked thus at her, reflecting, he noticed that she was frowning.

"What is it?" he said.

She shook her head, slowly.

"I don't know."

"Tell me."

"Nothing. It just occurred to me that perhaps you weren't looking quite so well."

Mr. Arcularis was startled. He straightened himself up.

"What nonsense! Of course this pain bothers me—and I feel astonishingly weak——"

"It's more than that—much more than that. Something is worrying you horribly." She paused, and then with an air of challenging him, added, "Tell me, did you?"

Her eyes were suddenly asking him blazingly the question he had been afraid of. He flinched, caught his breath, looked away. But it was no use, as he knew: he would have to tell her. He had known all along that he would have to tell her.

"Clarice," he said—and his voice broke in spite of his effort to control it—"It's killing me, it's ghastly! Yes, I did."

His eyes filled with tears, he saw that her own had done so also. She put her hand on his arm.

"I knew," she said. "I knew. But tell me."

"It's happened twice again—*twice*—and each time I was farther away. The same dream of going round a star, the same terrible coldness and helplessness. That awful whistling curve . . ." He shuddered.

"And when you woke up"—she spoke quietly—"where were you when you woke up? Don't be afraid!"

"The first time I was at the farther end of the dining saloon. I had my hand on the door that leads into the pantry."

"I see. Yes. And the next time?"

Mr. Arcularis wanted to close his eyes in terror—he felt as if he were going mad. His lips moved before he could speak, and when at last he did speak it was in a voice so low as to be almost a whisper.

"I was at the bottom of the stairway that leads down from the pantry to the hold, past the refrigerating-plant. It was dark, and I was crawling on my hands and knees . . . *Crawling on my hands and knees! . . .*"

"Oh!" she said, and again, "Oh!"

He began to tremble violently; he felt the hand on his arm trembling also. And then he watched a look of unmistakable horror come slowly into Clarice's eyes, and a look of understanding, as if she saw . . . She tightened her hold on his arm.

"Do you think . . ." she whispered.

They stared at each other.

"I know," he said. "And so do you . . . Twice more—three times—and I'll be looking down into an empty . . ."

It was then that they first embraced—then, at the edge of the infinite, at the last signpost of the finite. They clung together desperately, forlornly, weeping as they kissed each other, staring hard one moment and closing their eyes the next. Passionately, passionately, she kissed him, as if she were indeed trying to give him her warmth, her life.

"But what nonsense!" she cried, leaning back, and holding

his face between her hands, her hands which were wet with his tears. "What nonsense! It can't be!"

"It is," said Mr. Arcularis slowly.

"But how do you know? . . . How do you know where the——"

For the first time Mr. Arcularis smiled.

"Don't be afraid, darling—you mean the coffin?"

"How could you know where it is?"

"I don't need to," said Mr. Arcularis . . . "I'm already almost there."

Before they separated for the night, in the smoking-room, they had several whisky cocktails.

"We must make it gay!" Mr. Arcularis said. "Above all, we must make it gay. Perhaps even now it will turn out to be nothing but a nightmare from which both of us will wake! And even at the worst, at my present rate of travel, I ought to need two more nights! It's a long way, still, to that little star."

The parson passed them at the door.

"What! turning in so soon?" he said. "I was hoping for a game of chess."

"Yes, both turning in. But tomorrow?"

"Tomorrow, then, Miss Dean! And good night!"

"Good night."

They walked once round the deck, then leaned on the railing and stared into the fog. It was thicker and whiter than ever. The ship was moving barely perceptibly, the rhythm of the engines was slower, more subdued and remote, and at regular intervals, mournfully, came the long reverberating cry of the foghorn. The sea was calm, and lapped only very tenderly against the side of the ship, the sound coming up to them clearly, however, because of the profound stillness.

" 'On such a night as this——' " quoted Mr. Arcularis grimly.

" 'On such a night as this——' "

Their voices hung suspended in the night, time ceased for them, for an eternal instant they were happy. When at last they parted it was by tacit agreement on a note of the ridiculous.

"Be a good boy and take your bromide!" she said.

"Yes, mother, I'll take my medicine!"

In his stateroom, he mixed himself a strong potion of bromide, a very strong one, and got into bed. He would have no trouble in falling asleep: he felt more tired, more supremely exhausted, than he had ever been in his life; nor had bed ever seemed so delicious. And that long, magnificent, delirious swoop of dizziness . . . the Great Circle . . . the swift pathway to Arcturus . . .

It was all as before, but infinitely more rapid. Never had Mr. Arcularis achieved such phenomenal, such supernatural, speed. In no time at all he was beyond the moon, shot past the North Star as if it were standing still (which perhaps it was?), swooped in a long, bright curve round the Pleiades, shouted his frosty greetings to Betelgeuse, and was off to the little blue star which pointed the way to the unknown. Forward into the untrodden! Courage, old man, and hold on to your umbrella! Have you got your garters on? Mind your hat! In no time at all we'll be back to Clarice with the frozen time-feather, the rime-feather, the snowflake of the Absolute, the Obsolete. If only we don't wake . . . if only we needn't wake . . . if only we don't wake in that—in that—time and space . . . somewhere or nowhere . . . cold and dark . . . *Cavalleria Rusticana* sobbing among the palms; if a lonely . . . if only . . . the coffers of the poor—not coffers, not coffers, not coffers, Oh, God, not coffers, but light, delight, supreme white and brightness, and above all whirling lightness, whirling lightness above all—and freezing—freezing—freezing . . .

At this point in the void the surgeon's last effort to save Mr.

Arcularis's life had failed. He stood back from the operating table and made a tired gesture with a rubber-gloved hand. "It's all over," he said. "As I expected."

He looked at Miss Hoyle, whose gaze was downward, at the basin she held. There was a moment's stillness, a pause, a brief flight of unexchanged comment, and then the ordered life of the hospital was resumed.

Interpretation of a Dream

JOHN COLLIER

~~~~~~

A young man entered the office of a well-known psychiatrist, whom he addressed as follows: "Doctor, save me!"

"By all means," responded the mind specialist suavely. "After all, that is what I am here for."

"But you can't," cried the young man distractedly. "You can't! You can't! Nothing can save me!"

"At all events," said the psychiatrist soothingly, "it will do no harm to talk it over."

With that he waved his hands a little, smiled with a rather soapy and ingratiating expression, and before he knew it the young man was seated in a deep armchair, with his face to the light, pouring out his story.

"My name," said he, "is Charles Rotifer. I am employed in the office of an accountant, who occupies the top storey of this skyscraper. I am twenty-eight years of age, single, engaged to be married. My fiancée is the best and dearest girl in the world, beautiful as an angel, and with lovely golden hair. I mention this because it is relevant to my story."

"It is indeed," said the psychiatrist. "Gold is a symbol of

money. Have you a retentive attitude toward money? For example, you say you are employed in an office. Have you saved anything considerable out of your salary?"

"Yes, I have," replied the young man. "I've saved quite a bit."

"Please continue, Mr. Rotifer," said the psychiatrist, benevolently. "You were speaking of your fiancée. Later on I shall have to ask you one or two rather intimate questions on that subject."

"And I will answer them," returned the young man. "There is nothing in our relationship that needs to be concealed—at all events from a psychologist. All is complete harmony between us, and there is nothing about her that I could wish altered, except perhaps her little habit of gesturing rather too freely as she speaks."

"I will make a note of that," said the other, scribbling on his pad.

"It is not of the least importance," said the young man. "I hardly know why I mentioned it, except to indicate how perfect she is. But, Doctor, thirty-eight nights ago I dreamed a dream."

"Thirty-eight, indeed!" observed the mind doctor, jotting down the figure. "Tell me frankly, when you were an infant, did you by any chance have a nurse, a teacher or a female relative, on whom perhaps you might have had a little fixation, who happened to be thirty-eight years of age?"

"No, Doctor," said the young man, "but there are thirty-nine floors to this skyscraper."

The psychiatrist gave him a penetrating glance. "And does the form and height of this building suggest anything to you?"

"All I know," said the young man obstinately, "is that I dreamed I was outside the window of our office at the top, in the air, falling."

"Falling!" said the psychiatrist, raising his eyebrows. "And what were your sensations at that moment?"

"I was calm," replied the young man. "I imagine I was falling at the normal rate, but my mind seemed to work very fast. I had leisure to reflect, to look around me. The view was superb. In a moment I had reached the ornamental stone-work which separates our windows from those immediately below. Then I woke up."

"And that simple, harmless, perfectly ordinary little dream has been preying on your mind?" asked the psychiatrist in a jocular tone. "Well, my dear sir . . ."

"Wait a moment," said his visitor. "On the following night I dreamed the same dream, or rather, a continuation of it. There I was, spread-eagled in mid-air—like this—passing the ornamental stonework, looking into the window of the floor below, which is also occupied by our firm. I saw my friend, Don Straker, of our tax department, bending over his desk. He looked up. He saw me. His face took on an expression of the utmost astonishment. He made a movement as if to rise from his seat, no doubt to rush to the window. But compared with mine, his movements were indescribably slow. I remember thinking, 'He will be too late.' Then I dropped below his window, and down to the dividing line between that floor and the next. As I did so, I woke."

"Well," said the brain doctor. "What have we here? The dream of one night is resumed on the night following. That is a very ordinary occurrence."

"Possibly," said the young man. "However, on the next night, there I was, having just passed the dividing line between that floor and the floor below it. I had slipped into a recumbent posture, with one leg slightly raised, like this."

"Yes, yes," said the psychiatrist, "I see. It is not necessary to demonstrate. You nearly knocked over my ash-tray."

"I'm sorry," said the young man. "I'm afraid I have picked up the habit from Maisie. Maisie is my fiancée. When she wants to say how she did a thing, she just shows you. She acts it out. It was the night she told me how she slipped and fell on the icy pavement on Seventy-second Street, that we became engaged. Well, as I say, there I was, falling past another floor, looking about me in all directions. The hills of New Jersey looked magnificent. A high-flying pigeon coasted in my direction, and regarded me with a round eye, devoid of any expression whatsoever. Then he banked and sheered off. I could see the people in the street below, or rather their hats, jammed as closely as black pebbles on a beach. Even as I looked, one or two of these black pebbles suddenly turned white. I realized I was attracting attention."

"Tell me this," said the psychiatrist. "You seem to have had a good deal of time for thought. Did you recollect why you were falling; whether you had thrown yourself, or slipped, or what?"

"Doctor, I really don't know," said the young man. "Not unless my last dream, which I had last night, sheds any light on the matter. Most of the time I was just looking around, falling faster all the time, of course, but thinking faster to make up for it. Naturally I tried to think of subjects of importance, seeing it was my last opportunity. Between the seventeenth and the sixteenth floors, for example, I thought a lot about democracy and the world crisis. It seemed to me that where most people are making a big mistake is . . ."

"Perhaps, for the moment, we had better keep to the experience itself," said the brain doctor.

"Well," said the young man, "at the fifteenth floor I looked in at the window, and, really, I never believed such things happened! Not in offices, anyway. And, Doctor, next day I paid a visit to the fifteenth floor here, just out of curiosity. And those offices are occupied by a theatrical agent. Doctor, don't you think that confirms my dream?"

"Calm yourself," said the psychiatrist. "The names of all the firms in this building are listed on the wall directory on the main floor. You no doubt retained an unconscious memory which you adroitly fitted into your dream."

"Well, after that," said the young man, "I began to look down a good deal more. I'd take just a quick glance into each window as I passed, but mostly I was looking downwards. By this time there were big patches of white among the dark, pebble-like hats below. In fact, pretty soon they were clearly distinguishable as hats and faces. I saw two taxi-cabs swerve toward one another and collide. A woman's scream drifted up out of the confused murmur below. I felt I agreed with her. I was in a reclining posture, and already I felt an anticipatory pain in the parts that would touch the ground first. So I turned face downwards—like this—but that was horrible. So I put my feet down, but then they hurt. I tried to fall head first, to end it sooner, but that didn't satisfy me. I kept on twisting and turning—like this."

"Please relax," said the psychiatrist. "There is no need to demonstrate."

"I'm sorry," said the young man. "I picked up the habit from Maisie."

"Sit down," said the psychiatrist, "and continue."

"Last night," said the young man despairingly, "was the thirty-eighth night."

"Then," said the psychiatrist, "you must have got down to this level, for this office is on the mezzanine floor."

"I was," cried the young man. "And I was outside this very window, descending at terrific speed. I looked in. Doctor, I saw you! As clearly as I see you now!"

"Mr. Rotifer," replied the psychiatrist with a modest smile, "I very frequently figure in my patients' dreams."

"But I wasn't your patient then," said the young man. "I didn't even know you existed. I didn't know till this morning, when I came to see who occupied this office. Oh, Doctor, I was so relieved to find you were not a theatrical agent!"

"And why were you relieved?" asked the specialist blandly.

"Because you were not alone. In my dream, I mean. A young

woman was with you. A young woman with beautiful golden hair. And she was sitting on your knee, Doctor, and her arms were around your neck. I felt certain it was another theatrical agency. And then I thought, 'That is very beautiful golden hair. It is like my Maisie's hair.' At that moment you both looked toward the window. It was she! Maisie! My own Maisie!"

The psychiatrist laughed very heartily. "My dear sir," said he, "you may set your mind entirely at rest."

"All the same," said the young man, "this morning, in the office, I have been a prey to an unbearable curiosity, an almost irresistible urge to jump, just to see what I should see."

"You would have had the mortification," said the psychiatrist, "of seeing that there were no grounds whatever for your rash act. Your fiancée is not a patient of mine; therefore she could not have had one of those harmless little transferences, as we call them, which have been known to lead to ardent behaviour on the part of the subject. Besides, our profession has its ethics, and nothing ever happens in the office. No, my dear sir, what you have described to me is a relatively simple condition, a recurrent dream, a little neurotic compulsion—nothing that cannot be cured in time. If you can visit me three or four times a week, I am confident that a very few years will show a decided improvement."

"But Doctor," cried the young man in despair, "I am due to hit the ground at any moment!"

"But only in a dream," said the psychiatrist reassuringly. "Be sure to remember it clearly, and note particularly if you bounce. Meanwhile, return to your office, carry on with your work, and worry as little as possible about it."

"I will try to do so," said the young man. "But really you are astonishingly like yourself as I saw you in my dream, even to that little pearl tie-pin."

"That," said the psychiatrist, as he bowed him smilingly out, "was a gift from a very well-known lady, who was always falling in her dreams." So saying, he closed the door behind his visitor, who departed shaking his head in obstinate melancholy. The psychiatrist then seated himself at his desk and placed the tips of his fingers together, as psychiatrists always do while they are pondering over how much a new patient may be good for.

His meditation was interrupted by his secretary, who thrust her head in at the door. "Miss Mimling to see you," she said. "Her appointment is at two-thirty."

"Show her in," said the psychiatrist, and rose to greet the new entrant, who proved to be a young woman with the appearance of a rather wild mouse, upon whose head someone has let fall a liberal splash of peroxide. She was in a very agitated state. "Oh, Doctor," she said, "I just *had* to telephone you, for when I saw your name in the book, of course I knew it was you. I saw your name on the door. In my dream, Doctor. In my dream."

"Let us talk it over very quietly," said the healer of souls, trying to manoeuvre her into the deep armchair. She was fidgety, however, and perched herself upon the corner of his desk. "I don't know if you think there is anything *in* dreams," she said. "But this was such an extraordinary one.

"I dreamed I came up to your door, and there was your name on it, just as it is out there. That's how it was I came to look you up in the telephone book, and there it was again. So I felt I just had to come and see you.

"Well, I dreamed I came into your office, and I was sitting here on the desk, just like this, talking to you, and all of a sudden—of course I know it was only a dream—I felt a feeling . . . well, really I hardly know how to tell you. It seemed to me as if you were my father, my big brother, and a boy I once knew called Herman Myers, all rolled into one. I don't know how I could feel like that, even in a dream, for I am engaged to a young man I love with all my conscious mind, and I thought with my unconscious, too. Oh, it's awful of me!"

"My dear young lady," purred the psychiatrist, "this is nothing more or less than the phenomenon of transference. It is something which can happen to anybody, and usually it does."

"Yes," said she, "but it made me transfer myself to your knee, like this, and put my arms around your neck, like this."

"Now! now!" murmured the psychiatrist gently, "I'm afraid you are acting out a neurotic impulse."

"I always act things out," she said. "They say it makes me the life and soul of a party. But, Doctor, then I happened to look out of the window, like this, and . . . Wow! There he is! There he was! It was Charlie! Oh, what a terrible look he gave us as he went by!"

The Secret Songs

FRITZ LEIBER

~~~~~~

Promptly after supper, before Gwen had cleared away the dishes, Donnie began the Sleep Ritual. He got a can of beer from the refrigerator, selected a science-fiction magazine, and shut off the TV sound.

"The picture too?" he asked. "Might as well."

Gwen smiled at him as she shook her head. With the gesture of one who eats peanuts she threw her right hand to her mouth, swallowed, then dropped her hand with the tiny bottle it held back to the pocket of her smock.

Donnie sighed, shrugged his shoulders, settled himself in the easy chair, opened his magazine, and began to read and sip rapidly.

Gwen, who had been ignoring the TV, now began to study the screen. A kindly old rancher and a tall young cowpoke, father and son, were gazing out across broad acres framed by distant mountains. Gwen tuned her ears and after a bit she could faintly hear what they were saying.

THE OLD RANCHER: *Aim to plant her to hemp and opium poppy, Son, with benzedrine bushes between the rows.*

THE YOUNG COWPOKE: *Yeah, but what legal crop you fixin'
to raise, Dad?*

THE OLD RANCHER (smiling like God): *Gonna raise babies,
Son.*

Gwen looked away quickly from the screen. It never paid to
try to hear too much too soon.

Donnie was studying her with a teasing grin.

"I bet you imagine all sorts of crazy things while you watch
it," he said. "Those terrible bennies get your mind all roiled
up."

Gwen shrugged. "You won't allow any noise while you're
putting yourself to sleep. I have to have something," she said
reasonably. "Besides," she added, "you're having orgies out in
space with those girls in fluorescent bikinis."

"That shows how little you know about science fiction,"
Donnie said. "They dropped the sex angle years ago. Now it's
all philosophy and stuff. See this old guy?"

He held up the magazine, keeping his place with his forefinger. On the cover was a nicely drawn picture of a smiling
intelligent-looking young man in a form-fitting futuristic uniform and standing beside him, topping him by a long head, a
lean green-scaled monster with a large silver purse slung over
his crested shoulder. The monster had a tentacle resting in com-
radely fashion across the young man's back and curling lightly
past his feather epaulet.

"You mean that walking crocodile?" Gwen asked.

Donnie sniffed. "That walking crocodile," he said, "happens
to be a very wise old member of a civilization that's advanced
far beyond man's." He lifted his other hand with two fingers
pressed together. "Him and me are like that. He tells me all
sorts of things. He even tells me things about you."

"Science fiction doesn't interest me," Gwen said lightly, looking back to the TV. There was a commercial on now, first a
white-on-black diagram of the human body with explosions of

bubbles occurring in sequence at various points, then a beautiful princess in a vast bathroom, then a handsome policeman. Gwen expertly retuned her ears.

VOICE OF MEDICAL EXPERT: *Benzedrine strikes at hidden sleepiness! Tones muscles! Strengthens the heart! Activates sluggish wake centres . . . One . . . Two . . . Three!*

THE BEAUTIFUL PRINCESS (looking depressed): *Yesterday I was overweight, listless, intensely unhappy. Mother called me The Ugly Dumpling. Now* (becoming radiant) *I build beauty with benzedrine!*

THE HANDSOME POLICEMAN (flashing badge with huge "N" for Narcotic Squad): *You're all under arrest! Grrr . . . aarrar-rgghhh!*

Gwen quickly looked away. It was the only thing you could do when you got static or the wrong voice channel. She began to carry the supper dishes to the sink.

Donnie winced violently without putting down his beer can or looking up from his page. "Don't clank them," he said. Gwen removed her shoes and began to do the dishes as if she were a diver in the silent world under the surface of the sea, ghosting between table, sink and cupboard.

She was still lost in this rather fascinating operation and even beginning to embroider it with little arabesques when Donnie continued the Sleep Ritual by opening his second can of beer, this time a warm one by choice. Before taking the first sip he swallowed a blue capsule of amytal. At the *kerzing!* of the opener Gwen stopped to watch him. She carefully dried the suds off her right hand, popped onto her tongue another benzedrine tablet from the bottle in her smock pocket, and still watching him thoughtfully, rinsed a glass, ran an inch of water into it and drank it.

If Donnie had his Sleep Ritual, she told herself in not exactly those words, she had her Vigil.

Donnie stood shaking his head at her.

"I suppose now you'll be wandering around all night," he said, "making all sorts of noise and disturbing me."

"I don't make any more noise than a snowflake," Gwen countered. "Not one-tenth as much as the autos and streetcars and planes. Almost every night the people next door have their TV on high."

"Yes, but those noises are outside," Donnie said. "It's your noises that bother me—the inside noises." He looked at Gwen speculatively. "Why don't you try a sleeping pill just for once?" he said with insidious appeal.

"No," Gwen answered instantly.

"A three-grain amytal," Donnie persisted, "would cancel those bennies and still have enough left over to make you nice and dozy. We'd go to sleep together and I wouldn't worry about noises."

"You don't want to go to sleep until you know everyone else is asleep," Gwen said. "Just like my mother. If I took one of your pills, you'd watch me sleep and you'd gloat."

"Well, isn't that what you do to me?"

"No, I do other things. By myself."

Donnie shrugged resignedly and went back to his chair and magazine.

Gwen wiped the itchy suds off her left hand, and leaving the rest of the dishes soaking, sat down opposite the TV. A curly-haired disk jockey was looking out thoughtfully across a record he was holding:

THE DISK JOCKEY: *Some might think it strange that with such divergent tastes in drugs Donnie and Gwen Martin should seek happiness together and in their fashion find it . . . but life holds many mysteries, my friends. I could mention Jack Sprat and wife. We'll all hope the Hubbard . . . oops! . . . Martin medicine cupboard is never bare. And now we will hear, by the joint request of Mr. and Mrs. Martin—are you out there, Don and Gwennie?—that popular old favorite* (glancing down at record) *The Insane Asylum Blues!*

The music was real gone.

Donnie leaned back from his magazine and looked up at the ceiling. Gwen wondered if he were watching one of the glittering stars he'd named and pointed out to her on one of the rare Saturday nights they got outdoors. But after a while he said, "Benzedrine is an utterly evil drug, worse than coffee. Other drugs soothe and heal, but benzedrine only creates tension and confusion. I'll bet if I ask the Wise Old Crocodile he'll tell me the Devil invented it."

Gwen said, "If we ever went out nights and did anything, maybe I wouldn't need so much benzedrine. Besides, you have your sleeping pills and things."

"You don't need less benzedrine when you go out, you need more," Donnie asserted unalterably. "And if I ever went out on week nights, I'd get excited and start to drink and you know what would happen. How often do I have to tell you, Woman, that the only reason I take my barbiturates and 'things,' as you call them, is to keep calm and get enough sleep. If I didn't get enough sleep, I wouldn't be able to stand my job. If I couldn't stand my job, I'd start to drink. And if I started to drink, I'd be back in the Booby Hatch. And since the only reason you're outside is that I'm outside, holding a job, why you'd be back in the Booby Hatch too and they'd put you on tranquilizers and you wouldn't like it at all. So don't criticize my sleeping medicines, Woman. They're a matter of pure necessity whatever the doctors and psychologists say. Whereas your bennies and dexies—"

"We've been through all this before," Gwen interrupted without rancor.

Donnie nodded owlishly. "Show we half," he agreed, his words blurring for the first time.

"Besides," Gwen said, "you're behind schedule."

Donnie squinted at the clock and snapped his fingers. The sound was dull but there was no unsteadiness in his walk as he went to the refrigerator and poured himself two fingers of grapejuice. Then he reached down from the top shelf of the cupboard the bottle of paraldehyde and poured himself a glistening tablespoonful. Swift almost as thought the intense odor, midway between gasoline and banana oil, leaped to the corners of the half-merged living-room and kitchen. Gwen momentarily wrinkled her nose.

Donnie mixed the paraldehyde with the grapejuice and licked the spoon. "Here's to the druggists and the one understanding doctor in ten," he said and took a sip.

Gwen nodded solemnly and swallowed another benzedrine tablet.

Donnie transported his cocktail back to the armchair with great care and did not take his eye off the purple drink until he felt himself firmly anchored. He found his place in the science-fiction lead novelette, but the print began to slip sideways and so, as he sipped his stinging drink, he began to imagine the secrets the Wise Old Crock might tell him if he were the young man on the cover.

THE WISE OLD CROCK: *Got a hot trip shaping for tonight, Son. Three new novas flaring in the next galaxy southeast-by-up and dust cloud billowing out of Andromeda like black lace underwear.* (Dips in his purse.) *Drop this silver sphere in your pocket, Son. It's a universal TV pickup on the old crystal-ball principle. It lets you tune in on any scene in the universe. Use it wisely, Son, for character building as well as delight. Don't use it to spy on your wife.* (Dips again.) *Now I want to give you this small black cylinder. Keep it always on your person. It's a psychic whistle by which you can summon me at all times. All you have to do is concentrate on me, Son. Concentrate . . .*

There was a courtroom scene on the TV screen. A lawyer

with friendly eyes but a serious brow was talking quietly to the jury, resting his hand on the rail of the box. Gwen had her ears fine-tuned by now and his voice synchronized perfectly with the movements of his lips.

THE FRIENDLY LAWYER: *I have no wish to conceal the circumstance that my client met her husband-to-be while they were both patients in a mental hospital. Believe me, folks, some of life's sweetest romances begin in the nut house. Gwen's affection inspired Don to win his release, obtain employment as a precision machinist, offer my client marriage upon her release, and shower her with love and the yellow health-tablets, so necessary to her existence, which you have watched her consume during these weary days in court. Needless to remark, this was before Don Martin began traveling in space, where he came under the influence of* (suddenly scowls) *a certain green crocodile, who shall be referred to hereinafter as Exhibit A. Enter it, clerk.*

Donnie rose up slowly from the armchair. His drink was finished. He was glaring at the TV.

"The Old Crock wouldn't be seen dead looking at junk like that," he cried thickly. "He's wired for real-life experience."

Donnie was half of a mind to kick in the picture tube when he looked toward the bedroom doorway and saw the Wise Old Crocodile standing in it, stooping low, his silver purse swinging as it dangled from his crested shoulder. Donnie knew it wasn't a hallucination, only a friendly faint green film on the darkness.

Fixing his huge kindly eyes on Donnie, the Wise Old Crock impatiently uncurled a long tentacle toward the darkness beyond him, as if to say, "Away! Away!" and then faded into it. Donnie followed him in a slow motion like Gwen's underwater ballet, shedding his shoes and shirt on the way. He was pulling his belt from the trouser loops with the air of drawing a sword as he closed the door behind him.

Gwen gave a sigh of pure joy and for a moment even closed her eyes. This was the loveliest time of all the night, the time of the Safe Freedom, the time of the Vigil. She started to roam.

First she thought she'd brush the bread crumbs from the supper table, but she got to studying their pattern and ended by picking them up one by one—she thought of it as a problem in subtraction. The pattern of the crumbs had been like that of the stars Donnie had showed her, she decided afterwards, and she was rather sorry she'd disturbed them. She carried them tenderly to the sink and delicately dusted them onto the cold grey dishwater, around which a few suds still lifted stubbornly, like old foam on an ocean beach. She saw the water glass and it reminded her to take another benzedrine tablet.

Four bright spoons caught her eye. She lifted them one by one, turning them over slowly to find all the highlights. Then she looked through the calendar on the wall, studying the months ahead and all the numbers of the days.

Every least thing was enormously fascinating! She could lose herself in one object for minutes or let her interest dart about and effortlessly follow it.

And it was easy to think good thoughts. She could think of every person she knew and wish them each well and do all kinds of wonderful things for them in her mind. A kind of girl Jesus, that's what I am, she told herself with a smile.

She drifted back into the living-room. On the TV a bright blonde housewife was leading a dull brunette housewife over to a long couch. Gwen gave a small cry of pleasure and sat down on the floor. This show was always good.

THE BRIGHT BLONDE: *What do you feed your husband when he comes home miserable?*

THE DULL BRUNETTE: *Poison.*

THE BRIGHT BLONDE: *What do you feed yourself?*

THE DULL BRUNETTE: *Sorrow.*

THE BRIGHT BLONDE: *I keep my spirits high with benzedrine. Oh happy junior high!*

THE DULL BRUNETTE: *What was happy about it? I had acne.*

THE BRIGHT BLONDE (bouncing as they sit on the couch): *You mean to say I never told you how I got started on benzedrine? I was in junior high and unhappy. My mother sent me to the doctor because I was fat and at the foot of my class. He gave me some cute little pills and zowie!—I was getting slim, smart and giddy. But pretty soon they found I was going back for an extra refill between refills. They cut me off. I struck. Uh-huh, little old me called a lie-down strike. No more school, I said, unless I had my pills. If the doctor wouldn't give them to me, I'd forage for them—and I did. Two years later my mother had me committed. If I hadn't become a TV star I'd still be in the Loony Bin.*

THE DULL BRUNETTE: *Did they give you electroshock?*

THE BRIGHT BLONDE: *Think happy thoughts. What do you do for kicks? Are you on bennies too?*

THE DULL BRUNETTE: *No.* (Her face grows slack and subtly ugly.) *I practise witchcraft.*

Gwen switched off her ears and looked away from the screen. She did not like the thought that had come to her: that she had somehow planted that idea about witchcraft in the brunette's mind. It was months since Gwen had let herself think about witchcraft, either white or black.

There came a long low groan from the bedroom, adding to Gwen's troubled feeling because it seemed too much of a coincidence that it should have come just after the word witchcraft had been spoken.

DONNIE was twisting on the bed, going through hell in his dreams. The Wise Old Crock had abandoned him in a cluster of dead stars and cosmic dust on the far side of the Andromeda Galaxy, first blindfolding him, turning him around three times, and giving him a mighty shove that had sent him out of sight of whatever asteroid they had been standing on. Floating in space, Donnie went through his pockets and found only a Scout knife and a small silver sphere and black cylinder, the purpose of which he had forgotten. A cameo-small image of Gwen's face smiled at him from the sphere. He looked up. Worms twenty feet long and glowing dull red were undulating toward him through the dusty dark. He had an intense sensation of the vast distance of the Earth. He made swimming movements only to discover that a cold paralysis was creeping through his limbs. Eternities passed.

GWEN had got out her glue and glitter and sequins and had spread newspapers on the table and was making a design on a soup plate that she hoped would catch something of the remembered pattern of the bread crumbs. The idea was to paint with glue the design for one color of glitter and then sprinkle the glitter on it, knocking off the excess by tapping the edge of the plate on the table. Sprinkling the glitter was fun, but the design was not developing quite the way she wanted it to. Besides she had just discovered that she didn't have any red or gold glitter, though there were three bottles of green. Some of the green glitter stuck to the back of her finger where she had got glue on it.

She stole a look over her shoulder at the TV. The two women had been replaced by a large map of the United States and a rugged young man wearing glasses and holding a pointer. The first word she heard told her she wasn't going to like it, but she hitched her chair around just the same, deciding that in the long run it would be best to know the worst.

THE THINGS FORECASTER: *A witchcraft high is moving down from Western Canada. Werewolf warnings have been posted in three states. Government planes are battling in the black front with white radio rays, but they're being forced back. Old folks who ought to know say it's the end of the world.* (Scans sheet handed him by page girl.) *Flash from outer space! Don Martin, famed astronaut, is facing nameless perils in the Lesser Magellanic Cloud!*

DONNIE had just blown the psychic whistle, having remembered its use only as the red worms began to spiral in around him, and the Wise Old Crock had appeared at once, putting the worms to flight with a shower of green sparks flicked from the tip of his right-hand tentacle.

THE WISE OLD CROCK: *You passed the test, Son, but don't pride yourself on it. Some night we're going to give it to you without paraldehyde. Now it's time you returned to Terra. Think of your home planet, Son, think of the Earth. Concentrate. . . .* (They are suddenly in orbit a thousand miles above North America. The larger cities gleam dully, the moon is reflected in the Great Lakes. Donnie has become a green-scaled being a head shorter than the Wise Old Crock, who weaves a tentacle majestically downward.) *Observe the cities of men, my Son. Think of the millions sleeping and dreaming there, lonely as death in their apartment dwellings and all hating their jobs. The outward appearance of these men-beings may horrify you a little at first, but you have my word that they're not fiends, only creatures like you and me, trying to control themselves with drugs, dreads, incantations, ideals, self hypnosis and surrender, so that they may lead happy lives and show forth beauty.*

GWEN was looking intently in the living-room mirror, painting evenly-spaced bands of glue on her face. The bands curved under her eyes and outward, following the line of her jaw. She painted another band down the middle of her forehead and continued it straight down her nose. Then she closed her eyes, held her breath, lifted her face and shook green glitter on it for a long time. At last she lowered her face with a jerk, shook it from side to side, puffed out through her nostrils what breath she had left, and inhaled very slowly. Then she looked at herself again in the mirror and smiled. The green glitter clung to her face just as it had to her finger.

A feeling of deadly fatigue struck her then, the first of the night, and the room momentarily swam. When it came to rest she was looking at a flashing-eyed priest in a gorgeous cloak who was weaving across the TV screen.

THE GORGEOUS PRIEST: *The psychology of Donnie and Gwen must be clear to you by now. Each wants the other to sleep so that he may stand guard over her, or she over him, while yet adventuring alone. They have found a formula for this. But what of the future? What of their souls? Drugs are no permanent solution, I can assure them. What if the bars of the Safe Freedom should blow away? What if one night one of them should go out and never come in?*

DONNIE and the Wise Old Crock were hovering just outside the bedroom window three stories up. Friendly trees shaded them from the street lights below.

THE WISE OLD CROCK: *Goodbye, my Son, for another night. Use your Earthly tenement well. Do not abuse your powers. And go easy on the barbiturates.*

DONNIE: *I will, Father, believe me.*

THE WISE OLD CROCK: *Hold. There is one further secret of great consequence that I must impart to you tonight. It concerns your wife.*

DONNIE: *Yes, Father?*

THE WISE OLD CROCK: *She is one of us!*

DONNIE flowed through the four-inch gap at the bottom of the bedroom window. He saw his body lying on its back on the bed and he surged toward it through the air, paddling gently with his tentacle tips. His body opened from crotch to chin like a purse and he flowed inside and the lips of the purse closed over his back with a soft *click*. Then he squirmed around gently, as if in a sleeping bag, and looked through the two holes in the front of his head and thrust his tentacles down into his arms and lifted his hands above his eyes and wriggled his fingers. It felt very strange to have fingertipped arms with bones in them instead of tentacles. Just then he heard laughter from the living-room.

Gwen was laughing admiringly at the reflection of her breasts. She had taken off her smock and brassiere and painted circles of glue around the nipples and sprinkled on more glitter.

Although her ears were switched off, she thought she heard the priest call from behind her, "Gwen Martin, you ought to be ashamed of yourself!" And she called back to the TV, "You shouldn't peek, Father!" and she turned around, haughtily shielding her breasts with a forearm held crosswise.

The bedroom door was open and Donnie was standing in it, swaying and staring. Gwen felt another surge of deadly fatigue but she steadied herself and stared back at her husband.

Woman, the Cave Keeper, the Weaver of Words, faced Man, the Bread Winner, the Far Ranger.

They moved together slowly, dragging their feet, until they were leaning against each other. Then, more slowly still, as if they were supporting each other through quicksands, they moved toward the bedroom.

"Do you like me, Donnie?" Gwen asked.

Donnie's gaze brushed across her glittering green-striped face and breasts. His hand tightened on her shoulder and he nodded.

"You're one of us," he said.

The Circular Ruins

JORGE LUIS BORGES

*Translated from the Spanish by Norman Thomas di Giovanni
in collaboration with the author*

~~~~~~

And if he left off dreaming about you . . .
Through the Looking-Glass, IV

Nobody saw him come ashore in the encompassing night, nobody saw the bamboo craft run aground in the sacred mud, but within a few days everyone knew that the quiet man had come from the south and that his home was among the numberless villages upstream on the steep slopes of the mountain, where the Zend language is barely tainted by Greek and where lepers are rare. The fact is that the gray man pressed his lips to the mud, scrambled up the bank without parting (perhaps without feeling) the brushy thorns that tore his flesh, and dragged himself, faint and bleeding, to the circular opening watched over by a stone tiger, or horse, which once was the color of fire and is now the color of ash. This opening is a temple which was destroyed ages ago by flames, which the swampy wilderness later desecrated, and whose god no longer receives the reverence of men. The stranger laid himself down at the foot of the image.

Wakened by the sun high overhead, he noticed—somehow without amazement—that his wounds had healed. He shut his pale eyes and slept again, not because of weariness but because he willed it. He knew that this temple was the place he needed for his unswerving purpose; he knew that downstream the encroaching trees had also failed to choke the ruins of another auspicious temple with its own fire-ravaged, dead gods; he knew that his first duty was to sleep. Along about midnight, he was awakened by the forlorn call of a bird. Footprints, some figs, and a water jug told him that men who lived nearby had looked on his sleep with a kind of awe and either sought his protection or else were in dread of his witchcraft. He felt the chill of fear and searched the crumbling walls for a burial niche, where he covered himself over with leaves he had never seen before.

His guiding purpose, though it was supernatural, was not impossible. He wanted to dream a man; he wanted to dream him down to the last detail and project him into the world of reality. This mystical aim had taxed the whole range of his mind. Had anyone asked him his own name or anything about his life before then, he would not have known what to answer. This forsaken, broken temple suited him because it held few visible things, and also because the neighboring villagers would look after his frugal needs. The rice and fruit of their offerings were nourishment enough for his body, whose one task was to sleep and to dream.

At the outset, his dreams were chaotic; later on, they were of a dialectic nature. The stranger dreamed himself at the center of a circular amphitheater which in some way was also the burnt-out temple. Crowds of silent disciples exhausted the tiers of seats; the faces of the farthest of them hung centuries away from him and at a height of the stars, but their features were clear and exact. The man lectured on anatomy, cosmography, and witchcraft. The faces listened, bright and eager, and did their best to answer sensibly, as if they felt the importance of his questions, which would raise one of them out of an existence as a shadow and place him in the real world. Whether asleep or awake, the man pondered the answers of his phantoms and, not letting himself be misled by impostors, divined in certain of their quandaries a growing intelligence. He was in search of a soul worthy of taking a place in the world.

After nine or ten nights he realized, feeling bitter over it, that nothing could be expected from those pupils who passively accepted his teaching, but that he might, however, hold hopes for those who from time to time hazarded reasonable doubts about what he taught. The former, although they deserved love and affection, could never become real; the latter, in their dim way, were already real. One evening (now his evenings were also given over to sleeping, now he was only awake for an hour or two at dawn) he dismissed his vast dream-school forever and kept a single disciple. He was a quiet, sallow, and at times rebellious young man with sharp features akin to those of his dreamer. The sudden disappearance of his fellow pupils did not disturb him for very long, and his progress, at the end of a few private lessons, amazed his teacher. Nonetheless, a catastrophe intervened. One morning, the man emerged from his sleep as from a sticky wasteland, glanced up at the faint evening light, which at first he confused with the dawn, and realized that he had not been dreaming. All that night and the next day, the hideous lucidity of insomnia weighed down on him. To tire himself out he tried to explore the surrounding forest, but all he managed, there in a thicket of hemlocks, were some snatches of broken sleep, fleetingly tinged with visions of a crude and worthless nature. He tried to reassemble his school, and barely had he uttered a few brief words of counsel when the whole class went awry and vanished. In his almost endless wakefulness, tears of anger stung his old eyes.

He realized that, though he may penetrate all the riddles of the higher and lower orders, the task of shaping the senseless and dizzying stuff of dreams is the hardest that a man can attempt—much harder than weaving a rope of sand or of coining the faceless wind. He realized that an initial failure was to be expected. He then swore he would forget the populous vision which in the beginning had led him astray, and he sought another method. Before attempting it, he spent a month rebuilding the strength his fever had consumed. He gave up all thoughts of dreaming and almost at once managed to sleep a reasonable part of the day. The few times he dreamed during this period he did not dwell on his dreams. Before taking up his task again, he waited until the moon was a perfect circle. Then, in the evening, he cleansed himself in the waters of the river, worshiped the gods of the planets, uttered the prescribed syllables of an all-powerful name, and slept. Almost at once, he had a dream of a beating heart.

He dreamed it throbbing, warm, secret. It was the size of a closed fist, a darkish red in the dimness of a human body still without a face or sex. With anxious love he dreamed it for fourteen lucid nights. Each night he perceived it more clearly. He did not touch it, but limited himself to witnessing it, to observing it, to correcting it now and then with a look. He felt it, he lived it from different distances and from many angles. On the fourteenth night he touched the pulmonary artery with a finger and then the whole heart, inside and out. The examination satisfied him. For one night he deliberately did not dream; after that he went back to the heart again, invoked the name of a planet, and set out to envision another of the principal organs. Before a year was over he came to the skeleton, the eyelids. The countless strands of hair were perhaps the hardest task of all. He dreamed a whole man, a young man, but the young man could not stand up or speak, nor could he open his eyes. Night after night, the man dreamed him asleep.

In the cosmogonies of the Gnostics, the demiurges mold a red Adam who is unable to stand on his feet; as clumsy and crude and elementary as that Adam of dust was the Adam of dreams wrought by the nights of the magician. One evening the man was at the point of destroying all his handiwork (it would have been better for him had he done so), but in the end he restrained himself. Having exhausted his prayers to the gods of the earth and river, he threw himself down at the feet of the stone image that may have been a tiger or a stallion, and asked for its blind aid. That same evening he dreamed of the image. He dreamed it alive, quivering; it was no unnatural cross between tiger and stallion but at one and the same time both these violent creatures and also a bull, a rose, a thunderstorm. This manifold god revealed to him that its earthly name was Fire, that there in the circular temple (and in others like it) sacrifices had once been made to it, that it had been worshiped, and that through its magic the phantom of the man's dreams would be wakened to life in such a way that—except for Fire itself and the dreamer—every being in the world would accept him as a man of flesh and blood. The god ordered that, once instructed in the rites, the disciple should be sent downstream to the other ruined temple, whose pyramids still survived, so that in that abandoned place some human voice might exalt him. In the dreamer's dream, the dreamed one awoke.

The magician carried out these orders. He devoted a period of time (which finally spanned two years) to initiating his principle into the riddles of the universe and the worship of

Fire. Deep inside, it pained him to say goodbye to his creature. Under the pretext of teaching him more fully, each day he drew out the hours set aside for sleep. Also, he reshaped the somewhat faulty right shoulder. From time to time, he was troubled by the feeling that all this had already happened, but for the most part his days were happy. On closing his eyes he would think, "Now I will be with my son." Or, less frequently, "The son I have begotten awaits me and he will not exist if I do not go to him."

Little by little, he was training the young man for reality. On one occasion he commanded him to set up a flag on a distant peak. The next day, there on the peak, a fiery pennant shone. He tried other, similar exercises, each bolder than the one before. He realized with a certain bitterness that his son was ready—and perhaps impatient—to be born. That night he kissed him for the first time and sent him down the river to the other temple, whose whitened ruins were still to be glimpsed over miles and miles of impenetrable forest and swamp. At the very end (so that the boy would never know he was a phantom, so that he would think himself a man like all men), the magician imbued his disciple with total oblivion of his long years of apprenticeship.

His triumph and his peace were blemished by a touch of weariness. In the morning and evening dusk, he prostrated himself above the stone idol, perhaps imagining that his unreal son was performing the same rites farther down the river in other circular ruins. At night he no longer dreamed, or else he dreamed the way all men dream. He now perceived with a certain vagueness the sounds and shapes of the world, for his absent son was taking nourishment from the magician's decreasing consciousness. His life's purpose was fulfilled; the man lived on in a kind of ecstasy. After a length of time that certain tellers of the story count in years and others in half-decades, he was awakened one midnight by two rowers. He could not see their faces, but they spoke to him about a magic man in a temple up north who walked on fire without being burned. The magician suddenly remembered the god's words. He remembered that of all the creatures in the world, Fire was the only one who knew his son was a phantom. This recollection, comforting at first, ended by tormenting him. He feared that his son might wonder at this strange privilege and in some way discover his condition as a mere appearance. Not to be a man but to be the projection of another man's dreams —what an unparalleled humiliation, how bewildering! Every father cares for the child he has begotten—he has allowed— in some moment of confusion or happiness. It is understandable, then, that the magician should fear for the future of a son thought out organ by organ and feature by feature over the course of a thousand and one secret nights.

The end of these anxieties came suddenly, but certain signs foretold it. First (after a long drought), a far-off cloud on a hilltop, as light as a bird; next, toward the south, the sky, which took on the rosy hue of a leopard's gums; then, the pillars of smoke that turned the metal of the nights to rust; finally, the headlong panic of the forest animals. For what had happened many centuries ago was happening again. The ruins of the fire god's shrine were destroyed by fire. In a birdless dawn the magician saw the circling sheets of flame closing in on him. For a moment, he thought of taking refuge in the river, but then he realized that death was coming to crown his years and to release him from his labors. He walked into the leaping pennants of flame. They did not bite into his flesh, but caressed him and flooded him without heat or burning. In relief, in humiliation, in terror, he understood that he, too, was an appearance, that someone else was dreaming him.